She was all alone in the Klondike.

Perhaps what Genevieve needed most was a proper husband who would hold her and love her and tell her everything would be fine. But when Luke reached out with a firm hand, his warm touch was reassuring. Despite herself, she wished he'd let his hand lay.

She could be in such terrible trouble if Luke let his hand linger. And yet, as she stared at the rugged beauty of his tanned fingers curling over her arm, she was rooted by the heated connection. The improper connection.

She allowed his hand to remain. When he drew her somewhat closer, she didn't voice a complaint. He rocked her arm then, as if he wished to pull her tightly to his chest.

Please don't.

Please do.

* * *

Klondike Wedding
Harlequin® Historical #863—September 2007

KATE BRIDGES

KLONDIKE WEDDING

HARLEQUIN®

TORONTO • NEW YORK • LONDON
AMSTERDAM • PARIS • SYDNEY • HAMBURG
STOCKHOLM • ATHENS • TOKYO • MILAN • MADRID
PRAGUE • WARSAW • BUDAPEST • AUCKLAND

ISBN-13: 978-0-373-29463-3
ISBN-10:   0-373-29463-8

KLONDIKE WEDDING

www.eHarlequin.com

Printed in U.S.A.

DON'T MISS THESE OTHER NOVELS AVAILABLE NOW:

#864 A COMPROMISED LADY—ELIZABETH ROLLS

Thea Winslow's scandalous past has forbidden her a future. So why does her wayward heart refuse to understand that she cannot have any more to do with handsome Richard Blakehurst?

#865 A PRACTICAL MISTRESS—MARY BRENDAN

She was nearly penniless, and becoming a mistress was the only practical solution. The decision had *nothing* to do with the look in Sir Jason's eyes that promised such heady delights....

#866 THE WARRIOR'S TOUCH— MICHELLE WILLINGHAM

Pragmatic, plain Aileen never forgot the handsome man who became her first lover on the eve of Bealtaine, the man who gave her a child without ever seeing her face. Now that he has returned, how can she keep her secret?

The MacEgan Brothers

This book is dedicated to all of my readers,
in various countries. For your letters, your e-mails,
your kind words in person or your silent support in
simply picking up this book. Thank you.

I would also like to thank my editors, Ann Leslie Tuttle
and Linda Fildew, for being so encouraging and always
making me strive for my best. And to my agent,
Charles Schlessiger, for being a part of my world.

Chapter One

Dawson City, Yukon, July 1898

"I now pronounce you man and wife." The old judge coughed. "Sort of."

Genevieve Summerville felt like a fraud. She didn't normally dress in such rich clothing. She clutched at her much-too-expensive bouquet of fresh-cut pink roses, white chrysanthemums and stag's-horn moss. Ribbons of organza streamed below the stems, lily of the valley perfumed the air and she could barely breathe in a corset laced too tight for this heat. She glanced up from the banks of the rushing river to the judge. His black robes flicked in the breeze. Dots of sweat gave sheen to his forehead and caused his spectacles to slip down his nose. Behind him sprawled the tents and new plank buildings of Dawson City, center of the Klondike gold rush, at the juncture of the Yukon and Klondike Rivers.

She couldn't bring herself to look at the tall, intimidating man standing to her right, a position normally reserved for the groom. Dressed in the handsome red uniform of the North-West Mounted Police, he wasn't hers.

She'd only been in town for three days, but she'd already heard the rumors about him.

A light breeze lifted her loose black hair and swirled around her bodice, around the see-through lace overlay, the twenty-four tiny buttons that plunged down her spine, the low-cut neckline she'd picked out because she'd thought she'd be wearing it for another man. Beneath the silk and chiffon and her lengthy tulle veil, she wore homemade bloomers and drab stockings she'd mended many times over.

Thank goodness, some things remained private.

"You may now…um—" Judge Donahue strained to be heard above squawking ducks "—shake hands."

Genevieve turned to the Mountie inspector.

Luke Buxton Hunter didn't smile when he took her hand, gloved in white satin. His grip was a bit too firm, like the man himself. The officer wore no hat and his shiny black hair sparkled in the sun. She bet *his* underclothes matched the state of his fine-looking uniform.

She bet *he* was what he appeared to be.

"Congratulations," said the stand-in groom. "I hope you two will be very happy."

"Thank you."

"Whenever he makes it back to town."

"Hopefully Joshua will return…before the end of the month."

Sunshine caught the jagged scar beneath the officer's left eye. She wondered how he'd got it. Is that why he never smiled?

"Unless he strikes gold first."

The statement cheered her. It was the whole point of Joshua's absence, and why he hadn't been here to meet her three days ago when she'd arrived. Most of the lucrative gold claims in Dawson City had already been staked. Joshua was trying his hand panning farther up river, working hard to support her and any future children.

"Yes…well…well, thank you for filling in for Joshua."

"Least I can do for an old friend. I must admit, this is my first proxy wedding."

"Mine, too. Well, save for my parents' back home, but I didn't attend their wedding." Anxious, she chattered on. "I wasn't born for another two years."

When she stared into his dark and serious eyes, that pang of loneliness hit her again. What this man had done for his friend, Joshua McFadden, reminded her of the dear friendships she'd left behind in Montana.

But she should count her blessings. She was getting a whole new start in a beautiful new country, with an upstanding man she'd briefly known in her childhood. He came highly recommended by her aunt and uncle here in Dawson.

In his letter to her, Joshua had written that he was supportive of her new profession. She didn't recall exactly what he looked like, but she remembered his kindness when once taking her to the country fair, and how ambitious he'd seemed telling her of his big dreams to see the world and make a fortune.

His ambitions were what had attracted her as an adolescent. That's why she understood his absence today.

Her puppy yelped at her boots, biting at the buttons, breaking her spell. Genevieve smiled. She bent forward in the intricate gown she'd hauled over the Chilkoot Pass, careful to hide the scuffed boots that didn't match her gown, and scooped up the frisky white pup.

"Nugget, can't you sit still for ten minutes?"

The inspector leaned over and, with two broad fingers, stroked Nugget's head. The gesture seemed too intimate, seeing how the puppy was pressed so close to her bosom. Genevieve flushed, but then recalled that the inspector was a veterinary surgeon. A doctor of animals. He looked after the horses and livestock at the Mountie outpost. Hence his interest in puppies was genuine.

"How'd you get her here?" he asked.

"In my pocket, the whole climb up." All three pounds of her. Now she was four. The tiny white lapdog had French heritage, Genevieve had been told by the steamship captain who'd donated her, like Genevieve herself.

Her aunt was the first to bounce over from the handful of witnesses.

"Congratulations, my dear." Abigail Thornbottom, as wide as she was tall, cupped her niece's face in her hands and kissed her cheek. "Your mother would be so proud. And your father, my goodness, may God rest their souls." She lowered her head—and her magnificent felt hat in the process—to smell the bridal bouquet. "Worthy of a princess."

"Much too extravagant flowers," murmured Genevieve. They'd sent the money for her wedding gown, as well, and she'd be forever grateful.

"Nonsense. We bought them from the best Dutch florist in town—"

"The *only* florist," said thin Uncle Theodore, dressed in his tight wool suit.

Aunt Abigail whispered with pride. "His gardens are full of imported seeds all the way from Rotterdam."

Genevieve knew they meant well, but she lowered her lashes. She wished they'd stop boasting. Especially in front of the officer.

Two steps away, Judge Donahue moaned. When he coughed again, his face turned patchy red.

Inspector Hunter put his hand on the frail man's shoulder. "Are you all right, sir?"

He rubbed his temple. "It's this…heat…."

"Come. Let's get you a glass of water." The Mountie led the gent to a table and chair, set up beneath a gnarled willow tree. The officer's wide brown Stetson lay on the table.

While he took care of the judge, some of the other witnesses stepped forward to congratulate Genevieve. They were all strangers to her, except for her smartly dressed seventeen-year-old cousin, Milly, Aunt Abigail and Uncle Theodore.

A rugged man in his thirties, a casino owner and friend of her uncle's, removed his gold pocket watch and looked at the time. He'd brought his two brothers to the wedding out of respect for her uncle, she'd been told. Uncle Theodore, a rope and broom salesman who'd only arrived weeks ago himself, seemed to know almost everyone in town.

They were the Cliffton brothers, Genevieve recalled. Burt, Vince and Ripley Cliffton had been introduced to her as the saloon keeper, casino owner and gold prospector. In addition to their good looks, they had sandy-brown hair in common, shaggy to their shoulders. One of them, Burt the saloon keeper, wore a mustache.

"Miss, are you sure this is legal?" asked Vince Cliffton. "A proxy ceremony without your groom?"

She took her hand off the elegant bouquet and pressed it to her nervous stomach. "As legal as any country wedding."

Some of the weddings on the long journey here, Genevieve recalled, hadn't bothered to use a preacher *or* a judge. There were simply none available. Her folks had told her that on the frontiers of Montana, too, on the trails riding West, couples solemnized their nuptials by themselves, using friends as witnesses. The couple would then register the marriage at the courthouse— when and if they could; otherwise, saying their sacred vows aloud and moving in under the same roof meant they were married.

"You know, English royalty have been using proxy weddings for centuries." Aunt Abigail shook her head so hard that her plumed hat sprang forward on her head, like a chipmunk about to pounce.

"You don't say," said Burt Cliffton.

"And we mustn't forget Napoleon to his archduchess." Beaming, Aunt Abigail pressed her gloved hand to her throat.

Ripley Cliffton, the third youthful brother, not nearly as finely dressed as the other two but just as handsome, strummed his fingers along his shabby wool overalls. "If it's good enough for emperors, it's good enough for your niece."

They laughed.

"But to just to make sure," Genevieve declared, "Joshua and I plan on a church ceremony as soon as he returns."

She smoothed her wedding gown and attempted to step forward, but her boot snagged the train.

"Let me help you." Cousin Milly, in an apricot dress and white picture hat, scooted to the grass and picked up the ballooning silk.

Genevieve scanned the gathering to locate the sturdy Mountie. She looked over the heads and shoulders of the other men—an older fellow who worked in the livery stables, as muscled as a horse himself and his scalp as shiny as a cabbage; a quiet jeweler she'd met only yesterday and whose head was shielded by a bowler hat; and a tall blond constable who was the veterinarian's apprentice.

Her gaze found the officer. He was giving his apprentice direction, pointing to the horses hitched at the riverside.

She tried to ease her jitters. Her new life with Joshua would work out fine. She'd just been married to a man who'd take good care of her. She'd do her best to make their home a center of comfort and, hopefully sometime in the future, of love.

"The proxy is only a formality," Uncle Theodore explained to the guests. His long white ponytail ruffled in the wind. It hit the spine of his plaid wool jacket. "It was our idea. Genevieve, well-bred lady that she is, didn't want to move into his cabin while he was gone, without the proper title of being his wife."

"Of course," said Burt Cliffton, the saloon keeper.

Aunt Abigail caressed the silk on Genevieve's mutton sleeve. "And Joshua insisted she be looked after in fine style while he was away. He wasn't quite sure when she would arrive in the Klondike. But he begged us to move in with her, in that gloriously large home he built last year."

"I can hardly wait," whispered Milly.

"We bought her a little bell," said Aunt Abigail.

"A bell?" asked the men.

Aunt Abigail giggled. "To call the maid."

Genevieve blushed. "There's no maid, Aunt Abigail. I've told you, there's isn't that type of money—"

"There will be. There will be. Just you wait until Joshua comes back with sacks full of gold."

"But—"

"I picked up the bell from a shop across the street from ours. The shopkeeper is the only Englishman in town who imports directly from London."

Inspector Hunter looked up from the judge's side, straight at Genevieve. He'd removed an envelope from his uniform and was pointing to it as the judge took quill in hand, signing the marriage certificate. Had the inspector overheard?

Genevieve prickled with discomfort right down to her toes. What did it matter what he thought of her or her family?

She would enjoy this moment. She inhaled air as fresh as morning dew, sensed a breeze warming her throat, tasted the mint powder she'd brushed her teeth with only an hour ago.

It occurred to her that the officer had taken extra care to dress, as well. His hair, dark above his temples, shone with freshness. His cheeks were smooth due to a morning shave, his uniform neatly pressed. A shoulder harness was strapped across his broad chest and fitted with a gun. He was well groomed, she thought, out of respect for his friend, Joshua.

Still, she pondered the incongruous nature of the polished details set against the scarred face.

There was no getting around the daunting presence of the officer looking her way. She was in her early twenties, but he was likely in his late thirties. More experienced in the world. She wondered about the rumors, the whispers she'd heard about him. It was said that Inspector Luke Hunter was a man who highly savored his bachelor days.

Her breath quickened. And nights.

She was a lovely bride, thought Luke, and Joshua McFadden was a lucky man. If a man went for that sort of thing. Marriage.

Watching her from beneath the willow tree while he stood over the judge, Luke straightened in his uniform. A warm summer breeze filtered through his dark hair. Amusement tugged at his lips as he watched the dark-haired beauty with her aunt and uncle. Only a few weeks ago, Luke had traveled with the Thornbottoms on their journey here, and he considered himself damn fortunate the journey was over. He had been traveling incognito with five other Mounties, disguised as brothers to infiltrate a crime ring. The Thornbottoms were unsuspecting stampeders they kept bumping into.

He'd never met a woman who talked so much as Abigail Thornbottom, usually utter nonsense.

Her pretty niece, Genevieve, however, seemed to take after her Uncle Theodore. Quiet and watchful. And a little bit scared. But you never knew with women—sometimes the quiet ones turned into Abigail Thornbottoms when you least expected them.

Luke surveyed the bride. He took in the curves of her silky gown, the large bosom, the pinched waist, the long length of her hidden legs. But it was her face that drew him. Her sharp green eyes, the arched black eyebrows, straight nose, glowing skin, the eager lips. Hair a mile long.

What a shame she would be spending her wedding eve alone.

If she were his, he'd be keeping her up all night.

Luckily, though, Luke wouldn't be thus constrained. Sure, the wedding night would be easy. Spending a night with her would be more pleasure than any man could fathom. Especially in this harsh land where women were few and far between. It would be the other forty years that would be trying. He'd witnessed *that* with his own eyes.

Good luck to Joshua McFadden and Miss Genevieve Summerville.

This evening, Luke would be enjoying a get-together of his own, with an enchanting woman who worked at the casino.

Luke's apprentice, Weston Williams, approached him and the judge, swinging a canteen.

"It's empty," said Weston.

Luke frowned. "Judge Donahue could use a sip of cool water."

"It's…it's…all right." The judge's face dripped with sweat. "I'll just finish with this paperwork and sit here a spell."

"It's no trouble." Luke gazed up the slope to the Mountie outpost. It was right on the edge of town, two blocks up from Front Street from where the banging and hammering on the new wharf echoed day and night. Beyond the boardwalk that ran past the outpost, several log cabins were perched on a grassy slope, along with stables and corral. The place was deserted because most of the Mounties were out on duty.

A well stood in the center of the courtyard.

"Let me go to the well," said Luke. "I'll be right back."

He took the empty canteen and strode up the hill. He twitched with discomfort, feeling as though he was being watched. He scanned the outpost, between the buildings, but there was no one around. Smoke puffed from the chimney of the commissioner's cabin. The man was likely preparing himself coffee.

Luke turned his head to the wedding crowd by the river. No one was looking back at him, so he trudged upward.

The sooner this ceremony was finished, the sooner Luke could return to more vital tasks.

There weren't enough Mounties to deal with everything that needed attention.

First off, the measles scare. Everyone in town was fearful and watching out for symptoms of the deadly disease. Two gold miners, found dead last week at their campsite, had caused near hysteria. Near as Luke could tell, the men hadn't been in contact with any townspeople, so it had to be passersby who'd spread the disease.

Then the usual bout of crimes and misdemeanors. The ongoing investigation of the armed robbery two days ago of the jewelry shop—belonging to the very man who stood as witness to the wedding today—plus suspected arson of one of the town's livery stables. There was Luke's personal overseeing of the construction of a new bridge over the Klondike River, two miles out of town. Then there were the gold disputes. Hell, those never seemed to go away on their own. So many folks, all claiming someone else infringed on their claim.

Luke reached the well, hauled up a bucket of cool spring water and filled his canteen. When he returned to the judge's side, Luke tingled with warning again.

Someone was watching him. And something wasn't quite right with the judge. His color was off; his eyes looked hollow.

Bloody hell, did he have a fever?

"Your Honor, have a sip of this."

The judge looked up from the marriage certificate. He clutched the letter he had removed from the envelope Luke had given him yesterday. In it, Joshua had asked him to take care of Genevieve if she arrived before he returned.

Luke glared at the names on the certificate and froze.

"What in God's name?" he whispered, thunderstruck.

The judge groped for the canteen, rose to his feet and immediately fell over.

Ducks quacked.

Abigail Thornbottom screamed.

Genevieve dashed to help.

Luke dropped to his knees beside the old man. The marriage paper fluttered to the grass. With racing fingers and pounding heart, Luke clawed at the old man's cravat.

Eyes closed, the judge lay as still as a board.

Luke ripped open his robe and then his shirt. Buttons flew. Although Luke struggled to shake life back into him, the poor man was dead. His chest was covered in tiny red dots.

Measles.

Luke took a moment to fathom it.

Then he was suddenly aware of her. Genevieve, on her knees beside him in a cloud of creamy silk, trying to help the judge. It took her seconds to realize, looking up at Luke's solemn face, that the judge had passed on.

She sank back onto her heels, speechless.

The marriage certificate blared up at them from the grass, as though it had a voice of its own.

Dumbfounded, Luke stared at the white parchment riddled with drops of water. There, in the shaky penmanship of the judge's hand were the names of the new bride and groom.

Miss Genevieve Summerville and Dr. Luke Hunter.

Genevieve gazed at it long and hard. She blinked and stared at it some more. Then with a trembling to her lips, she turned slowly, stiffly, to face Luke.

Holy hell, thought Luke. *What had just occurred?*

Chapter Two

Commotion swirled around Genevieve as she tried to compose herself. Breathe in. Breathe out.

Strangers hustled around her, trying to stir the judge for themselves, but to no avail. Aunt Abigail, who'd fainted beyond the willow tree, was lifted from the ground by Uncle Theodore. Milly paled to the color of a dull moon. She fell on Genevieve from behind, and pressed her face into Genevieve's back as if afraid of looking at a dead man.

The officer said nothing.

Genevieve got to her feet.

Why couldn't someone say something? The inspector, rising to his full height, his broad shoulders blocking out the sun, stared down as Nugget raced around and around the outer edges of Genevieve's wedding gown.

Trying to act composed, Genevieve swept a strand of hair off her temple. She adjusted the lace tulle of her headgear. Sorrow touched her heart at the judge's passing.

"Now then, what can we do for this poor man? I feel awful for him."

Surely, surely, the incorrect marriage record was null and void. It meant nothing. There was no need to panic.

But the poor judge could be helped. Not to bring him back to life, unfortunately, but to lay him gently to rest. To tell his next of kin—if he had any in town—and to thank them for his…presence at the ceremony. It didn't matter about the mistake on the marriage document. She'd fix that later. What mattered was the judge, and notifying the folks who loved him.

His age and his thin figure reminded her of her father when he'd passed away, and the wake she'd held in Montana several years ago. Her father's passing had quickly been followed by her mother's, then her grandmother's. Genevieve had more experience in wakes than most women her age.

The inspector covered the judge's face with the judge's broad black hat, gently tucked the dead man's shirt back into position over his chest, and pressed the black robes shut.

"We'll need someone to go up the hill and inform the commissioner."

"Right," said the saloon keeper. "I'll go."

"No, it's best you stay here." The Mountie eyed the group. "Weston, you go. Throw some pebbles on the door to attract his attention. When he opens up, you're not to get within thirty feet of him."

"Thirty feet?" asked Weston. He dropped his hand to the side of his brand-new blue jeans. New cowboy boots squeaked on the grass.

"That's right. You've been exposed to the illness."

Genevieve shifted her weight as Nugget nipped at her boots. What exactly did this mean?

Weston tore up the hill.

"Well, we best be goin', Luke." Burt Cliffton, the saloon keeper, had stood listening to the exchange. "Shop's about to open. Things to do."

"Hang on a minute, Burt," the Mountie said but was ignored.

"I've gotta run, too." Ripley Cliffton, the gold miner, adjusted his spectacles. "Back to digging my claim."

Vince Cliffton, the casino owner, looked at his gold pocket watch again, turned and left.

"Hold it right there," said the inspector.

The Cliffton brothers all kept moving, as if they hadn't heard. Inspector Hunter stared after them in silence, but Genevieve noted the twitching jaw and slight flush of anger creeping up his neck. The brothers kept walking, two toward the center of town, the prospector toward a stallion hitched at the river.

Uncle Theodore, bracing Aunt Abigail, who was breathing easy now, set her down on the chair formerly used by the judge. They both listened quietly to the officer.

Clyde Orman, the freckled jeweler with his bowler hat and handlebar mustache, backed out of the crowd. "I've got an appointment."

Kirk Kendall, who was older and had a shiny head and thick muscled neck, hiked his hands into his pockets, headed toward his horse tethered next to the prospector's and made his excuse. "I'm sure the commissioner will find some men to help you bury this poor fellow."

Every guest wanted to leave. Not one wished to stay a moment longer. How could Genevieve blame them? She wanted to run, too.

She turned and embraced Milly. The puppy, lying at their feet, chomped on a stick.

With a deliberation that frightened her, Inspector Hunter pulled his handgun from his holster. She gasped as he hoisted it to the air and pulled the trigger.

The explosion ripped through sunshine and pulsed down her spine.

"I want everyone to turn around, right now, and come back. Do you hear me? If you take one more step, Burt, I'll haul you up that hill and throw you into jail so quick your boots won't touch the ground."

The three brothers and two other men froze in position. Slowly turning, they faced the panting Mountie.

"We can do this peacefully," said the officer, glaring at them, "or we can do it by force."

Aunt Abigail groaned and slumped her head onto the table.

"Listen up." The Mountie swept his gaze over the group, ending on Genevieve, making her shiver at the magnitude of his power. "This wedding party's in quarantine for the next fourteen days."

Four hours later, Luke hoisted a shovel into dirt. He had examined the body and found measles.

The three Cliffton brothers assisted him in the digging, while the other two men helped the Thornbottoms and their displaced niece—the new bride—gather their things beneath the willow tree. A crowd of about twenty folks with nothing better to do watched from the boardwalk, not daring to cross the white line Luke had one of the shopkeepers paint on the planks. Some were saddened about Judge Donahue. Some were curious about who exactly would be kept in quarantine. Most were still murmuring about the scandalous news.

Had Luke and the Summerville woman been accidentally married?

Luke cursed beneath his breath. There'd be time to sort it out later. Now was the time to bury the dead.

Reverend Murphy, thirty feet away, standing behind the painted white line alongside Mountie Commissioner York, read from the Bible and the service began.

The quarantined group gathered around the riverbank and lowered the casket. Heads bowed, they prayed for the judge's soul. The three women brought out their hankies and sniffled when it was over. Mrs. Thornbottom wailed the most, but to Luke, quiet Genevieve seemed most affected.

She'd barely spoken for four hours. Adrift in her silent thoughts, she looked out of place at the funeral, standing in her silken wedding gown.

Luke's heart tugged with a softness he hadn't felt in a long time. He stared at her swollen eyes, the soggy cheeks, the gentle turn of her lips as she reprimanded her pup. Even the little dog seemed to sense this was serious business, for she'd simmered down at her mistress's feet.

When it was over, Luke approached Genevieve. Still in uniform, he towered above her. "Do you have a change of clothes?"

"Pardon?" She looked up from the grave as the Cliffton brothers poured dirt onto the casket. Holding her pup to her chest, she seemed not to notice its paws were soiled. At some point earlier, the bride had removed her veil.

"I'm sorry I never thought of it before." Luke ran his hand along his sleeve. "Can you get out of that gown? Do you have a change of clothes?"

"Yes. Yes, I think so." She squinted up at him, the light breeze blowing tendrils of black hair across her forehead. Somewhere behind them, ducks squawked on the river. "Someone went to my home…Joshua's home…and packed my…my suitcases, as you ordered." She craned her neck to the willow tree. The soft muscles at her throat tugged gently when she spotted her two suitcases. "There they are."

"I'll bring them to my cabin for you."

"Your cabin?" Genevieve leaned back. "Now just a moment. If you think I'm going to hop into your—"

"Hold on. Hold on." He raised his palm and nodded to the large log cabin on the edge of the Mountie outpost. "Those are the Mountie barracks. One of three cabins. The commissioner and I have decided it's where the eleven of us will spend our quarantine. Men in one room. Women in another."

"Oh."

"The other buildings are far enough away—forty and fifty feet—that the troops will be safe. We'll have a cook at our disposal. Can't get close to him, but he can deliver meals."

She clutched Nugget. "Yes, I suppose…I suppose that'll work well."

"I've ordered my men to check into all the other people the judge may have been in contact with in the last four to five days. If he had a fever then, he would have been contagious." Luke inclined his head to get a better look at her solemn face. Sunshine warmed his cheek. "How are you feeling?"

She raised her chin. Her eyes flashed a new depth of green. "I'm better than the judge. But not great."

"Do you have any symptoms? Headache? Fever? Itchy—"

"*No.*" Her eyes widened. "Nothing like that." When she pulled away, the sun's rays cut her in two. "Don't be digging another hole just yet."

He stared. Obviously upset, she took in a deep breath. He waited for her to relax.

"I'm sorry," she offered. "I shouldn't have said that. It's just that…I'm…I'm…"

Luke lowered his voice. "If it makes you feel any better, I'm scared, too."

She sighed.

They waited, quietly fidgeting while the Cliffton brothers finished the burial.

"Did he have any next of kin?" she asked.

"Not here." Luke retrieved his shovel. "He came from the East Coast. His wife passed on ten years ago, I'm told, but he still has his grown children. I'll be writing to them first chance I get."

"Oh."

"It wasn't a bad way to go, as far as departures. He lived a long, productive life. He was likely frail to begin with and succumbed to the symptoms."

"…not a bad way…" She stared at the heap of newly turned soil.

Something about her manner didn't sit right with him. "Are you sure you're all right?"

"It reminds me of too many other funerals I've been to."

"Ah, I see." But he didn't really. He knew almost nothing about her. Whether she still had family in Montana, or what she planned on doing in the future.

Her coal-black hair flickered across her face. The sharp black features, set against smooth creamy skin, were riveting.

"Luke!"

He heard his name called and spun around toward the boardwalk and the crowd.

Commissioner York held up the marriage certificate. "I've had a look at it. And just spoke to the reverend here."

Luke glanced at Genevieve. He pressed his fingers into

her spine and led her two steps closer to the two men who were deciding their fate but still at the safe thirty-foot distance to protect them. The crowd was dispersing, but some folks fell back to listen to the commissioner's verdict. Luke winced, but there was nothing he could do to control the busybodies.

"What do you think?" Luke hollered. "Big mistake, right? We can just tear it up and walk our separate ways."

"I'm afraid not!"

Genevieve eyed the commissioner. "What do you mean, sir?"

"Well, the reverend and I…we went over it very carefully…and I'm afraid we must consider this certificate to be a legal document."

Luke's heart took a leap. "But it was a proxy wedding—"

"Yours was no proxy. You were there in person. There are nine remaining witnesses who saw you take your vows."

Luke's heart drummed. "But I said them on behalf of Joshua McFadden."

"That's how it was *supposed* to work. But that was verbal. We've never come across anything like this before, so we have to take the judge's written decree as valid."

Luke's face heated. "But he was ill. He wasn't in his right mind."

"That's exactly why you should have no problem in dissolving this union, when a new judge arrives."

Genevieve's voice was shaky. "When will that be?"

"Who knows? There may be one on his way here already, in a natural course of events. One should have arrived in early spring, but we don't know what happened to him."

Luke rubbed his cheek. "Wonderful. Just wonderful."

"Or, the other option…"

Genevieve rose eagerly on tiptoe. "Yes?"

"When the quarantine's over, you two could travel out of the Yukon and see a judge on your own."

"That would take half a year," said Luke.

"Now," Genevieve demanded. "I want this settled now."

"I'm afraid that's not possible."

With frantic appeal, she addressed the clergyman. "Reverend, can you please help us?"

He adjusted his clerical collar and shrugged his shoulders. "Nothing I can do. Right from the beginning, I counseled you to wait until your groom returned. If you recall, I advised you to marry properly in the church. Not by a judge."

Genevieve groaned. Reverend Murphy was too far away to hear the grumble, but Luke heard.

"You young people are always in such a hurry," the reverend added. "I shall use your unfortunate situation as an example in my sermon on Sunday."

Genevieve gasped.

"Look at the bright side," hollered the commissioner. "The new judge will no doubt dissolve this marriage very quickly when he arrives. Or give you a divorce."

"Divorce?" She stumbled back a step. Yards of white silk pooled at her feet. "I haven't been properly married and you're talking of divorce?"

"Sorry, ma'am. On second thought, divorce is not something you'll have to trouble yourself with. It'll be out of the question because it's not like you'll be consummate—" The commissioner suddenly seemed to notice the inquisitive faces lining the boardwalk. He cleared his throat. "Divorce won't be necessary. It'll be a simple dissolution of marriage. Annulment. Whatever you want to call it."

And with that shocking assessment, the two men turned and walked down the boardwalk.

The remaining folks dispersed, whispering and shaking their heads. Gossip and rumor and scandal. Luke couldn't contain it.

"It'll run its course," he whispered to Genevieve, who was staring at them with mouth agape. "They'll tire of it."

"What am I supposed to do when Joshua finds out I got married without him?"

"Well, no one knows quite where he is. He's off panning for gold in the middle of the wilderness. It's not likely he'll hear until he returns to town. And then you'll be here to explain it to him directly."

"So will you."

"Right." Luke gulped. "So will I."

They strode to the trees. He lifted her two suitcases, watched her pick up her pup and waited for her to fall into step beside him. She hiked her wedding gown to her ankles. He glanced away at the impropriety of looking beneath her skirts.

"And how, Inspector Hunter, do you suggest we explain this to my real groom when we do see him?"

"I'm not sure. Hopefully the new judge will get here before Joshua does and clear up this mess." He felt his heart still pounding, and she looked out of breath. "And under the circumstances—" he tried to be humorous "—seeing that you're my wife, you might as well call me Luke."

Her eyes misted with tears. He'd never seen a woman look at him with more displeasure. It was a disquieting sensation and one he was unsure how to handle, for most women, in the heat of the night, looked at him as though they couldn't get enough.

Chapter Three

Wife.

Inspector Hunter...*Luke*...had called her his wife. The sound of it made Genevieve nauseous. How on earth was she going to explain this to her dear Joshua without making herself and Luke appear to be nitwits?

They trudged up the hill toward their cabin, the others slowly following. The weight of her wedding gown pulled at her waistline. The scooped neckline bulged open, and the gold chain she wore at her throat hovered above her breasts.

"Luke!" called a pretty brunette woman from the board-walk.

When he halted to look, Genevieve did, as well. She had to glance past his wide shoulders, in full red uniform, to get a good view.

The first thing Genevieve noticed was her striking hat. Sunshine caught the brim of the green felt, tipped at the front and embroidered with colorful little birds. Pigeon feathers, tucked smartly at the side, whirred in the breeze. Everything about her said money. The matching green cape, the leg-of-mutton sleeves of her crisp white blouson, the abundant use of fabric in her green wool skirt. She would have made a very elegant, high-society woman, save for the overly done rouge and painted eyes. Nonetheless, the pretty brunette woman turned the heads of every man in the vicinity.

"Penelope, how are you?" Luke called.

Was that a smile gracing Genevieve's so-called husband? The scar beneath his eye nearly disappeared with his grin. The done-up woman got a smile from the inspector, but in the hours Genevieve had spent with him, she hadn't got a one?

The woman's painted cheeks pinched with alarm. "I just heard. How are you feeling, luv? Have you got any symptoms?"

"No, I'm fine."

"Thank goodness." She cast her eyes at Genevieve. Her gaze traveled down and then up the silky wedding gown. "Tell me the other rumor isn't true, luv."

Luke stammered. "Um…yeah." He set down the suitcases. "Let's see…how can I explain this?" He scratched his dark cheek, standing a foot above Genevieve, his razor-sharp eyes searching hers for assistance.

She pursed her lips together, determined to say nothing. Let him talk his way out of this.

Two men on the boardwalk leaned over the rail, watching and listening as if this was some sort of staged play.

"Can you or can you not make it to dinner this evening?" asked his Penelope.

"I'm afraid I can't." Luke took a deep breath and planted his hands on his slim hips. "I'm married."

Penelope burst into a chuckle of humor, disbelieving at first, then simmering when she saw neither Luke nor Genevieve smiling.

"How do you do," said Genevieve, nodding with a smile. "I'm his wife."

Penelope gasped. She turned and stumbled. Luke tried to stop her from fleeing by calling out, but she continued running.

"Penelope! It's not what you think! We can still see each other!"

Struck with an incredulous sense of insult, Genevieve reeled toward him. "I beg your pardon."

"Oh, we're not truly *truly* married. You know that. You're having a bit of fun at my expense. But this is a private matter you're ruining."

Genevieve snatched one of her suitcases. She clamped a fist on her skirts and whirled up the hill. "And I, in contrast, am having the time of my life!"

They entered the barracks without speaking.

It took her an hour in the cabin, alongside Aunt Abigail, Milly and Nugget, unpacking her suitcases into an armoire and arranging her things, before her temper abated. How could he possibly think this affected him more than her?

Genevieve folded her wedding gown neatly onto the top shelf of the armoire and sighed. She'd wear it again for Joshua, she told herself, trying to cheer up. She'd already placed her wedding bouquet above the fireplace mantel, so that everyone might enjoy its beauty and scent.

"I can't believe we have to suffer like this." Aunt Abigail heaved herself onto a lower bunk.

Milly shoved her flannel nightgown onto the upper bed above her mother. "This is so…unexpected…and dangerous. Not knowing who might get the measles next."

"It won't be you, Milly," said Genevieve. "Don't worry. None of us got close enough for the judge to breathe on."

"Except maybe you and the inspector."

When her mother glowered at her, Milly clamped her mouth. That heavy foreboding in Genevieve weighed her down again. She hadn't really gotten *that* close. And there had been a breeze swirling around them during the entire ceremony, pushing away any possible germs. Wasn't that right?

Wasn't it?

When the two other women left to join the men in the sitting room, Genevieve unbuckled her second suitcase. She lifted the flap and stared at the nightclothes intended for her wedding eve. The nightgown smelled of fresh white cotton. Pretty eyelet lace ruffled its neckline and hem. There was a new black corset and shimmering silk stockings.

Gently, Genevieve pulled out the corset. She'd saved for two months just to buy the raw silk fabric. It had taken her a whole day to insert the whalebone strips. The scooped neckline was low enough to show her cleavage, and when she'd sewn the tiny pearls along the cups of the bosom, she had hoped that dear Joshua would appreciate the time and care she'd taken to look her best on their wedding night.

Nugget barked beside her. The door creaked open as the pup jumped through it, and there *he* stood.

Luke. Staring at her as she held up the most intimate undergarment she owned.

The heat of her blush surged to the roots of her hair. Genevieve slapped the door closed, but not before she witnessed the sparkle of amusement in his face.

Ignore him.

She tried to, as she changed into more sensible clothing, but she couldn't rid herself of his image. Perhaps she'd have better luck if she stepped outside to catch a breath of fresh air.

Horses in a corral fifty feet from the cabin attracted her attention. Two mares were ripping at fresh grass in the corner when Genevieve hiked her worn-out cotton skirts and hitched her foot on the bottom rung of the wooden fence. She stroked the bay. So soft and warm.

A movement beside her caused her to jump.

Luke, dressed in denim jeans and white shirt, wearing his broad Mountie Stetson, hiked his boot next to hers.

She huffed. "I came here for some fresh air."

"Nice, isn't it?"

Obviously, he was too obtuse to catch her meaning, so she had to be more direct. "I was hoping to be alone."

"I'm sure you were."

"Who was the woman?"

"Penelope Wick."

"Your companion for the evening."

"Not anymore."

"I'm *sorry*."

"You don't sound it."

She burst out with the thought that had weighed on her mind for hours. "The paperwork was your responsibility."

"You're blaming me for this fiasco?"

"As a woman, I have no say in the paperwork or the proceedings. Joshua left it with you. You were to take care of it all."

"He left me that envelope. He wrote my name on the outside, and his note on the inside. It's not my fault the judge copied the wrong name onto the marriage certificate."

"Then whose fault is it? Mine?"

The fine line of his scar drew a ridge down his cheek. "It's the judge's fault."

"Don't speak ill of the dead. It's bad luck."

"Bad luck? How much more bad luck can we have?"

"Listen, I'm sorry you can't go out for dinner with your…your companion. Marriage can be such an inconvenience." She realized she was angry about her situation more than at him, but he wasn't helping matters.

"It's not the marriage that's stopping me. It's the quarantine."

She gasped. "You mean if we weren't quarantined, you'd still see her tonight?"

"Why not?" He reached into his shirt pocket and removed the certificate. "It's just piece a paper. Nothing more. Here, let me tear it up right now and we'll pretend this whole thing never happened."

She leaped for the page. "No."

Without effort, he held it above her head. She accidentally bumped her body into his, trying to maneuver. The touch of his biceps grazing her shoulders sent a rush of sensation through her limbs.

She panted. "Everything I've heard about your reputation is true."

He held the certificate higher.

Stepping back in defeat, she crossed her arms against her chest. Her everyday cotton corset, beneath her linen blouse, strained to contain her.

"If you tear it up, we'll have no chance of rectifying this situation. You'll put any further marriage of mine into dispute forever. And right now, I wouldn't be able to *stomach* the thought of being married to…to…"

She whirled to the feeding mares.

"You might not think a lot of me," he said with restraint, "but Joshua did. He trusts me."

"For all the good it did him."

"He's got a good sense of humor. At least he did have once. Maybe he'll understand."

"What do you mean, did have?"

He blinked, then ran his hand along the railing. "I mean…maybe he'll laugh at this."

She uncrossed her arms and stepped closer, ignoring the sheer size of him. "You think this is funny? Joshua won't, I assure you. He'll react in the same manner as any red-blooded man would. More so, I'm told, because of his Irish temper."

Luke's mouth tightened, as though he found it difficult to respond. She noticed the wind puffing through the dark hair at his temples. Late-afternoon shadows crisscrossed his shoulders.

She turned and stomped away.

"Where're you going?"

"To get word to the cook to send up the bottles of wine we set aside for the reception. Wine for all. It's my wedding night, and I intend to drink myself out of this nightmare."

Five hours after dinner and a dozen wine bottles later, Luke peered up at the springs on the bunk above his head.

Sounds of insects buzzing and chirping outside filtered through the open window. The men in the spacious room with him were sprawled out on their various bunks, their suitcases kicked beneath their beds as they snored. Two of the Cliffton brothers snored the loudest. Clyde Orman lay silently facing the other wall. Kirk Kendall rolled his body beneath his sheets, trying to cram his muscled weight into his tight cot. Luke wasn't having any better luck fitting into his. He couldn't stretch out to full length or his feet would hang over the edge.

Sunlight poured into the room, even from around the cracks of the curtains. They were so far north, now, at the end of July, that daylight lasted twenty-one hours of every day. There were only two or three hours during the middle of the night where the sky remained an unusual twilight blue. There was never complete darkness. Luke had grown accustomed to it, but it drove some people mad.

Abigail and Milly Thornbottom had retired to sleep when the men had, but Genevieve had insisted she wanted to take a walk on the grounds. Alone at night was the best time to avoid the other Mounties, seeing how she was quarantined. A fence around the outpost ensured her safety.

Physical safety, thought Luke, but her inner tension was more worrisome.

His own wasn't much better, but he could hide it.

Couldn't he? The guilt of letting down his friend washed over Luke. How could he have been so careless to let this happen?

But there was nothing Luke or Genevieve could do about this ludicrous marriage until a new judge arrived, so she might as well sit back and let the time pass.

Maybe he should tell her; maybe it would help ease her disquiet if he stated it aloud. Working silently, he rose to sitting position, pulled on his jeans and boots, grabbed his leather duster at the back of the door, and walked out into dimming sunshine.

It was close to midnight, and the night was chilly.

He found Genevieve sitting on a swing tied beneath a cottonwood, curled inside a sheepskin coat.

"Can't sleep?" he asked, taking the swing next to her.

"Guess not."

Waning sunlight outlined the gentle curve of her cheeks. The scent of summer grass and wild raspberries mingled between them. He planted his boots on the hard ground and rocked back and forth, easing his shoulders sideways between the ropes to make them fit.

"Look, I'm sorry. I'm sorry you're stuck here with me."

Her dark lashes flickered on her cheeks. The swell of her lips rose as she spoke softly. "I should apologize. I took my frustrations out on you. You don't want this any more than I do."

He murmured in sympathy.

His heart tugged for her. At the beginning of the proxy ceremony, her optimism for a future with Joshua McFadden had shone in her eyes. Now there was nothing but sadness.

At least she'd changed out of the wedding gown. The clothing she wore now was not nearly as affluent. Her skirt pockets were well worn at the edges—obviously from years of use. Her blouse had a collar that was nearly threadbare. This was the clothing she'd picked out for her honeymoon with Joshua? This was the best she had?

"I came out here," he said, "to tell you we can't change what happened with the judge. But we can try to come to terms with what we're going to do in the future."

"Which is?"

"We ride this out. We wait for the new judge. As soon as he arrives, we cooperate as quickly as we can to dissolve this thing."

She smiled then, very softly. Her skin sparkled and changed her entire demeanor.

"Yes, well, that is a sensible plan." She rose, still smiling, as if wanting to make amends. At some point in the evening, she had braided her hair into a single plait. It rolled down her shoulder as she held out her hand. "I suppose we should shake on it. That we both agree to cooperate as quickly as we can."

Whatever wine she'd consumed had long ago left her. She was steady on her feet, although a tinge of red wine graced the air around her. He liked the scent. It mingled with the scent of the grass and her laundered clothes.

Rising to his feet, he took her hand in his. Her grip was warm and soft but decisive as she squeezed.

She wobbled, and he realized the effects of the wine hadn't left her.

"Easy now. You've probably had a bit much."

"Just three glasses."

"But at the end of an exhausting day." He noticed an empty wineglass at the base of the tree.

"So you promise, then?" she asked.

He responded to her grip with a gentle shake. "Promise. We'll call a truce." Then for some unknown reason, he swooped down to kiss her cheek. Innocently, like a brother to a sister.

But she stepped aside unexpectedly, maybe thinking the handshake was over, and his lips landed on her throat instead.

Warm velvet skin met his. A delicious sensation burned through his body. He moved his lips slightly and inhaled the scent of her. Unable to stop himself, he grazed her with his lips again. The pulsing hollow at the base of her throat pulsed against his mouth.

A shock of want surged through him. His breathing stopped. His pulse tripled.

He felt her breath at his ear. A soft gasp. A whisper of no.

Raising his head from her flesh, he gazed into her green eyes. The heady sensation of his lips against her throat left him yearning for more.

Speechless, she stood frozen with her mouth an inch away from his.

He couldn't have kissed her in a more intimate place than if he'd kissed her naked breast.

The thought of her naked breasts made his senses roar. Cold night air filtered through his lungs. A songbird called above them. The taste of her skin lay moist on his mouth. The smell of rich red wine permeated his air.

She said nothing.

The accusations were ripe in her gaze.

What have you done? she seemed to ask.

Do you feel it? came his reply.

It was something about the night, he told himself. Not something about her.

It was something *he* was lacking, mourning the loss of an intimate evening with Penelope.

It was not this woman before him.

Bursting with the perception of a man who'd just felt and witnessed something extraordinary, he disengaged his hand and took a step back. He was married to *her?*

Genevieve dropped his hand, as though it was a heavy anchor, and rubbed her throat at the spot he'd kissed. She was trying to erase his touch, he thought, and as she raced back to the cabin, he wondered how on earth he might do the same.

Chapter Four

What sort of a man kissed a woman's throat upon a first meeting? Of all places, how could he kiss her there?

Sitting at the crowded breakfast table in the officers barracks the next morning, Genevieve shoved a spoonful of porridge into her mouth. She avoided looking directly at *him*. The notion that Luke Hunter assumed she would be another one of his willing women in bed left her speechless. Let him have his pretty Penelopes, or his…his buxom Belindas, or his audacious Annabelles…he would never have *her*.

Encased in long skirts and a country blouse, Genevieve reached over the rough wooden table for a jar of honey. She dabbed another spoonful onto her oats, enjoying the scent and flavor of the golden liquid.

Since it was Sunday, Uncle Theodore had read from the Bible earlier, and it had given Genevieve some comfort. But she was still praying this ordeal would be over soon.

In the far corner at the cast-iron stove, pouring himself a cup of coffee, Luke turned his head in her direction.

Beneath his discomforting scrutiny, she lowered her eyes to her meal and rotated on the hard bench seating.

Did his bold maneuvers actually thrill Penelope?

Probably yes, thought Genevieve, munching on her oats. She recalled the lady's painted, puckered mouth and how it had sprung to life with a special smile directed at Luke. Penelope likely thought his advances were exceedingly pleasurable.

The bench rocked as Aunt Abigail heaved in beside Genevieve with a platter of beef hash and two fried eggs. She glanced with approval at the full plates her husband and slender daughter carried as they nudged in around the end of the table. Food was more plentiful at the Mountie barracks than most other homes in town, but just like everywhere else, most of the Mountie food came from canned and dry goods that had been trekked over the mountains, or hauled in along the natural waterways.

Genevieve took a moment to look around the dining room, trying to get to know the faces and recall the names.

Sunlight flooded through the log frame window of the massive room, spilling over the shoulders of the folks making their way around a table and its colorful spread of food. One part of the room, roughly twenty feet by forty feet was used for dining. The other side, equally large, was set up as a cozy parlor. There were some luxuries for the officers that enlisted men likely didn't have in their quarters: two plush Oriental rugs, a chiming wall clock, magazines from London and Toronto, two horsehair sofas and five soft leather wing chairs. The items had likely been delivered by the narrow steamboats, the paddle wheelers.

Their wedding party always seemed to subdivide into the same groups. Luke and his young apprentice, Weston, who were standing by the coffeepot. The three Cliffton brothers yawning at the opposite end of the table. Milly,

Aunt Abigail, Uncle Theodore, Genevieve and Nugget, who formed their own group at this end. And then the two men who seemed the loners, drifting in among the others whenever it suited them: Clyde and Kirk.

"Apparently," said Aunt Abigail, "the whole town's talking about it."

"About what?" Genevieve turned to her aunt.

Aunt Abigail's voice dimmed to the wattage of a candlelit whisper. "The impropriety of marrying a stranger. The *wrong* stranger."

"Oh." Genevieve plopped the tip of her spoon into her porridge and mixed, going over and over the missteps of yesterday and still coming up with frustration and disappointment.

"How do you know they're talking, Mother?" Milly chewed daintily on a piece of bacon. Her dark brown hair hung loosely over her slender shoulder.

Uncle Theodore reared back his head, white ponytail curving down his spine as he stared at his full platter of scones and jarred fruit, as though wondering what to target first. "I overheard the cook tellin' the stable man. Kirk Kendall."

With a flutter of nerves, Genevieve glanced up at the thick-necked Mr. Kendall, who was collecting his tray of food at the far end. Did it matter what he thought of her? He didn't even know her.

Aunt Abigail patted Genevieve's arm and gave her one of those sentimental looks. "Never you mind. What do they know? This whole town is full of gossips. I've never seen the likes of such speedy mouths. Honestly. We made the right decision in choosing Joshua for you. Let them all talk about that."

"Amen," said Uncle Theodore.

Milly smiled and lowered a scrap of smoked bacon to the puppy beneath the table.

The porridge in Genevieve's throat stuck like a lump of glue. She tried to swallow past it, and wished her coffee cup wasn't empty.

"Coffee?" Luke walked up from behind, holding the tin pot.

Nugget whipped out from beneath the table and bit the tip of Luke's cowboy boot.

The boot was longer than the puppy.

Luke shook his foot, trying to maintain his balance while gently shrugging off Nugget. "Get off my leg. Watch out, this coffee's hot."

Nugget growled and continued to attack the boot.

"She likes the shiny tip." Genevieve darted around Luke's long legs for Nugget, but missed. "She's teething and bites into everything she sees."

Luke held still while Genevieve maneuvered. He was dressed in denim this morning. Blue denim pants, blue cotton twill shirt. All two hundred pounds of muscle. All blue. All man.

Genevieve's throat ached, looking at him. She grabbed hold of Nugget. "Got her." She placed the pup onto her lap and brushed away the loose hair from her own flushed face.

Luke peered at the lengthy black braid that flipped over her shoulder and tumbled across her bosom. Why did he make her feel so self-conscious of everything she wore? Right down to her undergarments. At least the threadbare cotton against her breasts felt warm and familiar and comforting this morning.

Drifting away into explicit thoughts, she wondered how many women he'd disrobed in the past. How his hands might feel upon her naked skin. How he might look, fully unclothed and waiting beneath rumpled sheets. Would he be a good lover?

"Hold it up, please," said Luke, cutting through her secret images.

She bristled with the reminder of where she was and how inexcusable her thoughts were. She shoved her cup upward and he poured steaming coffee into it. She nodded in thanks and refused to look at him as he moved on, instead asking the Cliffton brothers to pass the mound of sugar from their end of the table.

Vince, the gentleman with the gold pocket watch who was the finest dressed of the three, in neatly pressed shirt and cravat, handed it to her.

"Are you done with it?" she asked, desperately trying to pretend she was as interested in sugar as she was in Dr. Hunter's love affairs.

"Please go ahead, I'm not partial to sweets." Was he subtly smiling at her?

She took the sugar and minded her own affairs. Nothing like a little sugar to perk one's spirits. Although no amount of sweets could overcome the difficulty she had in grasping the outrageous nature of her circumstance.

Married to the wrong man.

Would it be in the newspaper? Under what headline?

Idiot Bride Mistakenly Weds Stranger.

Or perhaps, Dimwitted Man and Idiot Woman Say "I Do" as Judge Falls Down Dead.

"Are you all right?" Luke stared at her from across the table. He'd finished pouring coffee and had a forkful of scrambled eggs poised to enter his mouth.

Genevieve nodded. She brought her linen napkin to her

mouth, avoiding Nugget's open jaws on her lap, and dabbed the side of her mouth.

Mr. Kendall chewed on bacon. "She's just enjoyin' your honeymoon, Luke. It's not every day that a bride spends it with ten other people."

Well, didn't that wisecrack set off everyone's bells.

Stifled laughter grew deeper. Smiles turned into chuckles, chuckles into snorts, and Genevieve's face burned with humiliation.

She was supposed to have married another man. One who was more suited to family life. One who didn't have the reputation of being a wild and unencumbered bachelor.

But would her real husband look as provocative, naked in her daydreams?

When she finally dared to look at Luke, he drew back his lips into a sullen line and simply mouthed the word *sorry*.

Sitting across the table from her, Luke reminded himself after the laughter died down that Genevieve belonged to Joshua. Heaven help Luke when the jilted man returned.

If the shoe were on the other foot, and it was Luke who'd left Genevieve in another man's care for the proxy wedding, how would he respond to the accidental marriage?

Like any red-blooded man, he supposed, just like Genevieve had said.

Accident or no, Luke was married to the striking black-haired woman in the clinging lace blouse and black cotton skirt. Her large green eyes shimmered with the reflection of sunlight, and the disappointment of being teased by Kendall.

There wasn't much more Luke could do except apologize. And...what had happened to him last night with that kiss? Had it been an accidental slip, or wishful thinking?

Had he been sexually overpowered by the friendliness of her smile, the high cheekbones, slender curve of her jaw, the proud way she walked even though she dressed as though she didn't have a nickel in her thin pocket?

How on earth could he be so drawn to a woman completely different from anyone he'd ever courted? Most of the women he fell for…well, dressed differently. They dressed in a way that captured a man's eye from fifty paces. They talked differently, too. More direct…more focused on what *he* said than in trying to communicate how *they* felt.

For God's sake, Genevieve was his friend's intended wife.

Bursting with the vow he'd made to Joshua to look after her, Luke turned his attention to his breakfast. He gulped the rest of his meal, then rose and headed for the door.

"When you're done with your breakfast," he told the group, "I'd like you all to join me outside."

"What for?" asked Orman from the corner. "Need some help out there?"

"We're going to discuss how we'll pass the time during quarantine."

Folks groaned. Luke left the cabin, but not before he noticed Orman helping Genevieve up from her seat. Was every man in the room enamored with her? Why wouldn't they be? She was a pleasure to the eye. Women—especially women like her—were rare in the Klondike.

"Last month," Orman said to her as Luke was walking through the door, "I paddled for an hour upstream to a new roadhouse, just to be served a cup of coffee from a woman's hands. And you have such lovely hands."

Luke didn't wait to hear the rest. He stepped into morning sunshine. His spurs jangled with his long stride. The sky was clear, and so his boxy shadow fell crisply to the ground.

When the others joined him, he gave his orders. The men would tend to the horses. The animals would be in no danger of measles, since the illness couldn't affect them. Luke knew the men would enjoy stretching their muscles, pitching hay and exercising the animals. There would be firewood to chop, and the odd chore of fixing a wagon wheel, or carpentry to be done.

The women would tend to the vegetable gardens, hoeing and weeding. There would be laundry to wash, hang and iron. The cook would handle most of the meals, but both men and women would be responsible for cleaning up.

Genevieve listened with an eye turned toward Nugget, keeping watch as her puppy raced up the hill.

She entranced him. A gentle breeze blew up from the river, hugging her black cotton skirt against her thighs, pressing her creamy lace collar to her throat, and pressing her full sleeves against the curve of her upper arms. The smooth lines of her body were silhouetted against the slope. A grass-covered mountain ridge formed her backdrop.

She was luscious. Her mere presence sent his mind whirling in the wrong direction. And his blood throbbing.

He was lecherous.

Trying to control himself, Luke walked over to a pile of shovels, gripped one, but then recalled the taste of her throat. Sweet and soft and oh so very feminine.

He plunged his shovel into the vegetable patch, willing his body to behave. Their quarantine would be over in less than two weeks' time.

Thirteen days. All he had to do was stay away from her for thirteen days.

* * *

"It's a shame that a young woman, with such a privileged background like yourself, has to stoop to such mundane tasks." Aunt Abigail wrenched another weed from among the onions and stood up to face Genevieve, roots in hand.

Privileged? Genevieve? Hardly.

Genevieve kneeled into the dirt, her eyes shielded from the late-afternoon sun by the brim of her beautiful straw hat. The sun's rays heated her shoulders. She still delighted in the fabric she'd chosen to trim the hat. A wide band of gathered cotton was anchored at her throat—a rich green paisley with teeny white flowers that complemented her skin tone. When she'd made the hat three months ago, she'd envisioned wearing it for the first time in front of her husband, perhaps in a vast garden of their own, stepping outside a grand home bought by Klondike gold.

Instead, she was on her knees in the hot sun, being watched by a group of strangers who were watching each other for signs of spots, and one particular Mountie who spoke to her only when he wanted to direct her to a new task.

Or perhaps the single men were watching her and Milly for different reasons. Mr. Orman, the jeweler, was particularly attentive to Genevieve.

"How's the sun over there?" he hollered to her from outside the stables.

"Hot!"

What a daft question.

The smell of the earth hit her nostrils. Lichen and moss and purple fireweed clung to the mountain slopes as far as she could see. Beyond the edge of town, past the boardwalk and the painted canvas signs—Shaving Parlor, Eldorado Saloon and Laundry Done Here—hawks circled the hills.

The garden had been seeded more than a month ago by the other Mounties. Genevieve didn't mind weeding the onions and garlic bulbs. It gave her something to do. She was amazed to learn that onions, dirt cheap in Montana, were worth a fortune here because of their ability to fight scurvy. The garden was heavily fenced to avoid theft of the precious vegetables. She'd been told scurvy was a common ailment that attacked the gums and teeth of mountain men and gold miners, who survived on nothing but the game they caught all winter. She hoped Joshua had never suffered from it.

The inspector—Luke, if she could grow accustomed to the name—was busy tending to the horses behind the stables. Men scattered about him. He stood beside a gorgeous gray stallion that looked almost purple in the sunlight, with its striking black mane and tail rustling in the breeze. Luke lifted one of the stallion's hind legs— inspecting horseshoes. He looked primitive himself, sleeves rolled up past his muscled and hairy forearms, thick thighs wrapped in denim and braced to withstand the power of the horse, the black stubble of his jaw in bad need of a shave.

Lord have mercy, he was her husband. Her stomach dipped in another bout of nerves. Her skin burned with her racy thoughts. A man who no doubt loved to share his bed.

Frustrated by the heat, she reached the end of her row of onions and started on a row of garlic sprouts.

To top off her burdensome day, her aunt and uncle were wickedly twisting the facts of her life.

"Your mother always told me you were destined for greatness," Aunt Abigail said.

Genevieve lowered her lashes and hoped Luke couldn't overhear. "She did?"

"Mmm-hmm. And your father always predicted you'd marry a rich man. That's where we come in." She laughed and nudged her husband with her heavy arm.

The blow nearly sent thin Uncle Theodore falling over his row of corn. Bracing himself against his hoe, he glanced at his niece. "Sure doesn't seem right, you two young ladies having to work so hard."

Milly, bent at the waist, walked along the corn row beside him, yanking at the obnoxious grasses that were fighting to take control of the vegetable patch.

"I don't mind, Pa. I'd rather be outdoors than in. And later, Weston's going to show me how to saddle a horse."

"Hmm," said her father. "You best stay away from the men."

"But how will I learn how to handle a horse?"

"I'll show you what you need to know."

"When, Pa?"

"After dinner."

Milly smiled, unable to contain her pleasure. "And then maybe Dr. Hunter can show me how he tends to the animals. Apparently, there's a horse that's not feeling well."

"I said you best stay away from the men."

Bending over the garden, Milly braced her hand on her knee. "Genevieve can come with me, then. We'll go together and we'll be safe from…from anyone's attention."

Genevieve startled at the thought. "I'm not so sure."

"Please come. It'll be such a pleasure. You adore animals. Why, just look at how much you're attached to that little dog."

Nugget yelped around her skirts and Genevieve laughed at the muddy condition of her paws. "How can one little pup get so dirty so quickly?"

Nugget barked with delight at the attention.

For the first time in twenty-four hours, the first time since Genevieve had said her marriage vows, she felt all right. Decent, even. Optimistic. For golden sunshine was pouring down on her, Nugget was wagging her tail, Milly was delighting in the surroundings, and perhaps the quarantine would end up totally without merit. Perhaps the judge was the sole victim, and none of them here would be touched by the fatal disease.

The others turned their attention to the garden again, while Genevieve stood captivated by the view.

She'd never get over the breathless beauty of the Yukon. A vast ridge of mountains crisscrossed the country, their bulky dark shadows contrasting with the sky's intense blue. The rich vegetation had surprised her. She had predicted the Yukon would be barren, perhaps even filled with ice and snow year-round, but it was nothing of the sort.

An array of trees sculpted the mountains—spruce, scrub pine, willow, aspens and cedar. Shades of green grasses and wild mountain flowers competed for her eye—jades, emeralds and deep moss-greens. It was as though an artist had painted an oil canvas before her, using only shades of green and blue. Even the rivers were an unusual turquoise color, due, she'd been told, to the silt runoff from mountain glaciers. Trapped specks of silt in the waters caught the sunlight and spun it into turquoise.

Alaska had been just as magnificent.

On the ship, they'd sailed along her jagged coastline, with ice-laced mountains so tall and pointy they pierced the clouds. Bottomless ocean waters had swirled below them, and whales, otters and fish had filled every eyeful.

But the air is what struck her most. The richness of the

oxygen felt heavy in her lungs. It carried the fragrance of flowers and trees she'd never seen in such abundance, and frigid rivers that churned up heady scents from the bottom of century-old riverbeds.

"Genevieve?" Milly called her name.

Genevieve felt a nudge on her elbow.

"Cousin?" Milly said again.

Genevieve stepped out of her mental paradise and squinted at the youthful face framed by rich dark hair. "What is it?"

Milly nodded toward the stables, where two armed Mounties were approaching the cedar fence. They stopped forty feet away.

Luke left the side of his gray stallion and shouted to them. "What news do you bring?"

The muscles in Genevieve's stomach tightened into a rock of nerves. The news wasn't good. She could see it in their grim expressions. She could see it in the way Luke burst forward, broad shoulders tipped toward the men as if ready to do battle.

One of the Mounties shouted, "Another case of confirmed measles. And one other person who came in contact with the judge. Two women, to be precise."

Genevieve caught her breath. The disease she'd hoped wouldn't spread was here at their door.

Chapter Five

Standing beside his restless stallion, Luke watched with a curiosity that consumed him. The spread of this nasty illness was growing bigger by the minute, and he wondered where it would end. The stallion snorted and lowered his head to graze. The weight of hooves rumbled through the ground beneath Luke's boots. Luke shifted his weight; his spurs clattered. He stared as an unsmiling, smartly dressed woman in her early fifties walked gingerly through the pathway between the stables and barracks. Her face was covered in tiny reddish-brown splotches and she looked as though she'd been crying. The judge's housekeeper. Miss Greta Norris.

Knowing how close she'd been to the judge, Luke wasn't sure if she'd been crying due to his passing, or crying due to her illness and the resulting stress.

There was another, more familiar woman, dressed in a low-cut peasant's blouse and swirling calico skirt, sauntering behind her.

Good Lord. Penelope Wick.

Penelope wasn't covered in any spots. How had she come in contact with the judge?

Miss Norris glanced apologetically at the staring group, as though she was a tiger in a circus who'd just been summoned to do a trick but was unable to perform.

Penelope's look was more defiant. She had a fire in her eyes when she glared at him. Luke sighed. She was still annoyed at him for yesterday. Well, it wasn't his fault; he was still annoyed at the whole damn marriage situation himself.

For a moment, he wondered what Genevieve thought. He stole a glance in her direction.

Her cheeks grew flaming red at the sight of Penelope.

Oh, wonderful, he thought. Contending with measles was difficult enough, but trapping these two women together was an added complication he wasn't prepared for.

The two Mounties leaning over the fence watched Luke approach Miss Norris. She sniffed into a neatly pressed handkerchief. Her brilliant red hair was pulled tightly into a bun. She wore a stiff burgundy jacket with matching skirt, ironed with the heavy creases he was so accustomed to seeing whenever he'd dropped by the judge's house on Mountie duty.

In contrast, Penelope's long skirts and carefree white blouse swirled around her, catching the wind.

"I'm sorry for your loss," he said to Miss Norris. He rubbed the back of his neck beneath his blue denim collar. "I know how good the judge was to you."

A sheen sparkled in her clear eyes. "Fergus was a lovely man."

"I didn't see you at the funeral yesterday."

"I just couldn't…couldn't bring myself…"

It was a good thing she hadn't come, for half the town would now be in quarantine if they'd come in contact with her.

"Goodness gracious." Mrs. Thornbottom drew closer, leaning her weight against her hoe, fingers dirtied with mud. "You're as spotted as one of those South American lizards we saw once in a traveling show in Montana."

Genevieve pressed her fingers to her throat at the indelicate comment.

"How do you do," Miss Norris replied coldly to the aunt. Her haughty gaze lingered on the woman's hoe, as if to make a point that who was she to label anyone.

Mrs. Thornbottom, flustered by the slight, grappled for words.

Luke was watching the awkward moment, wondering how best to handle them, when Genevieve stepped forward. "I wish these were better circumstances, but welcome, Miss Norris. Somehow, I feel responsible for this whole matter. It was my wedding the judge was attending to when he collapsed and—and now the entire wedding party has to be quarantined."

The strain in Miss Norris's face lifted slightly.

Genevieve studied the woman's pretty suit. "Are you related to the judge?"

Luke wiped his sweaty palm on his thigh. "Sorry, I should do the introductions. This is…*was*—" he tilted his head at the slipup "—Judge Donahue's housekeeper, Miss Greta Norris. And I think you all know Miss Penelope Wick."

Mrs. Thornbottom reeled back slightly, narrowing her eyes at the older woman. "Housekeeper?"

Luke, too, had always been surprised at how done up Miss Norris was, as if there was more to her relationship with the judge than employer to subordinate. There had always been a warmth to the way Fergus and Greta exchanged glances when she'd served Luke and the judge coffee; a pleasing smile when she'd handed Fergus his wool coat for the courthouse; a lilt in the judge's voice when he'd summoned the housekeeper by her Christian name.

"I've been working for Judge Donahue for a year and a half," she said to the others.

Turning quiet, Genevieve fiddled with the waistband of her skirt, glancing at Penelope.

"You're welcome here, too," Genevieve told her. "I'm sorry about our conversation yesterday. It was a long day and I'm afraid the strain was showing."

Penelope nodded. At that, Genevieve stepped back to stand in line with her cousin Milly and Uncle Theodore. Apparently, she'd said all she intended to, Luke surmised.

He scrutinized the two newcomers, Penelope so eager to see him, Miss Norris trying to hide her sobs. "How are you ladies feeling, physically?" he asked.

Miss Norris ran her hand along the shiny buttons of her jacket. "I'm tired. The rash is itchy, I'm afraid," she said, scratching her chin, "but other than that, I don't seem to be too affected."

Penelope looked at Luke directly. "No sign of any illness. I don't think I should even be here."

"Why are you here?" asked Luke with concern.

Penelope smoothed her gaping neckline over the swell of her bosom. Luke tried not to stare, but felt the temperature rise at the back of his neck when he became aware Genevieve was watching for his reaction to Penelope's lovely chest.

"I served the judge drinks three nights ago. At the casino."

"Are you sure you're fine?"

Penelope's shoulders slackened at the tenderness in his voice. He prayed she wouldn't get the illness.

"Yes, thank you, luv," she said softly, only for his ears.

His luck hadn't been very good with this wedding. He and Penelope hadn't even courted once. He'd been looking forward to last night's dinner with her, to get to know her better. And perhaps more. And now they'd have to wait to be alone.

"What about the others who must've come in contact with the judge on that same night?"

Penelope glanced at Vince. "Well, the boss is here already. The judge dined privately that evening, in the private room, so I don't believe he came in contact with anyone other than us."

Luke turned to Vince, who nodded in agreement.

"I see," said Luke.

Nugget came racing from her shady spot beneath the trees to land at Genevieve's feet. She picked up the pup and wedged her onto her curvy hip. Luke eyed the gentle swell of her skirts. A physical awareness rippled through his body.

When he quickly turned away, this time Penelope was watching his reaction to Genevieve. The hairs on the back of his neck grew cold.

This was how it was going to be, then?

Being volleyed between two women for two weeks?

Normally, being volleyed between two women wouldn't bother him a bit; in fact, he'd rather enjoy it. But this... being trapped between...a would-be mistress and a would-be wife...would be insufferable.

Luke cleared his throat. "Genevieve, could you show these two ladies their quarters?"

"Me?"

"Yes. You. Please."

Fumbling, Genevieve led them toward the barracks. "Right this way, Miss Norris...Miss Wick."

"No need for such formality," said Penelope. "Simply Penelope will do fine."

The men around them smiled. She was a woman who was well appreciated.

Genevieve stomped past Luke, pup in arms, biting down on the side of one lip and looking as though she was walking toward her gallows.

Well, thought Luke, she'd have to make the best of things. It was damn hard for him, too.

The five women paraded past. The men openly admired the lineup as they walked back to the stables, leaving Luke alone with the two Mounties.

Luke turned toward the fence and interrupted Constables Enscott and Morgan as they stared at Penelope's receding backside.

Luke cleared his throat. "Anyone else affected by this?"

The younger constable, Enscott, shook his head. "On the housekeeper's side, no. She said she hasn't been feeling well for a few days and spent the time in her quarters. Said she did a lot of baking and cleaning, but saw no one other than the judge."

Luke nodded. "And Penelope?"

"Even though Miss Wick and Mr. Cliffton believe no one else at the casino came in contact with the judge, we're checking into it."

"Good. I didn't know the judge gambled."

"He didn't. Apparently, he sometimes ate at the casino restaurant."

"Ah, yes, one of the best chefs in Dawson. What about the two of you?"

"What about us, sir?"

"How close did you get to Miss Norris? And Miss Wick?"

"Maybe thirty or forty feet. We spoke to them from the sidewalk. They packed a bag each, and we took them around the countryside to drop them off here."

"Listen, this thing is spreading. There are bound to be more folks you'll be hauling into quarantine. Tell the commander we'll need to look for another house for quarantine, in case it's needed. Tell him I recommend the abandoned shack just past the wharf, on that deserted property."

"The old fish house?"

Luke nodded.

"Yes, sir."

"Have you found the original source for the judge's measles?"

"We think it was two gold miners who rode through here a couple of weeks ago. Miss Norris said they came knocking in the middle of the night, wanting the judge to write up some agreement between them for a gold claim."

"Did she get their names?"

"No, she didn't answer the door. The judge did. By their descriptions, we think they're the same two who turned up dead more than a week ago, the ones everyone was panicking about in the first place."

Luke rubbed his hand. "Then maybe this thing has been contained."

"Yes, sir."

"Be careful with the rest of your search."

The two constables left and Luke turned around and made his way toward the shack and the women, who had now reached the door of the barracks.

They didn't seem to notice him coming up from behind.

Squinting in the blue sunshine of high noon, Genevieve held the door. The sun's rays caught the back of her neck beneath the brim of her straw hat, at that delicious swell of flesh where the spine connected to the nape.

Miss Norris turned toward Genevieve and lowered her voice. "Is it true, my dear, you're married to that officer?"

The pink in Genevieve's cheeks intensified. Her eyelashes fluttered as though a piece of dirt had struck. She looked at Penelope, whose eyes had widened with dismay. Didn't the housekeeper realize he and Penelope were also suitors?

"I'm afraid we are married," Genevieve answered, "but I'm told it's something another judge can easily dissolve."

"Why Miss Norris," wailed Mrs. Thornbottom, obviously also unaware of the tense romantic situation, and that Luke was closing in behind them. "Genevieve would never in true life marry a man with *his* reputation."

Miss Norris leaned in. "Then it's best if you're never caught alone with him."

Both Genevieve and Penelope groaned, followed most distinctly by Luke. They all finally turned, noticed he was five feet behind them, and blushed to the base of their scalps.

Genevieve felt the barmaid's cool, assessing eyes on her back as she shoved her clothes aside in the armoire to make room for the added wardrobe. It was an uncomfortable feeling to be thrust together with this woman.

Genevieve wasn't really Luke's wife, but she felt stupid having to be polite to his lover. At least, she assumed they were.

"There you are, a full twenty-four inches." Genevieve's voice echoed into her hanging skirts and blouses. "I'm afraid that's all we get."

"It'll have to do then, I suppose. Thank you." Penelope wheeled around and unbuckled her fancy leather trunk. She'd brought a whole trunk full of clothing for only two weeks? Genevieve stood rooted to her spot by the sunlit window, curious to see what a woman of Miss Wick's stature carried in a personal chest of drawers. Things illicit? Perfumes and fancy lace corsets and silken underdrawers and perhaps even…even items that she might need in her line of work…personal toiletries and methods of controlling pregnancy. Genevieve turned away, shamed at thinking it.

Milly gasped at the sight of the opened trunk. A beaded gown came twirling out of the magical box, first to be placed in the armoire. A smartly cut hat, slender with ornate beading and sequins came next. High-heeled boots, five inches high, with an overlapping strap of leather and a multitude of covered buttons were laid into the bottom of the armoire.

Genevieve pressed a hand to her aching stomach. "Such beautiful things."

"Thank you."

"Where did you get them?" breathed Milly.

"Some were made especially for me. Others were imported from France."

Aunt Abigail stared, unimpressed. "You'll have no occasion to wear them here."

"I realize that."

"Then why on earth…?" Even Aunt Abigail didn't have the brazen quality needed to finish the question.

Why on earth would Penelope bring all her things here? To put on airs? Or sadly, perhaps, because they might be stolen if she left them behind where she worked and lived.

And what exactly was her line of work? She was a barmaid at the casino, but Genevieve wondered if she went one or two steps further.

Prostitution was illegal. Although Genevieve had heard

it whispered on the journey here that the Mounties generally turned a blind eye to the goings-on in the row of squalid homes known as Paradise Alley. There weren't enough lawmen in the Yukon to police everything, so they did what they could.

But by no means did Genevieve think Penelope was a…was one of those ladies. Joshua was Luke's friend, and that said more about Luke's character than anything. Also, Luke was a Mountie, for heaven's sake, an officer, a veterinarian who cared for animals. That type of man didn't correspond to a type who would use a woman like Penelope simply for one night of pleasure.

And why should Genevieve even care?

It was none of her business. Their situation—hers and Luke's—would soon be dissolved, and after she was married to Joshua, they might dine in the casino restaurant one night with Luke and Penelope, and share a round of laughter about it all.

Huh. That would never happen. She had nothing in common with this working woman.

Genevieve pivoted to fold her excess clothes neatly inside her luggage for later use. Penelope turned to watch her. She stood just as transfixed by Genevieve's clothing. While Genevieve draped her worn-out skirts over her arm, the other woman studied them as though she were getting an education in the proper attire for a proper lady.

Genevieve was so far removed from high society—if that's what the other woman thought—it was laughable. To look at her clothing was to see the genuine her.

Mended pockets, mismatched buttons, remnants of fabrics and colors from two seasons ago in London that she'd seen in catalogue illustrations. She was so far behind the times, to anyone who knew anything about clothing, that it was painful to display them. Even her new black corset, her honeymoon best, seemed embarrassingly homespun.

Bowing her head, she tucked the last of her five-year-old blouses onto the top of her skirts, above the hidden black corset, and quickly folded the flap to conceal the poverty.

Genevieve was mesmerized by his hands.

"Bring the brush down nice and slow. Nice and easy like this so you don't startle her." Standing in the stables, Luke groomed the beautiful bay as Milly and Genevieve watched. It was six hours later, nearly dinnertime, and Genevieve had been relieved when the other women—especially Penelope—had declined the invitation to see the stables.

Genevieve didn't wish to step too close to Luke, so she allowed Milly the front spot. She'd left the pup in the fenced-in area behind the barracks, away from the horses, for Nugget was liable to spook them. Genevieve shuffled in the fresh straw. The scent of newly pitched hay filled the air. In the cedar-rimmed stalls around them, six horses munched on their evening oats.

Animals were so simple. Their needs were transparent. All they wanted was fresh water and food, a dry space and some companionship.

Humans were much more complicated, she thought as she stared at Luke's angled back. His shoulder blades flexed beneath the fabric of his shirt. His forearms pressed toward the mare as he stroked her sides, conveying the opposite messages of tenderness and firmness all in the same touch.

Humans needed more. They needed to aspire to greater things.

Luke's hands, tinted golden by the sun, coaxed the fine beast to obedience. His long smooth fingers pressed downward into a gentle circle. Genevieve was mesmerized by the way his knuckles moved, synchronized in a lovely graceful sweep. Tiny gilded hairs accentuated the suppleness of his skin, the beautiful oval of his fingernails, the sensitive fingertips swirling down the mare. In the broad part of his hand, corded sinews and healthy veins flexed and twisted within the slender muscles.

The profile of his face portrayed the depth of his devotion. A straight nose, firm jaw, lips parted in concentration, a mellowing of the scar that marred his left cheek, then a swift furrowing of dark eyebrows and a keen focus to the dark eyes. All the muscles and nerves of his body worked in unison to guide his touch.

Oh, to be a horse beneath this veterinarian's loving hands.

Oh, to be Penelope.

"Would you like to try it?" Luke asked Milly, startling Genevieve into paying closer attention.

Milly smiled, wiped her fingers on her skirt and stepped forward to take the brush.

"That's it, slowly downward," Luke said. "The mare likes it. You're not only brushing her coat and removing burs and dust, you're massaging the muscles underneath."

Milly sighed. Genevieve stepped beside her to the right.

Young Weston, in his rugged stable clothes, was cleaning the empty stall next to theirs with a pitchfork. "Gettin' the hang of it, Milly?"

Milly giggled. "Yeah."

Her father scowled from twenty feet away as he hauled a saddle from the boards and dragged it over.

"Here." Uncle Theodore heaved it over their boards,

huffing and straining beneath the weight. "Anytime you're ready, Luke."

Luke helped to speed Milly by brushing the mare's tail. He then took the brush from her hand, set it down on his grooming tray and smoothed a blanket over the mare.

"When you've got it to this point, you can hoist the saddle," Luke instructed Milly.

"Mind if I show her?" her father asked.

"Sure, go ahead." Luke stepped back respectfully and allowed the father to carry on. "You look like you've handled a few horses in your time."

Uncle Theodore nodded and continued.

Feeling rather displaced, Genevieve stepped away and walked over to another horse. The gray stallion with the purplish mane and tail snorted in a friendly fashion.

"Well, hello to you, too." Genevieve patted the soft flank.

"Would you like to brush him?" Luke asked beside her.

Genevieve looked around his shoulder in time to see Milly and her father taking the bay outside.

Luke noticed them, too. "Every horse needs to be exercised as much as possible. Whether there's six feet of snow on the ground, or the fireweed's in bloom."

Genevieve hesitated.

"They're big animals with big muscles. They were born to run. Would you like to ride this one?"

"Not today."

"You can take him past the corral if you like. As long as you remain at the base of the hills where it's isolated, you can roam freely."

"Maybe another time." She didn't have much experience with horses.

Luke turned his attention to the gray coat. "He needs

brushing if you're interested. I've got to administer some medicine to that roan over there and I could use a spare set of hands on this one."

"I…I wouldn't mind." Her mind strayed. *Husband. Lord, don't even think of him in that way.*

Luke brought over his grooming tray, hooked it onto the boards and stayed to help her. Hadn't he said he was leaving?

She looked to his veterinary bag, propped in its position on the far wall. "What's wrong with the roan?"

"She cut her leg on a busted fence a few days ago. I apply a poultice every day to keep it from festering."

Genevieve glanced again at his suede bag on the wall. She wondered what other magical solutions he kept in there. A six-foot medicine cabinet sat tucked into the boards beside the bag. A lock on its door glinted in the light, and its heavy pine front was yellowed with exposure. Beyond the cabinet, a small hallway led to what looked like an office. She glimpsed the edge of a desk and lithographs of horses tacked to the walls.

She'd never met a veterinarian surgeon before. In fact, she'd only seen a medical doctor for *humans* twice in her life. Once when her mother got ill with pneumonia. The doctor couldn't save her anyway. The other time, when Genevieve had broken her wrist being chased and teased in school for wearing the same blouse and skirt a whole week running. That trip to the doctor to set the bones and the resulting medical fee had cost her parents any future clothing allowance she might have had, for the next year. Her parents' resulting argument had caused Genevieve to lose her sleep for a week. And it had caused her face to scorch with humiliation the following Monday at school when she had to wear the same, although newly laundered, clothing of the week before, the same garments that had initiated the whole incident.

Perhaps that's why she found such solace and pleasure in being a seamstress and milliner. One day, she'd make all the lovely clothes she could ever want.

"Use the large brush first," Luke told her, "then the finer ones."

"Okay." She wondered what Penelope was doing back at the shack. Likely enjoying her evening tea with the Cliffton brothers. A bit afraid of the large stallion, Genevieve stepped in tight, her skirt ballooning about her knees, her favorite, well-worn cotton blouse giving her the slack needed to move her arms and twist her torso up and over.

Luke pressed his hand on the horse's side. He was uncomfortably close, mere inches away, the sleeve at his shoulders grazing her soft cotton.

It felt silly. It felt very very silly to say so, but she felt at peace.

While she and Luke worked silently together, she noticed his hands were nearly twice the size of hers. Absently stroking the stallion, his fingers came within a breath of hers. Long and sturdy and full of strength. So very masculine and powerfully built compared to her slighter form. Her nails were trimmed neatly, and the soft hue of the sun from all the hoeing this afternoon had added color to her skin.

Luke's breathing suddenly fell in rhythm with her own. His chest rose, her lungs filled. He exhaled through his nostrils. *She* released it slowly through her mouth. And then he seemed to notice *her* hands, his face tilting as he followed her sweeping movements, his lips twitching in response to her gentle strokes.

He shuffled his positioning, his thigh perilously close to her own, all the time watching as though hypnotized by her touch.

A rising swell of emotion, unreleased tension, made it difficult for her to swallow. This was absurdly improper. For a man of Luke's reputation to be breathing so close to her ear. For her to be practically touching fingers with a complete stranger in a bed of straw. What would Penelope say?

"I better see to that roan," Luke finally whispered at her ear, staring at her gentle hands. "I better go."

Chapter Six

There was safety in being indoors, thought Genevieve, washing the dinner pots and pans two hours later in the barracks.

No decent woman should be caught alone with a man who had that mysterious gleam in his eyes, that open manner Luke had in speaking to her, of standing so mercilessly close when he shouldn't even be within reaching distance of a woman who belonged to another man.

Penelope might fall for his grooming techniques. Indeed, perhaps she had already. Perhaps Luke had shown the easily swayed Miss Wick how to brush the coat of his stallion in the same way he'd tried to enthrall her. Showing Penelope the way to hold the brush, how to massage the muscles beneath, all the while inching closer.

Uncle Theodore was so right to warn his daughter and niece to stay away from the men. It would be simpler. Men like Luke, who would eagerly court one woman while married—albeit accidentally—to another, obviously had one thing in mind for his…his women. How quickly to get them alone.

Here in the three-room barracks, it was practically impossible for Genevieve to be stuck with Luke alone. Here, thankfully, she wouldn't have the opportunity to study his agile hands or inhale the soapy scent of his shirt.

She blew the hair off her brow and lowered her fingers into cool, soapy dishwater.

She, Milly, Aunt Abigail and Miss Norris were nearly finished with the dishes while Penelope tended to the dessert. The aroma of fresh-brewed coffee and warm apple fritters wafted through the great room.

The men, including Luke and Uncle Theodore, had taken the dinner leftovers outside to feed the dogs. There was Nugget, plus a team of ten assorted dogs—huskies and one Saint Bernard used for winter dogsledding by the Mounties. Nothing went to waste in the Klondike, she'd quickly learned. Since the folks in quarantine couldn't pass down any germs to animals, Luke had told them, it was safe to continue with feeding them food scraps.

It was interesting that such a wayward bachelor had such considerable concern for his animals.

Perhaps the way he handled them was similar to how he handled women. Gentle hands, an easy caress, his undivided focus and an indescribable feeling that nothing else mattered at the moment than how the woman responded beneath his touch.

Embarrassed by the sexual nature of her thoughts, Genevieve glanced above the counter, through the square panes of the window, looking for distraction. But there he was again. Luke, speaking to the commissioner.

Ten yards separated the men. Both were rugged, one twenty years older with graying temples and a slight curve to his aging spine, the other as straight and thick as the cedar he stood beside.

Luke was handsome, no question, and she could see why women were drawn to him. Not only his dark, simmering stare, but the way he carried himself with pride and purpose. Even his scar seemed to disappear when he became enamored with his subject. She wondered, again, how he'd earned the mark.

Aunt Abigail's footsteps padded on the floorboards beside Genevieve. The older woman slid a dirty pot into Genevieve's dishwater, summoning her concentration back to her chores.

The Cliffton brothers had taken to playing cards—twenty-one and poker, and they had a big game slated for the evening.

Genevieve's special trunk, filled with her working supplies, had been delivered two hours ago by the young constables who'd escorted Miss Norris and Penelope earlier. The blue trunk with its scuffed silver buckles sat beside the fireplace.

Miss Norris rearranged the tea towel in her fingers to find a dry patch, then grabbed the cutlery.

"How long did you know the judge?" asked Genevieve.

Miss Norris blinked, as though surprised at the question.

From painful experience, Genevieve understood how welcoming it was to speak of newly departed loved ones. It was a comfort to share in their memory, not a burden. Most folks assumed death was too painful a subject to broach and therefore, out of kindness, avoided all talk of the departed.

"A year and a half," Miss Norris replied.

The enchanting tone in which she said it made Genevieve smile. "You got along well?"

Miss Norris glanced at Aunt Abigail, who was peering

over Genevieve's arm with a hint of suspicion creasing her mouth.

The housekeeper hesitated and lowered her enthusiasm. "Mostly." She rubbed a fork with her tea towel.

Still curious, Genevieve continued. "You started working for him as soon as you arrived?"

Miss Norris, with head lowered, bun slightly loosened at the back of her neck and red hair spilling, dragged her towel over a soup ladle and remained silent.

"It must be very difficult," Aunt Abigail said. "To be suddenly left alone with no job."

Genevieve winced at the clumsy comment.

Miss Norris puckered her mouth. Her brows twitched. Genevieve noted the two women were roughly the same age, so perhaps Aunt Abigail felt comfortable being this forward.

Her aunt didn't stop there. "But I'm sure you'll find more work in Dawson. Most of the town is male, and men are always looking for someone to cook and clean for them. You are a touch older than most, but you seem sturdy."

Miss Norris lowered her lashes to gaze at a pot lid, but not before Genevieve saw her eyes water. Any inroads Genevieve had made to comfort the woman were swallowed by her aunt.

Aunt Abigail, mouth still open, then turned to Penelope. Genevieve braced herself and tried to thwart the woman. "Aunt—"

Too late. Aunt Abigail barreled through her words. "You could learn to cook and clean, too, Miss Wick. It'd be a tad more honorable way to earn a living."

Penelope's rouged cheeks didn't move. "You have no idea, madam, how I earn my living."

Aunt Abigail colored profusely. She looked to her daughter Milly, who was listening.

"And furthermore, there is just as much honor in the way I lead my life as there is in the way you lead yours."

The older woman scoffed so loud the men at the far end of the table turned their heads. Genevieve cringed. How many more days of this?

Penelope opened her mouth, about to respond to Aunt Abigail's cry of indignation, when she looked over at Milly and must have thought better of it. Penelope closed her mouth, twirled on her high-heeled boots, her skirt shimmering in the evening light coming from the windows, and addressed the men. "Anyone for coffee?" She held up the pot.

"I'd like some," said Burt.

His brother and her employer, Vince, smiled at Penelope. "Here, too."

Mr. Kendall stared at her, beginning at her waistline and making his way up her peasant blouse. He held his tin cup. "Mmm-hmm."

Penelope smiled at the attention.

Genevieve turned away from the wolves and sloshed the brown dishwater into a bucket she'd take out later.

Just then, Luke burst through the door, bringing with him a gust of fresh-smelling Yukon air.

He was a brick of muscled denim.

Why did he always make his presence known in such a grand fashion? Why wasn't he here earlier, when she could have used his help in refereeing *his* Penelope and *her* Aunt Abigail?

Genevieve inhaled deeply and tucked her hands into her pockets, as if he might see them and remember how intimately close they'd come to his own.

When he kissed Penelope on the cheek, Genevieve felt awkward and hastily scrubbed the basin.

He made light conversation with the other men. She wondered what he'd think if he discovered how flirtatious they'd been with Penelope, and how she hadn't seemed to mind.

Genevieve rushed outdoors to empty her bucket. Upon her return, she took her coffee and apple fritter, being careful to sit apart from her husband.

Within the hour, she was seated in a rocking chair beside the rumbling heat of the fireplace to focus on her work.

She opened her trunk and searched through the fabrics—red felts, canvas ducking, black twill, plaid wool, sequins, buttons and thread. When her hand clamped around a partially constructed straw hat, she pulled it out and threaded a needle.

The four men playing twenty-one—Burt and Vince Cliffton, Mr. Kendall and Mr. Orman—called out their numbers.

"Fourteen."

"Seventeen."

"Twenty."

"Twenty-one," said Vince, chuckling.

His brother, Ripley, wasn't playing. He was reading a two-month-old newspaper from British Columbia. He looked over at his brother and scowled.

Miss Norris looked up from her ironing in the corner. Genevieve's aunt, uncle and cousin played checkers with Penelope.

Vince looked at his playing partners. "Are we going to sit around the table and play like a bunch of old women? Or do you fellas want to play for coin?"

Luke, standing at the fireplace speaking to Weston frowned. "There'll be no gambling on this site. You've got your license at the BlackJack Casino and that's where it'll stay."

"I'm losin' a lot of money as I sit here." Vince scoffed as Mr. Kendall dealt him a card he obviously didn't like. Or was he bluffing anger? The other players grinned at his misfortune.

"The casino's still open," said Luke. "I'm getting notes back and forth from the commander. Last I heard, you've got your dealers and your bartenders working full speed."

"It's not the same as me being there. Business is all about how clients feel. When they feel good, they spend more. And they feel looser with their chips when they see the owner. I got a note delivered from one of my men that business was down by two thousand dollars last night."

Genevieve gasped at the amount. Most men back home earned a dollar a day if they were lucky. Her aunt and uncle exchanged glances.

Luke pressed his hand to the mantel and peered at the roaring blaze. Above his dark head, Genevieve's wedding bouquet trailed down the fireplace's stone wall. The petals would dry nicely and be used for household fragrance later. Now, the flowers added a soft contrasting appeal against Luke's rugged charm.

"You make that amount of money just sweeping the spilled gold dust off the floor at the end of every night," Luke told him.

"Lost business is lost business."

"It's no easier for me," said his brother, Burt, fanning out his cards. "The Gold Digger Saloon doesn't have the staff Vince does. I've got to tend the bar myself to earn a living. And I can't do that here."

"You'll survive," said Luke. "Quarantine can't be helped."

Mr. Kendall heaved his burly shoulders as he leaned over the table and discarded two cards. "I'm not bloody well earnin' a paycheck, either, while I'm sittin' here playing blackjack."

The jeweler stared at his cards. "I was robbed two nights ago and there's no other place I'd rather be right now than protecting my store."

Luke addressed the jeweler. "I've ordered two of the Mounties to tour that area more often while you're in here. They're looking after you."

"Could have used their help two nights ago."

Luke sighed. "How about you, Ripley? And you, Theodore? Why don't you throw in your complaints, too?"

"Well," said Ripley, looking up from the newspaper and pinching the bridge of his spectacles, "I was supposed to head out for my new gold claim tomorrow morning. Can't see why I can't. It's in the middle of nowhere. I won't bump into anyone, and if I do, I'll tell 'em to stay clear of me."

"Can't take that chance," Luke said calmly. He peered at her Uncle Theodore, who leaned back in his wing chair, holding a black checker.

"Two weeks stuck in this place is a long time for a salesman, Luke. Every minute spent away from my ropes and brooms is another lost sale."

Luke took a moment to assess the group. Genevieve pressed a velvet ribbon to her straw hat and tried not to let his sultry gaze intimidate her.

"Okay, then," said Luke. "Everyone got it off their chest? How about the women? You ladies got any complaints?"

Aunt Abigail clicked her tongue. "What I miss most is going to the market. I like to do my own cooking, thank you very much, and pick out my own vegetables and cuts of meat. You never know if that cook of yours is trying to trim corners and save costs by giving us a poorer cut."

Luke's eyes widened as though he hadn't expected the blast. He said nothing in reply, and turned to Milly.

Milly patted Nugget's head and took her turn at checkers. "I miss my friends, Cora and Rose."

Luke turned to Penelope.

"I'm going to miss the excitement of the casino." She gazed pointedly at Aunt Abigail, who turned away flustered.

At last, he turned to Genevieve. "Your turn. Go ahead. Tell me you've got the worst deal here. Married to *me* and spending your honeymoon fortnight with a bunch of strangers."

She thrust her needle into velvet. "I can do my sewing just as easily in here as out there, waiting for Joshua to arrive."

Unlike the others, Genevieve had chosen not to complain.

His dark eyes flickered. He stared long and hard, and when the silence became unbearable, she looked away and lifted her trunk lid.

Trying to focus on her duties, she extracted mosquito netting she'd add to her hat. With its wide brim and bright sash, it would sell quickly. She could tell from Penelope's interested gaze that the design was appealing.

"Ah," said Aunt Abigail, eyeing it, too. "It's so much prettier than the hats available in town. All we have are men's work hats." She glanced at the animated faces. "My niece intends to open a milliner's shop. Men and women's hats, yes sirree. It's going to be the finest store this town has ever seen. As soon as Joshua comes back with all his gold."

Genevieve mumbled and tried to correct the impression her aunt was giving. "It's going to be a modest shop. I'll be working from my home—our home—for the first little while."

"You've got the hands of an angel," cooed Aunt Abigail.

Luke silently watched her the rest of the evening. Mostly, he conversed with Weston, explaining the finer points of heating horseshoes and branding cattle.

When her shoulders ached from working, Genevieve finally went to bed.

Her aunt snored from the far corner. Miss Norris sighed. Milly tossed beneath a quilt cover.

Nugget curled up at Genevieve's feet, creating a nice warm lump. Yet, perhaps it was Nugget's weight that made Genevieve's sleep fitful. Someone in the room got up and walked around. Or did Genevieve dream it? Later she dreamed someone was sitting on her chest, suppressing her lungs so hard she couldn't breathe.

Gasping, she awoke to early-morning sunshine.

Even though it was just past six, Genevieve was glad to rise. When she dressed and trudged into the kitchen, Luke was already there, seated at the table drinking coffee and reading the Monday morning newspaper. He'd asked the commissioner to send a man as soon as it came off the press. Mr. Orman was sleeping in a rocking chair by the gently crackling fireplace, his bowler hat shielding his face from view.

"Morning," Luke said to her.

"Morning." She poured herself a cup while he read from a selection of notes. "What are those?"

He fingered a coarse piece of paper. "Notes from the town doctor who's looking after us all. We've been communicating on paper. These are symptoms to watch for."

"Such as?"

"Fever. Sore throat. Runny nose. A red blotchy rash. There's not much we can do, though, to prevent measles if they're coming."

He continued reading his newspaper and she didn't interrupt. After fifteen minutes of quiet contemplation, looking out the window at the horses in the corral, she brought her coffee cup to the washbasin and noticed the morning headline.

Her stomach twisted.

Mountie Stuck in Quarantine with Another Man's Bride.

He saw her reaction and quickly folded it. He rose and tossed the paper into the fire. Flames ate it.

Mr. Orman didn't stir.

Luke nudged the man's boot. "Orman. Coffee's done."

The man didn't budge.

"Clyde. Your neck's going to be sore, kinked like that. Wake up and have a cup of coffee."

Genevieve watched Luke touch his shoulder.

The man's hat fell off, revealing a pale face.

Luke grasped a better hold of his shoulder and shook. Silence. Not a stir.

Pale himself, Luke reached down and placed two fingers at the man's throat. What was he doing?

Swiftly, Luke kneeled, gripped him by both shoulders and shook hard. "Orman. Orman."

Luke lifted the man's eyelid, and when it fell back with no response, he gulped and slowly rose. When he turned to look at her, her legs prickled. Her heart seemed to stall.

Oh, good Lord, no.

There was no safety in being indoors, either.

She waited for the words she knew were coming, and yet when they did, she was so horrified she dropped her coffee mug to the floorboards.

"The man's dead."

Chapter Seven

The sound of porcelain crashing on the floorboards rumbled up Luke's spine. Jarred by the noise, he withdrew from Clyde Orman and gave Genevieve a look of sympathy. She had to go through this again.

Trying to temper his own beating heart at the man's sudden death, Luke took a moment to absorb the situation.

There was nothing, unfortunately, he could do to help the jeweler. Orman had been gone for a while. Luke stared at the lifeless face. Orman's freckles had faded. It was a strange thing for Luke to focus on, but the dozens of tiny brown spots that had riddled the man's nose and cheeks while he was alive had paled to near invisibility.

Another dead man. Was it a coincidence?

When Luke had arrived in the Klondike, he'd been part of a team of six Mounties who'd infiltrated a ring of thieves, and Luke, as well as his brother, Colt, who'd commanded the team, had been promoted. Both were now inspectors. Luke's training and experience kicked in.

He went over the facts. The last time he'd seen the jeweler alive was at midnight when Luke had gone to bed. Orman and the three other men had remained, playing cards.

How did Orman die? There were no signs of wounds. No blood, no struggle. No measles, but then again, the judge hadn't had any spots on his face, either, but once they'd unbuttoned his shirt, his chest had been covered with it.

It was likely measles in its early stages for Orman, too.

But on the other hand, there'd been no sign of fever or perspiration or extreme thirst, like the judge had suffered.

How likely were two *accidental* deaths in the span of two days?

What was it with this wedding party?

Luke glanced up at the others rushing into the great room. Genevieve stood motionless, hand clamped to her throat. Behind her, her aunt stumbled in from the women's bedroom, heading to the coffeepot when she had to scoot around the broken cup on the floor.

"What happened here?"

Before Genevieve could answer, her aunt peered over at Luke and then Orman. She gasped and collapsed into a hard-backed chair. Milly entered and, noticing her mother, then Orman, stood dumbstruck.

Mr. Thornbottom slid out of the bedroom and caught on quickly to the events. "Oh, no."

Weston burst through the front door, lean and tall, letting in a flash of sunlight and swirl of wind. "Nugget's fed and roped up at the far end of the shack. Thought she'd like the chance to play in the grass." His smile faded as he took in the dead man in the rocker. His eyes shot to Luke.

Luke nodded to confirm the news.

"Where did his freckles go?" Staring, Milly rubbed her nose, covered with pretty freckles. "He had so many."

The young woman's comment seemed to awaken Genevieve. She looped an arm through Milly's. "Everything changes when a person dies, sweetheart. I imagine his freckles went with him to heaven."

Milly melted into Genevieve's shoulder. "Freckles in heaven."

Genevieve had put it kindly, thought Luke.

"Is there anything we can do, Luke?" she asked.

"I'm afraid not."

Blinking rapidly, she rubbed the crease between her eyebrows, her expression turning into one of concern for Milly. "Could you get the dustpan from the corner, please?" They stared at the splinters of white porcelain strewn about the floor and beneath the table. "I'll get the broom."

Luke knew Genevieve wanted to distract her cousin from the awful situation.

While they did that, Luke knelt at Orman's feet and examined the body more closely. He turned the man's face from side to side. Had his heart seized? The man was only in his early forties, but it was possible.

Did he have a nervous problem, perhaps with seizures, that no one had known about?

Had he been drinking heavily and perhaps had an unfavorable reaction to the alcohol?

Luke inhaled. No smell of alcohol.

Opium? Cocaine? The drugs were available in the back streets. Although to cross the mountains to get here, to navigate the rivers and lakes between Alaska and the Yukon, folks had to be in relatively good health. It was rare that someone would overtax their body with unnecessary toxins.

But something, something…and then Luke saw it. A red patch of skin at his collar.

Sweeping by them with the broom, Genevieve stopped. "What is it, Luke?"

"Measles." Luke was careful not to touch the patch. He stood up and stretched his legs.

She whispered, "Then any one of us could be next."

"Not necessarily. He had to have come in contact with it several days ago. He wasn't coughing last night, and he kept his distance from us, like I suggested we all do."

Luke's argument was weak and he knew it. Measles was highly contagious in its early stages.

Hmm. Odd that he hadn't been coughing. No red eyes last night, and Luke had sat right across the table from him when they'd played cards, so he would have noticed. No runny nose. No fever.

Something wasn't adding up.

But there was the rash.

A tin cup rested on a tray beside Orman. Luke picked it up. Empty. A few drops of brown liquid in the bottom. He sniffed. Coffee.

The outside door swung open again. A wall of light made Luke squint, and Kendall stepped through it, followed by Ripley Cliffton in his gold-digging overalls. The scent of cigar smoke clung to their clothing and filled the room. Kendall tossed his cowboy hat to a peg by the door and took a look at Luke bent over at Orman's feet, holding the coffee cup.

"You servin' breakfast, Inspector?"

"Orman's not having anything this morning."

"Why not? Too late a night last night? Is he mad 'cause I beat him out of all that mon—"

Ripley nudged Kendall to shut him up.

Money? They'd been gambling, after all? "No," said Luke. "He's not mad. He's dead."

Kendall froze. He simply stared from Luke to the dead man, to all the other folks in the room—Genevieve, her cousin, her aunt and uncle, and Weston, who'd joined everyone around the table.

Ripley, however, had a much stronger response. His eyes loomed wide. His face turned red and his upper lip twisted.

"Theodore," said Luke, watching the faces, "could you wake the other two men, please? Burt and Vince? Don't tell them what's happened. I'd like to do it." He turned to Genevieve. "And could you wake Miss Norris and Penelope? Same thing. Please don't tell them why."

Theodore rose from the table and rushed into the men's bedroom, hollering, "Time to get up, fellas."

Luke heard groaning and rumbling, but he couldn't make out the rest of the words.

Genevieve set down her broom and crossed the kitchen. Luke reached above the mantel, to another pine shelf beside the one holding her bouquet—pretty flowers that seemed so oddly out of place in these stark barracks—and pulled down his holster. He carried two Enfield revolvers. He'd tucked them away earlier, thinking he wouldn't need them.

"What is it?" Genevieve asked on her way to the women's bedroom. "What are you thinking?"

He strapped his guns to his hips, well aware all eyes in the room were upon him. "I've got a dilemma on my hands. But I won't know for sure until I examine the body." He turned to Weston. "Get your gun, Weston. I want you wearing it from now on." He addressed the group. "And I don't want any of you leaving this shack until I say so."

* * *

With trepidation at what Luke could possibly mean, Genevieve moved toward the lower bunk and touched Miss Norris's slim shoulder. She flinched beneath her white flannel gown. Although summer days were warm, nights could be much cooler, so thick nightclothes were a necessity.

"Rise and shine, Miss Norris." Genevieve pulled open the curtains. Sunlight poured into the room. "Inspector Hunter would like to see you."

The woman's hair, strands of orange and auburn, spread about her pillow as her eyelids quivered. It was past seven o'clock. For a housekeeper, Miss Norris certainly wasn't an early riser. Wouldn't most housekeepers rise around six to make breakfast, iron the laundry, feed the house pets, or anything else that needed doing to prepare for the day? Although the judge was gone, wouldn't Miss Norris's natural routine still cause her to awaken early?

Swallowing her own fears about the passing of Mr. Orman and the apparent spread of measles, Genevieve stood in the aisle. She stared at Penelope's back. She was tucked into a blanket facing the wall. "Penelope, time to rise."

Miss Norris rose on an elbow. "Huh?" She pinched her rigid nose and ran her fingers along either side of her lips, tugging them downward. "What is it?"

Genevieve stared at the dry splotches of reddish-brown spots covering the front plane of her face.

"A…a request of sorts. Inspector Hunter needs us all in the great room."

Penelope's bedsprings creaked. "Why?" She rolled to her side, hair spilling down her shoulders. Her flannel nightgown was cut low in the front, exposing much more flesh than Miss Norris. Genevieve turned away.

"Something important," she told them. "He wants you both right now."

"But I'm feeling rather flushed," said Miss Norris.

Of course, her illness. That would explain why she'd slept in later than expected. "May I get you a cup of tea while you get your robe?" The woman drank only tea, no coffee.

"That would be lovely." Her voice was coarse with sleep. "Thank you."

"Penelope?"

"Coffee, please."

"I'll meet you both in the kitchen."

Miss Norris gripped the collar of her neatly pressed gown. She ironed her bedclothes, too? "In my robe? Surely I have time to change."

"I'm afraid not. This is too important."

Miss Norris grumbled, but she swung her legs to the side of the bed. Genevieve left the bedroom and reentered the great room. Three minutes later when Genevieve was pouring a cup of tea, the two remaining Cliffton brothers came in. The casino owner, Vince, was buttoning his shirt and shoving his pocket watch into his wool vest. Burt stifled a yawn. They saw Mr. Orman seated in the chair, as still as stone, saw the faces watching them, turned back to Mr. Orman, and slowly came to a stop.

"Don't tell me…" said Vince, looking quickly to the others.

Burt frowned and said nothing.

Miss Norris shuffled in, her white night robe cinched perfectly at her waist, her hair brushed and clasped. She walked toward Genevieve, lifted her tea off the table, and swung around to see what was holding everyone's interest.

When she spotted pale Mr. Orman, the tea slipped. The liquid splashed over her arm, and she gasped. "Dear Lord."

Penelope followed in a red satin night robe and perfumed hair. She shrieked.

Genevieve slid around the table to help the housekeeper set down the tea, then turned to Luke.

He'd gotten what he wanted.

He wanted to see everyone's reaction to dead Mr. Orman. Now Genevieve waited for what he had to say.

Luke deliberated. Genevieve watched the morning light filter across his face. It dipped over his dark temples and made the scar beneath his eye shimmer like a thread of silk.

He pressed his hand to his holster and she felt a quiver of fear. Why the need for guns?

"Mr. Orman was poisoned," said Luke, looking around the room.

"Poisoned?" squeaked Milly.

"Good grief," exclaimed Aunt Abigail, still seated. She doubled over at the waist and groaned.

Genevieve's senses opened to the sights and sounds around her, as if ready to run. She heard the birds through the windows. She smelled the tea on the table. She tasted coffee on her tongue and felt a ripple of cold air racing over her skin.

Luke delivered a second blow as potent as the first. "I think Judge Donahue was poisoned, too."

It was more a hunch than medical reasoning. Medical reasoning told Luke the man had likely been coming down with measles. Luke's gut told him otherwise.

"Poisoned?" Genevieve stepped forward, the first to speak after Luke's announcement, her face creased with alarm. "What makes you think he was poisoned?"

He couldn't trust most people here; this included his lovely new wife.

"His lack of symptoms."

"But he's got a rash on his neck."

"A rash from poison."

"But the judge had measles," said Kendall. "Just look at Miss Norris here. She's got them, too."

Miss Norris sat down, cradling her head between the flat of her hands. She released a light sob. Standing beside her, Penelope ignored her at first, then with a frown, patted the woman's back.

"Yes, he had measles. But that's not what killed him."

"How do you know?" asked Vince.

"My gut."

Ripley laughed with disbelief. "Your gut, Inspector, is not admissible in the rule of law."

Luke turned to Weston. "Run and get the commissioner. Stay clear of him, like you did before. Tell him what's happened. Ask him to station two constables outside our door."

"Yes, sir." Weston tore off.

"Kendall, I need you to help me move Orman's body to the stables."

"The stables?"

"I need to examine it and I'd rather not do it here."

"Right."

"We'll wait till the guards arrive," Luke told him.

Minutes later, the Mounties arrived, along with the commissioner, who waited outside.

Inside, commotion ensued. The Thornbottoms voiced their fears loudly.

"I'm not staying here with a lunatic on the loose," bellowed the woman.

"No reason you should," said her husband.

The Cliffton brothers talked among themselves, but judging by the way they were staring at the outside door, Luke knew escape was on their minds, too.

"Calm down, everyone," Luke told them.

Penelope seemed to be the only one who looked relaxed, still patting Miss Norris on the back.

Even Genevieve was trembling.

Luke propped open the front door and told the two constables to take a seat on the fence, facing the barracks with a view straight in. No murderer would strike again while being watched.

Luke raced to accomplish what he needed to do, careful not to upset the delicate nature of dealing with a dead man in the middle of the barracks. He apologized to the ladies and spoke softly to everyone else as they inquired how and when Luke had discovered the body.

Luke then disappeared into the stables for an hour.

First, he located his veterinary bag. He rummaged through the tonics to see if he could determine what, if anything, was missing. Dammit, he should have locked up the bag. But who the hell could expect murder?

It was difficult to determine if anything was gone because most of the liquids and powders came in large jars. Many of them had been unsealed for months.

He removed a key from his office desk and unlocked the medicine cabinet. There were so many possibilities. The ether and mask he used for surgical anesthesia. Carbon tetrachloride used against the fluke organism. Ampoules of cocaine used as local anesthetic. Strychnine, liquid and tablet morphine, even the bottle of sodium chloride and potassium electrolytes could be used as instruments of poison. His gaze shot past his surgical instruments, the pill making machine, the ceramic mortar and pestles he used for crushing ingredients.

Nothing out of balance. But he'd left the key to this volatile mix of possibilities right in the top drawer of his goddamn desk.

He turned his attention to his other task and examined Orman's body. Thirty minutes later and after a thorough soaping of his hands and arms, he consulted with the commissioner—at thirty paces—telling the man nothing more than what he'd told the others.

Frustrated by his own confusion, Luke stepped back into the barracks.

"Now then, Genevieve." He buttoned the cuff of his sleeve. His fingers were still raw from scrubbing so hard. "I need you to come with me."

She wrapped her arms around her waist, as if protecting herself. "Where?"

"Outside for a moment." He nodded toward the open door and its view of the guards stationed outside. "If you please?"

Chapter Eight

Feeling Penelope's penetrating stare on her back, Genevieve stepped in front of Luke and walked out the door.

What could he possibly want from her?

She yanked on her straw hat as they hurried beneath a cluster of trees. The ribbons from her hat rippled down the back of her hair, mimicking the erratic beating of her pulse. Trying to calm herself, she inhaled the scent of scrub pines and cedars that the whispering wind carried from the far edge of the property, but the fragrance did little to subdue her trembling fingers.

The events of the past two days were too difficult to accept. Her marriage to this man, the deaths of Judge Donahue and Mr. Orman and now their possible…she couldn't even say the word. She swallowed hard. Murder.

She glanced up past the Mountie outpost, past the board-walk teeming with early morning shoppers and storekeepers, past the wharf crowded with workers who were bent over in the sun, hauling timber and sawing wood. To where could she escape? Could she flee on the next paddle wheeler out of here?

She wasn't safe. She was ready to run.

She craned her neck to look at Luke's face. His white shirt was a stark contrast to his tanned jaw, the black eyebrows, the acute depth of his dark eyes. Sunlight struck his shoulders from behind, creating a silhouetted form that accentuated his bulk.

He slid a hand into his pocket, looked down at his cowboy boots and frowned. "First off, I'd like to say I'm sorry."

With a nervous gesture, Genevieve rubbed her throat. Her scooped neckline soaked in the warm summer rays. Luke's gaze followed her fingers and lingered there.

"Sorry for what?"

"That all of this is happening on what should've been an occasion for you to celebrate."

She curled her shaky fingers into the front pleats of her skirt. "Thank you for saying as much."

"It doesn't help, though, does it?"

A cry of release broke from her lips. A letting go of all the emotion that had swelled in her since meeting this man. He understood. He understood what it was like for her.

Luke reached out with a firm hand on her arm and steadied her. "Are you all right?"

His warm touch was reassuring and, despite herself, she wished he'd let his hand lay. She was all alone in the Klondike. There were the Thornbottoms, yes, but she hadn't seen them in years. As grateful as she was for their loving company, she needed more. Perhaps what she needed most was Joshua, a proper husband who would hold her and love her and tell her everything would be fine. To quell her innermost fears of being trapped in quarantine with a murderer.

The comforting touch of this man was somehow absorbing the loss of the situation. She could be in such terrible trouble if Luke let his hand linger. And yet, as she stared at the rugged beauty of his tanned fingers curling over her arm, she was rooted by the heated connection. The improper connection.

She allowed his hand to remain. In fact, when he gently squeezed her arm and drew her somewhat closer, she didn't voice a complaint.

"Genevieve, are you all right?" he asked again.

She swayed in the sunshine. "I'll be all right, thank you."

He rocked her arm then, as if he wished to pull her tightly to his chest.

Please don't.

Please do.

He didn't. His focus dropped from her eyes, over her cheeks and lowered to her lips.

And in that instant, like an unexpected storm, she understood with her entire soul how a woman and a man, two strangers here in the Klondike, much like Luke and any one of his lady friends, might join together in a moment of passion and loneliness and heartache, to make love.

She breathed him in.

Catching herself, she stepped back into the shade of the trees, pulled her arm out of his grasp and cleared her throat. Her lashes flickered as she tried to drive away the indecent thoughts and any remnant of sentiment he might observe.

He, too, staggered back, as if snapped in two by the broken bond.

It was the distress of having witnessed Mr. Orman's death that caused her sanity to lapse. People said all sorts of things and acted in even stranger ways when faced with grief. She'd seen it herself when her parents had passed away. Grieving folks clung to hope and clung to strangers when suffering was at its greatest. Why, her Aunt Abigail had had hallucinations for several nights running that her sister, Genevieve's late mother, was serving her coffee in the kitchen while everyone else in the household was still sleeping. Delusions caused from grief. Temporary disorders of the nervous system.

Luke rubbed his wrist. "I asked you out here for a reason."

"Yes?"

"I don't know very much about you. Under the circumstances, I'd like to know more."

She tilted her head at him. His face was tanned by the wind and sun. He held himself with pride and never acknowledged the faint scar curling down his cheek.

Had he felt the pull, too, the subdued simmering of attraction that had raced beneath her skin and perhaps his own? Her cheeks heated at the thought that she might be discovered, at what he might confess, too. "Under the circumstances?"

The dark cut of his brow furrowed over even darker eyes. He looked out over the horizon. There was sudden distance in his manner. "I'm sure you understand. I need to know as much as I can about everyone here."

"Ah." Disappointment spiraled through her.

The wind lifted the weight of her hair. Of course he needed to know about everyone. Everyone here, in his eyes, was a potential killer.

"I'd like to know where you're from exactly, and how you came to marry Joshua."

"And I suppose you'll be asking these questions of everyone here?"

"Of course."

"Of course." She brushed her skirt of imaginary dirt, feeling the sting of…what? A rebuttal of an imaginary feeling that she'd stupidly assumed had sparked between them, when in fact, it had likely all been in her overactive mind?

"I'm from Montana. Southwest of Billings. Grew up on a strip of land my father mined for coal."

"Brothers and sisters?"

"None."

"And you came to know Joshua how?"

"He was a friend of my aunt and uncle's. Uncle Theodore first hired him as an assistant when he was seventeen to help him bind his brooms."

Was the information enough? Was he satisfied?

He didn't appear to be.

She stood rooted in shame, as though she were a criminal, while he continued his questioning.

"What was it like growing up in Montana? I hear it's remarkably beautiful."

The corner of her mouth tugged in surprise. The question was unnecessary to his cause, it was one born more of curiosity.

She turned and pressed a hand to the trunk of a nearby tree, etching her fingertips along the rough bark.

What was it like? They had scraped by on little more than food while her father had mined. There were many times when her parents had given her the last of the milk and potatoes and gone to bed hungry themselves.

Her parents had bickered and quarreled at every opportunity—at the price of fabric to sew clothing, at the cost of a new shovel when her father had worn through his, at the extraordinary cost of a mule to carry water from the river to the shack—a mule they could never afford and so

Genevieve had done all the carrying. Her mother had started using Genevieve, when she was only twelve, as a confidante for her troubled marriage. It had been a burden then for such a young girl to carry her mother's misery, praying that her folks would stop their shrieking and perhaps find some kind thing to say to each other, and it was a burden now to remember it when Luke asked.

Turning back to the tough officer before her, she talked past the sting in her throat. "The scenery was indeed magnificent. The same Rocky Mountains that soar in Montana are the backbone of those in Alaska."

He watched her hands on the willow's trunk as he listened.

It was the anguish of witnessing her parents' horrible marriage that had given Genevieve the determination that hers would be different. That she'd never succumb to bitterness; that her marriage to Joshua would be so much better than the example she'd been given.

Her marriage to Joshua would be the very reflection of herself, of the caring human being she aspired to be. Her marriage was everything to her. It was all she had and all she'd worked for, it seemed, since the age of twelve.

"How did you come to arrange it with Joshua?"

She fought for balance. "My Aunt wrote to me as she was leaving Montana. Said they were on their way to the Klondike and were meeting up with Joshua. He'd been asking about me in his letters to them, it seemed, and wanted to formally request my hand in marriage."

"And you said yes."

"I *shouted* yes."

"So you were waiting for him to ask you."

"I couldn't wait to start a better life. To leave the coal mines."

"But Joshua is a miner. A gold miner."

"That's different. When—*if*—he strikes it rich, he's going to open a shop next to my Uncle Theodore's. We're going to be shopkeepers, Joshua and I—he selling his wares, and me selling my hats."

"And if he doesn't?"

His dark presence melted into the space between them. Couldn't he stay his distance? Couldn't he keep his power and the scent of his skin to himself?

"Beg your pardon?"

"If he doesn't strike it rich?"

"It won't be the end of the world."

The intent way he studied her made her senses catch fire. "I've heard that said once or twice before. Especially on the trail leading to the Klondike. But once people get gold fever, it's hard to shake."

"I don't have gold fever. I have hat fever."

The outline of his shoulders flexed in the sun. "Your shop is a very nice dream."

It wasn't a dream. It was her life. "Don't you already know some of this? You're Joshua's friend. Didn't he tell you about me when you agreed to step in as proxy groom?"

"He told me some. I knew you were from Montana. I know he wants to open a shop of some sort."

She took a step and walked along the fence. Her skirts blew around her feet. "How did you become friends?"

Luke's heavy boots buckled the grass. "I looked after his two mares when he brought them in over the trails. They were in poor health. Most animals are, after the trek over the mountains."

"So you've known him for more than a year?"

"On and off. This is my second time here. I had to leave

for a special duty back to Vancouver, and just arrived again a couple of weeks ago."

She squinted in the sunshine. "That's when he asked you to act as groom?"

"That's right." He touched his revolver, reminding her he was the police. His demeanor shifted, his jaw flexed with restraint. "When did you meet the judge?"

His distrust was apparent. It sickened her, even though she understood it. "Five days ago."

"What sort of relationship did you have with him?"

She'd give him the same back. She lowered her voice and spoke as if she didn't care for his questions. "I met him only once before the ceremony. Joshua had requested the proxy wedding from him, so I only had to notify the judge when I arrived. He told me there was a Mountie who was stepping in as Joshua's replacement—*you*—and that he'd speak to you about the place and time. I couldn't locate you myself because you were out of town camping at some other site, looking after some problem with arson."

"I recall." He tapped his belt buckle with his tanned fingers. "And when did you first meet Clyde Orman?"

She looked away from his judgmental stare. Had it come to this? "I met him on the wedding day. *Our* wedding day."

If she expected the words might soften Luke, she was mistaken. His eyes remained penetrating, his lips tightly drawn, his shoulders pulled back squarely as if contemplating whether she might be a criminal.

It was demeaning to have her *husband* look at her in this manner. Demeaning to have a friend of Joshua's question her motives, and shameful to think of how only ten minutes ago, she'd felt an unbelievable connection to this stranger.

Stranger. Husband. Who was he to her?

Nothing.

A man who had neither the patience nor the kindness to give her the benefit of believing she was an innocent woman incapable of the horrible crimes he was investigating. Distrust was all she saw mirrored in his swirling brown eyes.

If there was a murderer among them, Luke was going to make damn sure everyone was safe while they completed their quarantine. He sure as hell was going to nail the killer.

While he stood beneath the trees with Genevieve, the unsettling Yukon wind ruffled the back of his hair. She drew her arms together, but the light hit her at just the right angle and erased the hardness from her face. It cast a golden sheen to her upturned lips. Who was she?

The murderer had the audacity to commit the crimes right beneath Luke's nose.

It was a personal slap in the face.

Because, dammit, the poison had likely come from his veterinary bag. Perhaps a horse medication, anesthetic or opiate painkiller the victims had ingested. He ruled out an injection. There'd been no needle marks on the bodies, no glass syringes missing from his supplies.

Why would someone want the judge and the jeweler dead? Did it have anything to do with the store robbery several days ago? They hadn't yet nabbed the thief and, according to the commissioner, had no leads.

The irony was, in this situation where he didn't know who was innocent or guilty, he had to physically protect the blasted killer as well as the others.

He blamed himself. He should have picked up on the judge's symptoms earlier, should have been more aware.

He'd been sidetracked by all the other blasted business—this damn marriage—that he'd come out looking so green at his job it filled him with shame.

And this woman standing before him. What was she all about?

He didn't know what to make of her. On one hand, she was a strong woman who'd set out for the Klondike to meet her husband. He didn't know of any other woman who'd had the drive, determination or guts to do that. She must have wanted her marriage badly.

She'd gotten *him* instead.

On the other hand, at times like these, Genevieve radiated softness and vulnerability, an uncertainty of what was expected of her and where her future was leading. Her blouse draped softly against her bosom, and as they strolled along, her skirts clung against her shapely thighs.

He realized he was angry at the situation and not at her. *Don't take it out on her.*

Sunshine spilled over her straw hat, filtering into tiny white flecks over her cheeks, shoulders, and an open neckline that gave him a glimpse of her skin. She dressed so differently than Penelope, yet both women lured him. One was conservative, hiding the outline of her body as though she didn't want anyone to witness its beauty; the other flamboyant and much more aware of her influence on the men around her.

For that matter, what really did he know of Penelope? He'd have a talk with her, too.

The breeze carried over them, bringing the faint sound of a yapping puppy who'd spotted them from her patch of grass where she was leashed.

Luke led the way along the stables toward Nugget. He had a few more questions for Genevieve. They walked in silence until they reached the puppy. Genevieve unleashed the jumping ball of white fur and the pup leaped around them, thumping her tail as if they'd been separated for weeks instead of minutes.

Genevieve laughed, and the richness of the sound made him aware of the elegance of the woman. Her color heightened. Her black hair shone like glass in the sun.

Her aunt and uncle never stopped talking about her privileged background; Genevieve must have had quite a wealthy upbringing. Her father, at one time, must have mined a fortune in coal. It didn't impress Luke. Money never had. Neither had gold, considering his own childhood connection to the unlucky yellow mineral.

They walked along the rim of the property, close to the fragrant pines and cedars. Luke nodded to the two Mounties stationed outside the barracks. All was quiet. To the other side of them, the town of Dawson was burgeoning with morning activity. The sound of hammers and handsaws echoed from the direction of the wharf. Shopkeepers were washing their windows. A new merchant was putting up a banner declaring Timepieces for Sale.

He ran a hand along his rough cheek and turned to Genevieve. "Who'd you travel with to get here?"

Her cheeks were as smooth as butterfly wings. "I answered an ad in the newspaper. There was a company of men and two of their wives who were traveling to the Klondike."

"You came with a group of strangers?"

"Well, they're not strangers anymore."

"Where are they?"

Thick feminine eyelashes caught the light. "Of the dozen of us who set out, only four of us made it. The others turned back."

Luke marveled again at her stamina. He knew from experience the bush she'd traveled through was untamed. It was filled with wild animals, blackflies and mosquitoes as thick as thunderclouds, mountain slopes that made your muscles ache until you swore they were being pulled out of their very sockets. There was never enough food and no civilized way to bathe.

"Where are they now, the other three who made it?"

"Two of the men stayed behind in Whitehorse, and the third one headed out to pan for gold as soon as we arrived." She cleared her throat and looked at him. "Partway through our journey, we banded up with another larger group, so we were never completely alone."

She hesitated over the words, as though she wondered what he might think of her, traveling with no other female, no proper chaperone. She'd set out with other women, though, and it hadn't been her fault they'd turned back.

He turned the topic back to the one at hand, feeling the anger swelling inside of him again. Who the hell had tampered with his medicines?

He asked directly. "Why was Orman at your wedding?"

She stiffened at his tone, her posture elevated. "Because Joshua invited him. He's a jeweler. Joshua had him make my wedding band."

She held out her hand and indicated the gold ring with its grooved circles. "Joshua had found the gold nugget himself and left instructions for Mr. Orman to get it fitted when I arrived. I consider it my good-luck charm."

Was she that naive? Luke cupped the bottom of her warm palm with his, studying the ring. He sensed the heated rush of contact. A jangle of nerves, a burst of desire. "And what kind of luck has it brought you so far?"

Astonishment caused her thick lashes to fly up. Her cheeks tightened as though she were insulted by his question. She snapped her hand out of his.

With a flip of her skirts, she turned and had the nerve to walk away. *From him.* An investigating officer of the North-West Mounted Police.

He reeled back in response as though he'd been slapped, and then lunged forward, his voice rumbling over the wind. "I'm not finished with you yet."

Chapter Nine

"Unless you'd like to charge me with the murder of Clyde Orman, I believe you are."

Luke panted through his teeth, more in annoyance with himself than at her. He couldn't seem to keep his thoughts in check around Genevieve, whether it was runaway thoughts of lust—*toward a woman who was promised to one of his friends*—or his anger at having been so stupidly wed.

Tricked by circumstance.

They stared at each other across a field of silence—she prim and withdrawn, her dog yapping at her feet, he solid and threatening and as silent as a hawk before its kill.

Startling them both, Penelope sauntered out of the barracks. "Luv, we must talk!"

Slowly, he raked his eyes over Genevieve. "No charges. For now."

The green in her eyes glistened. The soft vulnerability he'd witnessed earlier came out in the gentle curve of her cheek. She hesitated, watching Penelope approach.

"Luke!" Penelope called again. She wore a tightly knit sweater that scooped her bosom, a suede skirt that clung to her hips and came just short of her shins, and tall boots that covered her ankles. A scandalous length of skirt. Miss Norris and Abigail Thornbottom were likely having convulsions of dismay back in the barracks.

Nugget bounced past Penelope to the two Mounties who were leaning against the far post, watching the pretty barmaid stroll past.

Penelope sauntered toward them, well aware of the attention she was bringing upon herself, thought Luke, and finally reached him and Genevieve.

"Do you have time for me, now, luv?" Penelope glanced from one to the other. Her cheekbones, normally rouged in the evenings but without cosmetics this morning, needed no enhancement to make her pretty. Her full lips, slightly tinted with a pink sheen, puckered. He liked this cleaner look on her.

Self-conscious, Genevieve crossed her arms over her chest, hiding her body again, and placed the leash inside her skirt pocket.

"We'll continue this later," he said to her.

She brushed by him as if he were a fleck of dirt, peering past his shoulders for Nugget. "He's all yours," she said to Penelope. Then added to Luke, "Bye, luv."

He clenched his mouth.

"What did she mean by that?" Penelope watched her walk away.

"Nothing. We were arguing and she's making a point."

"What point?"

"That I'd rather be with you than her."

Penelope smiled. "Oh, that's all right then." She stared at his collar, as she liked to do, then down to see what boots he was wearing. Sometimes she stared more at his clothing than at his face. "Do you two argue a lot?"

"We never stop."

Penelope sighed with contentment. "I'm glad we never do." She linked her arm through his and they strolled along the property toward the boardwalk.

"We haven't known each other for that long, I suppose."

"We have nothing to argue about." She reached up and kissed him on the cheek.

Startled at the sudden gesture, Luke patted her hand. He hadn't minded her kisses two days ago. In fact, he'd been looking forward to them all week when she'd said yes to his invitation to dinner.

He didn't mind her kisses now, either. *Truly.* When she stepped away, he rolled his shoulders, willing them to relax.

"Timepieces for Sale," she read off the sign. "I do declare, I would love a pocket watch. One of those slender ones made only for women. Do you think they carry them, luv?"

"I suppose." He rubbed the back of his neck. "Penelope…did you have any recent conversations with Clyde Orman?"

"Last night, we said hello."

"I noticed you said it rather stiffly."

"Because he'd…several nights ago he'd invited me to the Community Social and I said no."

"He invited you?"

"Yes."

"And you said no."

"I couldn't very well say yes when I said yes to you for dinner."

"Right. How did he take it?"

"Like he never heard my answer. He kept asking all week long. He was there every evening I came on to serve drinks."

"And what happened?"

"Vince told me I should ignore him, but be polite. He was a good-paying customer, liked to gamble after drinking, and that…that I should say no but with a smile."

Luke fought through another rise in temper. First at Orman for pursuing her when she'd already said no, then at Vince for making her play along so he wouldn't lose any money at the tables. Penelope was a lovely woman, not a tramp. Simply a barmaid who'd once told him she made more in gratuities delivering drinks in one night than any other "regular" woman's job might earn in a week. She was smart *and* beautiful.

And he felt ten times more at ease with her than his accidental wife.

Penelope understood his need for quiet privacy, for an enjoyable conversation with a lively woman, for his desire to keep things simple and easy between them.

Luke patted her hand. "Thanks for putting up with my questions. I'll walk you back."

In comparison to Penelope, there was nothing simple or easy about Genevieve. He watched her retrieving her puppy from between the two Mounties who seemed to be joking with her, her shoulders stiff as planks, her pensive expression telling Luke she was ill at ease. Perhaps she knew she was being watched by both him and Penelope.

The friendly barmaid at his side always filled him with confidence, made him feel as though he were in control of every situation, made him aware of his need to be with a lovely woman whose attention was vied for by every man.

In contrast, Genevieve went everywhere alone, seemingly aloof from the others, not nearly as friendly or social, not nearly as carefree and proud of the way she turned the head of every man in her path. And aware of it or not, she most certainly did attract them all.

One of these people, thought Luke, was a killer. Beneath the pine trees, he stared at the barracks and the shadows passing in front of the open door, taking in every detail.

It was almost lunchtime and he was formulating a plan.

He turned to address his two constables, Enscott and Morgan, standing on the other side of the fence at a healthy distance. "I want you to ask every man in the force if they've ever had contact with measles."

"Yes, sir."

"Go to the commissioner. Tell him I need guards *inside* the barracks as well as out. I want round-the-clock surveillance to prevent any more poisonings."

Morgan scratched his chin. "You mean if someone's had contact with measles before, they're not in danger of getting it again?"

"That's right. Once you build up a resistance, you can't catch it again." Luke hadn't asked earlier for more guards because no one in the cabin had been in danger from a killer. He had been the sole Mountie inside, and thought that had been enough to keep order.

"My cousin had measles once," said Enscott. "Nearly killed him, but he survived."

"Is he here?"

"No, sir. He's in Ottawa."

"Well, find me a Mountie just like him."

Morgan looked dismayed. "It may take a while to go through sixty men. And half of them are out on patrol. Gone for days, sometimes weeks."

"I'll give you till the end of the day."

The constable frowned. "The end of the...?" He straightened and nodded. "Yes, sir."

The two left for the commissioner's cabin and Luke headed back inside in the barracks. He wanted to provide a calm example to the madness that was going on around them.

They'd left Luke a seat at the head of the table. Penelope squirmed in to his immediate right. On his left was Kendall, hungrily eyeing Penelope, to Luke's dismay, as well as the corned beef and hash.

No one ate.

At the other end of the table sat the Thornbottoms, and their niece, Genevieve. Abigail was still pale and quiet, but her husband, on the other hand, couldn't stop talking about nonsensical things. Milly clung to Genevieve and the puppy.

Genevieve wouldn't meet Luke's eye. Would she ever display any sentiment toward him besides anger?

Her shapely body pressed up against the table. The weathered fabric outlined a hint of the corset beneath. His pulse surged. Dammit, he was no better than the leering Kendall.

The Cliffton brothers had spread out in the middle of the table, Burt and Ripley on one side, staring at the warm buns the cook had delivered ten minutes earlier. Vince sat on the other side, beside Genevieve, not eating yet, staring at Luke.

No one trusted the food.

Miss Norris came out of her bedroom, dressed in a lacy white skirt and blouse, with matching white shawl. How could anyone stay so clean in the mud and wilderness of the Klondike? She nudged her way in beside Abigail, who mumbled hello.

Luke watched Miss Norris spread her linen napkin over her knees and swore, once again, that she *had* been romantically involved with Judge Donahue. Why had they never married? How did she feel about that?

He lifted a bowl of steaming peas, took a scoop and passed it to Penelope. She took it but didn't serve herself.

"Look," he said to the group. "If the cook wanted to poison us all, he would have done so already. And he can't target one person specifically, because how could he know what one person will choose to eat or not eat?" Luke shoved a forkful of peas into his mouth and chewed.

He pressed his palm to the table. "I want you all to continue with the routine. We've got to eat. We've got to chop wood. Go about your business, but always travel in groups of three."

"Three?" asked Ripley.

"Yeah. One might be the killer in the group, maybe even two. But not likely all three. Therefore, the killer won't try anything."

Abigail sniffled. Her husband comforted her.

"I can buy that," said Kendall.

"Good thinking." Vince reached for the peas. Others began to serve themselves, too, but not in heaping quantities. They murmured and shuffled on their seats, perhaps relieved that someone was in charge and telling them what to do. They reached for jugs of water, a basket of rye bread, the plate of corned beef, the salt and pepper shakers.

Luke spooned a heap of evaporated mashed potatoes onto his plate, followed by a river of gravy. "Now then. We're going to go around the table and I want you each to tell me how you knew Judge Donahue and what your relationship to Clyde Orman was."

Abigail brought her napkin to her lips and coughed.

Luke turned to his left. "We'll start with you, Kendall."

"I didn't know the judge well. He kept a horse at the livery stables."

"What happens to the horse now that he's gone?"

"I suppose that depends on what it says in his last will and testament."

"How did you come to be invited to the wedding?"

"I was delivering the judge his horse. He asked me to wait till the ceremony was over, said he wanted to ride in the country. Like he does every Saturday afternoon."

"You weren't even invited to the wedding?"

"No, sir. I was just waiting in the background for the judge to finish."

"How about Orman? Did you know him?"

"I think everyone in town knows him. Anyone who's ever found a nugget of gold sooner or later makes his way to the jewelry store."

Ripley bit into a piece of rye bread on the other side of Kendall. "I heard that Orman stiffed you once in a jewelry deal."

Kendall eyed him. "What'd you say that for?"

"Just keeping everyone honest."

Kendall stammered in Luke's direction. "Orman...he—he said my nugget wasn't pure and gave me half of what it was worth."

Luke blinked. "Did you argue?"

Kendall stopped chewing on his corned beef. "No. I needed the money."

"What about you, Ripley? What brought you to the wedding?"

"My brothers and I are acquaintances of Joshua's. And Theodore, here, who invited us." Ripley looked to his brother Burt, but avoided Vince's glare.

Luke kept going. "How did you know the judge?"

"Just like everyone else in town did, I suppose. I knew him by his stature and his business dealings. Never talked to him much."

"Yes, you did," said Miss Norris from the other side. "You knocked on his door three nights ago."

Ripley's gaze darted back to Luke. "I was delivering some paperwork from the Land Claims Office. I left the papers with you, Miss Norris. Something the judge had to sign on my gold claim."

"Which claim was that?" Kendall asked. "Your third or fourth?"

"What difference does it make?"

"Just keeping everyone honest." With a smirk, Kendall bit down on his bread.

Luke turned again to Ripley. "And how did you know Orman?"

"Met him once or twice at the casino."

Luke nodded and slowly turned to his brother, Burt. "Did the judge ever make it into your saloon, Burt?"

"Occasionally. Last year when I had that French Canadian cook. He came in for the garlic soup. Garlic soup and a beer."

"Talk to him much?"

"Not about anything important. We'd strike up a conversation, but most of the time my bartender took care of him."

"And did Orman ever come into your saloon?"

"Yup. He drank Scotch, straight up. He liked cognac, too, and sometimes a shot of peppermint liqueur."

Luke pivoted to the other side of the table. "Vince? I hear Orman was in your casino every night for the past week."

"How'd you know that?" Vince exchanged glances with Penelope.

"Did his presence make you mad?"

"*No.*"

Luke thought about how Orman had pounced on Penelope. "I was mad when I heard about it."

"Well, that's understandable...considering you and Penelope are...you know."

"How about the judge? How often did he come in?"

"Once a week or so. Late at night." Vince turned to stare at the other faces. "Could we do this in private? I'd like to think my patrons—dead or alive—have some privacy due. It's too late for the judge, but these fine folks here are gonna think I blab their secrets to anyone asking. I don't."

"Hmm." Luke glanced at the Thornbottoms. "Abigail and Theodore, who invited you to the wedding?"

"Well, Genevieve and Joshua, of course," said Abigail. "We set the whole thing up!"

"Did you know the judge?"

"Only...only in contacting him on Genevieve's behalf. We spoke to him the previous day with Miss Norris present in the parlor." She looked to the housekeeper. "Do you recall?"

Miss Norris nodded.

"And how about the jeweler?" Luke asked the Thornbottoms.

"Never met him before," said Theodore.

"Wasn't a customer of yours?"

"Oh, hold on now." Theodore's cheeks reddened. "Yes, well, he may have come into the store once to buy a broom."

"Yes, he did," said Abigail, suddenly enlightened. "He...he came in two weeks earlier, the day we opened. Introduced himself as one of the merchants in town and invited us to visit his jewelry store."

"Miss Norris," said Luke, suddenly changing tactics.

"Tell me where you first met Clyde Orman." Luke glanced at the necklace she was wearing—a fine gold chain with a nugget of gold dangling off the center. She rubbed her throat and played with the nugget.

"I was a patron of his store."

"That's where you got the necklace."

Her mouth slackened in surprise. "That's where it came from."

Had she bought it, or had the judge bought it for her? It was worth more than a regular housekeeper could afford. Luke decided not to embarrass her in front of the others, so moved on down the table.

He skipped over the people he'd already talked to—Genevieve and Penelope. There was also no sense in questioning Milly, not now, for he'd just scare the willies out of her. He overlooked Weston, too, since it was Luke who'd ordered Weston to accompany him to the wedding, pretty much ruling out Weston as a suspect.

Luke cleared his throat. "Does anyone here know how the two dead men knew each other? Orman and the judge?"

Forks and spoons stopped clinking. The group lowered their utensils and darted glances at Luke.

"That's the key to solving this thing," he told them. "Finding out how the two dead men were connected. If any of you would like to say anything now or tell me later in private, I'd be much obliged to hear you out."

He studied the faces for the effect his words had. Did the killer have nerves of steel, or was he or she the nervous type?

Three people avoided his stare: Milly, Weston and Abigail. Three men glared right back at him: Vince, Ripley and Kendall. Burt kept on eating. Theodore at the other end mumbled something to Genevieve, who glanced away from Luke quickly. Miss Norris reached for her glass of water, avoiding his appraisal. Penelope placed her hand on his.

The careful watch began, the sly glances, the scrutiny of everything put into their mouths, beginning with early-morning coffee and ending with late-night tea.

No one was exempt from suspicion.

Later in the evening, two Mounties surfaced from Luke's snare. Constable Franks, who'd been born in Ireland and as a child had crossed the ocean on a ship that was quarantined for measles outside New York City. And the other Mountie was Constable Zucker whose grandmother had died from the illness when he'd been but two. He'd come down with it as well, he'd told Luke, and had suffered through it.

Two extra guards weren't nearly enough for twenty-four-hour surveillance indoors, but better than nothing.

Luke introduced them to the group, then locked up his veterinary bag in its new spot—one of the kitchen cupboards. He scoured through his medical chest in the stables and locked up more bottles and tonics in the commissioner's cabin. Luke scrutinized every piece of equipment and read every label.

Two long days passed where Franks and Zucker rotated in twelve-hour shifts while keeping watch in the kitchen. When the cook brought their meals, folks relaxed enough to eat, but they poured their own coffee and tea and kept their glasses close to their chests.

On Thursday evening after dinner, a note was delivered to Luke. Someone needed his help with a sick filly. Two hours later came another note. An injured cow.

Around midnight, when everyone else had gone to bed

except for one of the new guards who was reading in the parlor and keeping watch while his partner slept, Luke tugged on his cowboy boots and unlocked his veterinarian bag from its cabinet.

The front door clicked and Genevieve burst through from the outside, surprising him. She tugged at the blue scarf wrapped around her throat. Her hair had caught in the wind, the single braid rolling over her shoulder. Lower still, her belted waistline attracted his eye.

Breathless and beautiful, she looked him over. "Where are you going?"

"I could ask you the same."

"I—I couldn't sleep and took a walk. The two constables outside kept me within sight the whole time. The rule of three."

She glanced up at him, her breasts and supple hips making his thoughts turn to something they shouldn't. Her face, tender and searching in the glow of the flickering lantern, was poised waiting for his answer.

"There's a sick cow at the far side of town that needs some attention. And a young filly." Before he had a chance to think it through, responding only to urgent male instinct, he asked her, "Care to come with me?"

In the glow of the flickering lantern, she glanced up at him, her face tender and searching for his hidden motivations. Her breasts and supple hips made his thoughts turn to something they shouldn't.

Chapter Ten

⧼⧽

Genevieve wanted to go with Luke. She didn't know why, other than perhaps curiosity at how he'd handle the animals—so tolerant and caring with them compared to how disciplined he was with people. There was also the splendor of being outdoors on a quiet Yukon night while others were in bed. Every sinew in her body pulled her toward the direction of the door, but she wasn't sure what others might think.

The guard in the far corner poured himself another cup of coffee, turning his back on their conversation. He nudged Nugget, who was sleeping in a straw basket.

The midnight sun slanted into the room from around the coarse canvas curtains and hit the muscled hollow of Luke's cheek.

"Shouldn't there be three of us going?" she asked.

"I can wake Weston."

She nodded but, truth be told, felt no need for accompaniment. Over the past couple of days, she'd deduced that if Luke was the guilty party, he would have tried to cover up the poisonings. He certainly wouldn't have announced them. But more than that, more than logic, her heart was telling her she could trust this man.

When Genevieve glanced hesitantly toward the bedrooms, Luke murmured. "They don't have to know."

"The guards will know."

"They won't care," he countered.

"What would...what would Penelope think?"

"Penelope's not much for animals, but I know you are. She cares about them—she just doesn't like to go near the big ones."

The mention of Penelope aroused Genevieve's guilt. She was driven, though, by the seductive charm of Luke and her desire to be alone with him. To hold a private conversation, perhaps. Nothing more.

"Horses *can* be intimidating."

Luke unclasped his veterinary bag and searched through it. "We've got to do this tonight while the town's sleeping so we don't spread measles. Coming?"

Genevieve hesitated. "How long would we be gone?"

"About two hours. Shall I wake Weston?"

Her gaze lingered on his face and dropped to his throat. "It's not necessary."

His mouth tugged upward into a smile that encompassed her with warmth and made her tingle. "Here, it might be chilly."

He tossed her one of his leather dusters, took another one for himself, and they stepped outside into quiet twilight. The night was rather warm. He wore his widebrimmed Mountie Stetson, but no uniform. In his ranching clothes and holstered guns, he looked tough and unbeatable. The sun was slung low in the sky and still burned brightly. She couldn't look at it directly, but watched the shadows play on Luke's broad shoulders as they made their way down to the river and an awaiting canoe docked by a cluster of woods.

Crickets sang, bullfrogs groaned and owls called to each other.

"Luke, aren't *you* concerned with the rule of three?"

He looked down at her waist and she tried to ignore how he caused her pulse to jump. "I think I can overpower you, no problem."

Genevieve hid a smile, strangely flattered.

"Unless you've got a gun under that skirt, strapped to your thigh?"

The devilish comment made her spin away. To comment upon her thighs!

While she waited for her pulse to return to normal, Genevieve inhaled pure air. She inhaled freedom. They'd been locked up for five days and she'd forgotten how good it was to venture wherever she pleased. She'd grown accustomed to the climate and had spent the past two months on the open trail getting here—camping in canvas tents, navigating the waterways in homemade scows, and sleeping beneath the sky. She'd lost twelve pounds doing it, but her weight had stabilized in Dawson. The journey had benefited her with a fine physical form, though, and clear, clear skin. She was stronger than she'd ever been.

To their left, the boardwalk led into town. It was almost silent, but many establishments were open twenty-four hours due to the Klondike's continuous summer sunlight. A few customers were making their way into the Waffle House. Lanterns glowed from store windows. Piano music—God only knew how they'd dragged that thing over the Chilkoot Trail and mountains—drifted from one of the grander saloons.

Luke tossed his medicine bag into the back of the canoe and climbed aboard first, hands sliding along the birch-bark edges till he reached the built-in plank seating at the back. He clung to the side of the dock, holding the canoe steady while she lifted her skirts and climbed into the front.

Yelping with a combination of surprise and laughter at how tipsy the canoe was, she perched on her seat with her back to Luke, facing the same direction he was. Reaching for her oar, she nearly jumped out of her skin when a strange gentleman called hello.

"Luke!"

Genevieve spun toward the dock. A man in similar leather duster and a Mountie Stetson waved from ten yards upstream. A blond woman, hiking her shawl around her slender shoulders, called beside him, her voice filled with teasing laughter. "Brother Buxton!"

Buxton? Genevieve frowned.

"My middle name," explained Luke. "That's my brother, Colt, and his wife, Elizabeth."

"He's a Mountie, too," Genevieve said with awe.

Her voice carried in the quiet air, for the man tipped the brim of his hat and replied, "Yes, ma'am. Inspector Colt Hunter. This is my wife, Dr. Elizabeth Hunter."

A doctor? Genevieve stared at the woman's smiling face. The distance was too great to see her eyes, but her silhouette leaned into her husband's in such a friendly and forthright manner, Genevieve felt at ease. So this was the female doctor Genevieve had heard about when she'd arrived. How unusual. How difficult had it been for the young doctor to pursue her career in such a male-minded profession?

Good heavens, what an enlightened age they lived in. Imagine going to another woman for care, someone who understood from firsthand experience the anatomy of the female body.

And she was part of Luke's family.

Was Luke this enlightened?

"I'd like you both to meet Miss Genevieve Summerville," Luke said in a rather hasty tone behind her. He added nothing to his statement, no explanation of why she was with him or what they were doing together. But his brother and sister-in-law had likely already read it in the papers.

Genevieve cringed at the impropriety of having no chaperone. But then, everything on the journey to the Klondike and in Dawson City itself was nothing close to a normally civilized life. The wilderness and physical constraints made some social rules obsolete.

"I see you found the canoe," Colt hollered after a moment, as if he'd been waiting for an explanation, too.

"Thanks for the note," said Luke.

"How is everyone feeling?" asked Elizabeth. "Any change in Miss Norris since you wrote this morning?"

"No change. She seems to be fine."

Luke had been exchanging notes with a *female* physician, thought Genevieve. She'd assumed it was a man. Knowing there were others outside of the barracks—including this doctor—who were following their progress and advising Luke on medical care was uplifting.

"And you, Miss Summerville?" asked the doctor. "How are you feeling?"

"Fine, physically, thank you. But it's a bit difficult in other regards." Now why had she admitted that? Why raise the topic with complete strangers who'd likely already heard the gossip of their accidental marriage?

The couple standing on the edge of the docks were staring and probably wondering what she and Luke were doing together. And what might Joshua think if he saw them.

"We heard about your situation," said the doctor. "And we're awfully sorry about the mix-up."

"I know Joshua," added her husband. "He's a fine man and—and when he comes back to town he'll…" The sentence went unfinished.

He'll what? What could Joshua do? Certainly nothing to speed along the dissolution. Only a judge could do that.

"We'll let you get on with your business, then," Luke's brother added, backing away. "The filly's gotten worse. You might want to tend to her first."

The doctor looped her arm through her husband's. "Keep us informed with the notes!"

Luke shoved his oar against the dock and the canoe glided down the river.

What *were* they doing together? The idea had seemed so carefree back at the barracks. But here in the isolated wilderness of the gently flowing river, Luke almost silent in his breathing behind her, the sound of his oar slicing the water, the sound of her stroke not nearly as powerful, she felt her stomach muscles squeezing at the thought that she was truly alone with her husband for the first time since they'd met.

Alone and scared.

Luke took his time examining the filly. He ran his hands down her neck and withers, marveling at the softness. "She's beautiful." There was no one to hear him inside the

stable except Genevieve, for the owner was inside his log
house where Luke had ordered him to wait.

"What kind of horse is she?" asked Genevieve.

"A golden palomino."

"I've never seen one like her."

"They've been prized for centuries. This little one was
born two weeks ago. She's the color of a golden nugget."

"Appropriate for this place." Genevieve smiled and
Luke appreciated her natural take to animals.

The filly flicked her white tail. Luke ran his hand along
her white mane. Her dark eyes were sunken, which worried
him, and her coat had lost its sheen.

"She's worth a fortune in gold herself. Horses don't
live this far north in the wild, so every last one of them has
to come over the trails."

Genevieve made a sour face. She'd obviously seen it
herself on the trek—three thousand horses hadn't been
able to make the steep climb. Many of their owners were
city folks, unaccustomed to caring for large animals, who'd
overtaxed them on the mountains, underfed them, and
didn't know they couldn't climb forever over rocks and
crags. Many of the horses, unfortunately, had died.

"What's wrong with her?" Genevieve patted her forehead, running a tender hand over the marking, a white star.
He liked the way Genevieve's hands moved.

"Lost her appetite. Won't eat." The filly was too thin.
Her ribs were showing and she had no energy.

Genevieve grew still as Luke pulled out his stethoscope
and listened to her heart. A bit fast, but it was strong. Didn't
seem to have a fever.

Luke didn't understand it. He straightened and looked
over the stalls to the broodmare. There was a palomino

stallion in the far end, next to a mule, with two goats in the corner, but the owner, Otis Rutledge, had only complained about the filly.

"Have you figured it out?" asked Genevieve.

"Not yet. Let's check her mother."

"But Mr. Rutledge said the broodmare's fine."

"He's not the vet. I am."

It took another twenty minutes for Luke to examine the mare. On the surface, she seemed fine. But she was developing the same symptoms as her foal—slightly sunken eyes and dry mucous membranes in her mouth.

"I think I know."

"What is it?" Genevieve asked, running behind him as he tidied up his things and headed outside. "Aren't you going to check the other animals? If two horses have the same thing, maybe it's passed on to the stallion and mule."

"Nope. Not necessary."

"Then tell me, what is it?"

"Mr. Rutledge is going to tell us."

Rutledge must have seen them coming out of the square pane of his window, for the cabin's front door opened and he stepped out in overalls, scratching his beard. They were careful to keep their distance. "What do you think?"

"The problem's not with the filly," Luke told him. "The problem's with the broodmare."

"How do you reckon that?"

"The broodmare's still nursing the filly, but her milk is drying up. Haven't you noticed?"

"No."

"That's why the filly's getting weaker. How much are you feeding the mare?"

"I've doubled her feed to account for the nursing."

"Doubling's not enough. You've got an active filly here that romps around for most of the day, and a mare who's attentive to her baby's every movement. The activity alone—never mind the milking—is draining the broodmare. She needs four times the amount of feed she usually eats."

"*Four?*"

"Yup. I've got some molasses back at the outpost. I'll have it sent tomorrow. You can add some to her feed to boost her energy and improve the condition of her coat."

"Much obliged."

"You got enough hay?"

"Yeah, my brother bought a shipment of seed hay that came in yesterday."

"Good. It's got more nutrition than meadow hay."

"We're intendin' on breedin' horses up here. We want the best care for 'em."

"Send for me again if things don't improve. Otherwise, I'll stop by when I can."

"Thanks, kindly."

Luke nodded and they were off again, he and Genevieve paddling into the night. The sun had hit the horizon and would hover there for a few hours before rising for the morning. It cast a pretty purple shadow on Genevieve's shoulder blades, on her long braid and slim waist.

He watched her movements in front of him, enjoying the way her hips rocked on her seat when she stretched her legs beneath her skirts, how the muscles beneath the back of her cotton shirt flexed and twisted with her strokes, the tilt of her rounded cheek, and the way the gentle sun struck the bend at her neck.

The neck he'd once kissed.

He wondered how her skin would feel beneath his lips if he had kissed lower. Warm? Inviting?

The growing fire inside of him intensified.

Willing his thoughts to leave, Luke turned away from her voluptuous figure. He steered the canoe to the banks of the next property.

"Do we have to do this in the middle of the night?" Henry Solbaucher lowered his rifle and called from his house.

"We're in quarantine. It's the safest time for us to travel."

The old man griped but nodded toward the small barn. "Cow's in there. Second one from the right. You'll see the bandage on her leg. I wrapped it, but it's not healing."

"What happened to her?"

"She came back from the pasture three days ago with a limp. Scraped her leg on something."

When Luke and Genevieve entered the barn, he took one look at the bandaging and realized it wasn't enough. The hock—the joint—was bandaged, but no support given above or below. He unwound the dry gauze and took a look.

The muscles above the joint were slightly swollen, red and hot. When Luke touched the spot, the cow flinched. Genevieve stepped into the stall and soothed the animal, stroking its forehead, murmuring quiet words, giving Luke opportunity to do his work.

The other leg was fine, and the straw bedding was thick enough that it wasn't the stall boards she was kicking up against that had caused the problem. It was indeed something in the pasture she'd stumbled upon. Luke opened his veterinary bag and removed a special paste made of dried beetles, called a blister. He rubbed it over the soreness. It soothed the cow, she relaxed and allowed Genevieve to continue stroking her.

Thirty minutes later, Luke told Solbaucher. "It's a strained tendon. I applied a blister and it seems to have done the trick. I'll be back in a week to do it again."

"Thank you," Solbaucher hollered as they left.

Luke checked his pocket watch. "Would you like to take a detour?" he asked Genevieve, back in the canoe once more. There was still no need for their dusters, for the air was warm. "We've got time."

"Where to?"

"Have you seen the gold pits yet?"

"I haven't been out of Dawson since I arrived."

"They're just around the corner."

She straightened on the seat six feet in front of him, eager to see the view. He turned at a fork in the river, and they were surrounded by a hillside of tents. Gravel chutes clung to the slopes on either side of them. Most men were sleeping, but some were still up, their voices rumbling over the landscape as they sifted through gravel they'd dug up earlier in the day.

But it was the tilled earth, overturned like a gopher might do as he was looking for a root vegetable, that captured Genevieve's eye. In awe, she stared at the mountain of manmade activity.

Thinking of his medicines and duties once again as they paddled away, he blurted out to her. "I've ruled out ether as the poison."

"Why?"

"For small animals like a cat or dog, it takes less than a minute to make them unconscious and ready for surgery when they inhale it. A horse needs two to three. A cow takes about fifteen. It would have taken too long for someone to gas Orman. There would've been a struggle and someone would've heard it."

"So ether's out. You think it was something else in your bag?"

"Had to be. It's full of poisons. Injections are out, too. There weren't any puncture wounds. So, no morphine or cocaine."

"What does that leave?"

"Carbon tetrachloride, but the bottle is still full and sealed. It could've been electrolytes. Special sodium and potassium tablets crushed into his coffee. They would've affected his heart in a major way. But the coffee would've tasted salty. He wouldn't have drunk it."

She lifted her oar and slid it into the water. "What else, Luke?"

"An overdose of just about anything in my bag. I've got a dozen more tonics. But most of them have strong smells. I didn't smell anything in Orman's coffee."

"You think the same poison was used on the judge and Mr. Orman?"

"Not necessarily."

"So what's your conclusion?"

"Don't have one yet. But I'm looking for a tonic that may leave behind a small rash."

"Mr. Orman's throat."

"That's right. And it's probably something that's as plain as day. I'll just have to go through them again. One by one."

They paddled for ten minutes against the current, the river narrowing, the gravel beds getting wider, the trees sloping toward them until he thought it best to turn around.

"We had better get home," he said, grateful that she'd listened to his reasoning, that he had someone to talk it through with.

They turned at a bend and the paddling became easier.

The still of the night engulfed them. Their breathing united. Their strokes became one.

Genevieve's silhouette against the aspens and willows became his focus. He watched the breeze pull at the scarf tied around her throat. Her hand came up to smooth the fabric, her mouth tilted at an angle toward the sunken sun. Her lashes flickered against the spray of water and her soft laughter coaxed him into a quieter mood.

They edged into the riverbank close to where they'd embarked. He couldn't return the canoe to the same spot due to the tide rippling against them. Instead, he turned into a cove nestled against the wind by a thicket of cedars. Inhaling the sweet scent of the wood, Luke stepped out of the canoe first, holding the edge as he slid toward her to give her a hand.

She embraced it, still smiling gently at their adventure, yanking at her scarf as she gingerly stepped out with one foot, then leaped out with the other.

"Oh," she said, laughing at the force of her own strength, bumping slightly into his elbow.

Holding her hand, feeling the warmth of her fingers tucked into his, Luke went suddenly still.

"I should…I should retrieve your coat…" She said it softly among the fragrant cedars but didn't move.

He slid his fingers deeper into hers, exploring the smooth underside of her knuckles, skin against skin, strength against tenderness.

"You never wear gloves," he said gently.

"They interfere with my duties."

"I've never seen that scarf before."

She ran her other hand over the blue linen and made a deep hum at the back of her throat. "It was my mother's favorite."

"When you catch sight of a hawk, you always make that same sound," he told her, still enjoying the feel of her fingers. "A low murmur, as though you're talking to it, saying hello."

"Do I? I...never noticed."

"When you think no one's watching, you sit back and simply listen to other people's conversation. You do that a lot."

"I...I enjoy listening to what they have to say. So many people from around the world."

He stroked her knuckles and she allowed him.

"When you drink your coffee in the morning," he added slowly, "you tap your toe and hum. You don't do it in the evening. Then you like to sip your tea slow and peaceful."

She continued to stare up at him, fingers entwined, panting to catch her breath.

"You do this little thing with Nugget. You scratch her belly and you come right up under her chin with two fingers...."

They stilled.

Her eyes shone with an appeal he found difficult to resist. "When you brush your horses," she said, revealing the details *she'd* noticed about *him,* "you always whisper in their ears. To every one of the animals you care for. It always makes you smile."

He smiled now, a slow and lazy warmth rising up his body. "I tell them how much they're appreciated."

She pressed her slender hands against her thighs, in that smooth alluring way that engaged him. "You drink your coffee black. You take no butter with your bread. Yet, you love the sweet pastries the cook brings around in the evenings."

"I come nowhere close to rivaling your sweet tooth," he whispered, stepping closer, cupping the side of her warm cheek, wondering what she'd do if he kissed her, slow and sensual. Unable to resist any longer, he leaned down to the curve of Genevieve's lips to discover for himself.

Chapter Eleven

The warm pressure of his mouth was intoxicating.

With eyes closed, Genevieve tilted her head and allowed Luke's bold advance. In the back recess of her mind, she knew it was shocking for her to stand here and allow this, but she'd been lulled by the midnight sun, spellbound by the warm Yukon wind and transported into his world tonight. It was a world where he cared lovingly for his animals, where beauty saturated every sense, where the solitude of nature melded into a yearning between a man and a woman.

With an unhurried manner, Luke looped his fingers at the back of her neck beneath her braid, softly urging her to draw forward, closer and closer yet. He kissed her mouth lightly, left a dampness on the swell of her upper lip, and the faint whisk of his shaving lotion on her skin, before he gazed into her eyes and they pondered where this union might lead. Where it must never lead.

"It's you and me right now," he whispered. "And I've been wanting to do this all night."

He angled his mouth and came down firmly on hers.

When his fingertips grazed the hollow part at the back of her neck, swirling in the soft tendrils, a feeling of heat and pressure surged through her limbs.

His kiss was unrestrained, and when his arms slid down her sides, she moved her own upward over his firm chest, eagerly cupping his throat.

"I like that," he murmured. It surprised her that he would speak such intimacies aloud.

She kissed the side of his mouth and then the other, the whole time being deliciously chased by his tongue. He licked her upper lip and their mouths lingered, tongues exploring tongues, the tips illicit messengers sending signals of sexual joy.

He murmured against her mouth. "So much nicer, even, than I thought."

He'd thought about her? *In that way?*

It was scandalous. Beyond wicked. She belonged to another man and this man had been dreaming of *her?*

Perhaps she was no better…having watched his hands glide along the muscles of his horses as he groomed them, wondering how those hands would feel upon her. How those fingers would knead her naked flesh and press against her hips.

With their mouths battling for expression, for a deeper connection and tighter fit, he slid his hand around her side, over her blouse and the mound of her corset, and found her breast. Her breathing grew fuller, richer, faster.

With a quick tug on her blouse, he pushed his hand beneath the fabric, between the cups of her corset, and aimed for bare flesh. She startled at the shocking contact between his fingers and her nipple.

Unable to control herself, she uttered a sound of pleasure.

Moaning into her lips, he nibbled the edge of her mouth and rolled the point of her budding breast between his fingers. When he gently tugged, she felt the resulting ripple of contact straight through to her thighs. She was moist for him, and ready for his touch there as well.

He was quick to receive the signal, for his other hand lowered to her hip. Trailing around her backside, he pressed her hips into his own, and when their centers met, she felt his rigid response.

She couldn't.

Bending away from him, she turned to look up at his face.

He was glazed by the golden rays, tall and proud, gasping for air as though she'd robbed him of breath.

No one had ever kissed her like this before. No one had ever made her feel so many things like this before.

She looked good, disheveled. Luke watched the unexpected beauty as she fought to regain her composure. Disheveled by his hand—her prim blouse tugged out of her proper skirt, pristine hair uprooted from its neat row of braiding, skin flushed with desire, lips bruised from his own.

"You haven't said a word," he said softly, regarding the tilted chin and the deliberate stare.

"Because I'm ashamed of what we're doing."

"There's nothing shameful in feeling how we feel."

"But there's shame in acting upon it."

"So you admit the feelings, just not the act."

"You're...you're putting words in my mouth."

He bit down on his jaw, tensing as he regarded her.

Light flickered in her eyes. Creases came to her forehead and worry grooved the lines around her lips.

"I certainly wouldn't want to do that," he said.

Luke could handle anything to do with crime. In fact, over the years, he'd seen many gut-wrenching crimes committed that would harden the toughest man. Some said he feared nothing. But he did fear this.

He feared reacting to Genevieve in a manner unfit for a gentleman. Unfit as a friend of her intended groom. Luke had lived in many cities and passed through many different homes, courting dozens of women along the way. But he'd never promised anything to any one of them. Not to *one*.

He lived a life without promises.

It was easier if people didn't expect things from him. Women expected nothing if he made it clear from the start how he led his life.

Wouldn't it have been easier for Luke's mother, if his father had made the same vow? No promises. No disappointments. She wouldn't have waited for him, then, struggling to raise two sons on her own while he gallivanted out of town for every vein of precious metal ever struck in North America—silver in the West, nickel in the North, gold in California.

Gold had been his downfall, coming home with a gold ore nugget the size of Luke's seventeen-year-old fist.

Gunned down in the back for that precious metal.

It stung like hell being in the Yukon where almost everyone had the same gold fever affliction, but Luke had come for precisely that reason. To try to see for himself what kind of a man his father might have been. And how odd it was that Luke was standing in as proxy groom for another man who had gold fever.

No promises, thought Luke, dusting off his hat. No promises.

This woman, so conservative compared to the women he usually sought, *already* staring up at him with the reflection of accusation and anticipation in her eyes, would expect big ones.

"I apologize." He swept the air with his Mountie hat, pointing toward the outpost, pushing away the memory of her soft naked breast and how he'd reshaped it in his palm. "Ladies first. We won't mention this again. I *promise*."

The memory tinkered in Luke's mind and wouldn't release him for the full ten minutes it took to get back to the barracks. The budding of her nipple, the warmth of her skin, but mostly her feverish response to *him*, when he'd touched and kissed her where he shouldn't be touching and kissing any woman, let alone Joshua McFadden's intended bride.

"Where were you two last night?" Penelope poured herself a cup of coffee as Genevieve sputtered hers at the unexpected question. She'd been avoiding Penelope since rising an hour ago.

The breakfast table was packed. The group passed around plates of flapjacks the cook and his assistant had brought in five minutes earlier. Steam rose from a basket of heated scones.

Genevieve decided to let Luke, seated halfway across the table from her, answer.

"We went for a tour of the outskirts of town. Were you up?"

"I couldn't sleep. Nugget woke me with her growling."

"Nugget growls?" Genevieve frowned at the pup.

Penelope puckered her mouth. "Evidently. She found a spider at three o'clock this morning."

Constable Zucker chuckled. "She doesn't like spiders."

"And Lord knows—" Penelope looked up at the cobwebs above the window "—there are enough of them around here."

"Zucker," said Luke, pouring himself another cup of coffee. "After breakfast I want you to take a broom and sweep them clear."

"Yes, sir."

Genevieve reached to the middle of the table for a bottle of maple syrup, poured it over her flapjacks and licked the spilled sweetness from her fingertips.

Mr. Kendall was seated next to Penelope, and seemed attentive to her every wish. "More coffee?" he asked her. Then, "Allow me to pass the scones." In return, Penelope giggled and pressed her shoulder onto his. At first, Genevieve thought it was escaping Luke's attention, but with the latest giggle, Luke shook his head.

Genevieve tried not to think of the burning kiss she'd shared with this woman's beau last night.

Luke was watching Genevieve. Instead of turning away, she stared back. Were the two of them any better than Penelope and Mr. Kendall? When a couple burned for each other's company, didn't their eyes meet at every opportunity? Didn't they make every excuse to be together?

She, however, didn't want to be like Penelope. So flirtatious. Genevieve would stay away from Luke. This would be her lesson from last night.

Penelope turned her lined lashes to Genevieve. "Where'd you go?"

"The inspector had a couple of visits to make."

"What visits?"

"On two very sick animals."

"Oh." Penelope spun to Luke. "Why didn't you ask me to go?"

"You would have been interested in sick cows and horses?"

"Well, I...I could have been of some help, I imagine."

Luke stared at her accepting yet another sliver of sugar from Mr. Kendall. "Right."

"I could have assisted you with whatever you needed assistance with." Penelope turned to Genevieve. "I'm sure you were right there, Miss Summerville, helping. Weren't you?"

Unnerved, Genevieve stopped eating. "Well...I sat with the filly while he examined her. She seemed rather agitated. And then later, the cow seemed to quiet down when I entered the stall."

Mr. Kendall smiled at Penelope. "I manage a large livery. Anytime you'd like to see the horses and mules..." His voice faded when he glanced at Luke, perhaps realizing he was overstepping his bounds.

Penelope's eyes sparkled. "There, you see, Luke. I'm interested in all sorts of animals."

"Right."

"Please, if you ever go out that late again, please wake me. I don't want to sit idle while I'm here."

"You weren't idle," Mr. Kendall teased her, quickly recovering from his temporary lapse of embarrassment in front of Luke. "You were sleeping."

"I can sleep anytime. If Luke needs me, he needs me."

"Right," said Luke.

Was that all he was going to say?

"Could you pass the sugar?" asked Ripley. Penelope slid it down the table. He hammered off a sliver from the top of the peak and dunked it into his coffee. His brother Burt did the same. Vince avoided the sweet, as did Uncle Theodore.

Five minutes passed when no one said a word. Perhaps they felt the tension between Mr. Kendall, Luke, Penelope and her.

Finished with his breakfast before the others, Luke took aside Uncle Theodore.

"You were the last person I saw close to my medical bag. Remember when we introduced Milly to the bay?"

Uncle Theodore's ponytail dangled along his arm when he stiffened. "I recall."

Genevieve, mouth agape, stirred her coffee. Luke thought her uncle was capable of absconding with horse medicine? That he might poison Mr. Orman?

What on earth for? What would her uncle gain?

"Now listen, here, Inspector." Aunt Abigail waltzed out from behind the pile of dirty dishes. "If you think I'm going to stand idly by and watch you tear my husband's character to shreds—"

"No, Mrs. Thornbottom, that's fine." Luke raised a hand in the air. "I have a question for Mr. Kendall."

The liveryman, in his clean overalls, shot up from Penelope's side. "I was just going out to enjoy a cigar."

"I heard the judge owed you some money on that horse you were holding for him."

Ah, thought Genevieve, Luke must have gotten the information from the other Mounties. She'd noticed that he was directing his men to question folks in town on his behalf. They were discreetly sending notes back and forth. It was insane how Luke was conducting an investigation at arm's length. Yesterday, he'd received a small box of documents. She'd glimpsed several before he locked them up—the judge's deed to his house, an old letter from his wife, outstanding legal work he was doing before he died.

"Yeah?" said Mr. Kendall. "The judge owed me money. So?" His tone was certainly different with Luke than it was with Penelope.

"I heard he wasn't that anxious to pay. There was a dispute about the horse's lineage."

Mr. Kendall lowered his empty coffee cup on the table and coolly declared, "Poisoning the son of a bitch wouldn't get me my money back any sooner, would it?"

The room hushed.

The air in the room stiffened.

Genevieve shuddered.

Penelope paled.

Mr. Kendall stalked to the door, lifted his jacket off a peg and turned around. "Sorry about the language," he said to Penelope, then turned back to Luke. "But I'm sure it comes as no surprise to you, Inspector, the judge and I had words that morning."

Aghast, Miss Norris sniffed into her hankie.

"Yes, I heard that rumor, too," said Luke calmly.

"You'd think a judge would be timely in his payments." Kendall opened the door and left.

Luke turned his attention to Vince Cliffton. "You and Orman were partners when you started out for the Klondike together. I heard you planned on opening that jewelry store together."

Vince sipped his coffee. "We had a falling-out."

"When?"

"When we reached Alaska."

"Over what?"

Vince's eyes narrowed. "I don't rightly recall."

"Let me understand this. You and Orman set out for a two-to-three-month journey to the Klondike, intending to stake a claim and use it to open a jewelry store, yet you forget what you argued about?"

His brother Burt spoke up to defend him, although his other brother, Ripley, lifted his coffee to his mouth and simply watched, it seemed to Genevieve, as though amused.

"There's plenty of folks who split up on the trail," said Burt. "You must have seen it yourself."

"Yeah, I saw some. Lots of folks can't handle the hardships."

"We argued about nonsense," said Vince, digging into his shirt pocket for a cigar. "We lost our temper so many times on the trail I lost count. On that particular morning, we were arguing over a jar of honey."

Luke strummed his fingers on the table, pondering it. "Honey."

"Yeah. We were both hungry."

The conversation seemed to be leading nowhere.

After a beat, Luke turned to Miss Norris. "I understand that on the night Mr. Orman passed away, you and Mrs. Thornbottom were up around three, having tea."

"We couldn't sleep," gasped Genevieve's aunt.

That would explain the noises she heard during her own restless night, thought Genevieve.

"What did you see?" asked the inspector.

"He…he was sleeping…and so we finished quickly and went back to bed."

Miss Norris lifted her handkerchief to her cheek. "Inspector, if you have any questions for me, please…please can we speak in private?"

He nodded. "All right. Let's step outside. You pick the other person you want to join us."

Miss Norris sighed. "The rule of three." She glanced

at the anxious faces and turned to Genevieve. "Miss Summerville?"

Why couldn't they all leave her alone? Didn't they know she had enough happening with her ill-gained marriage, that she just wanted to be left alone? Especially when it concerned Luke.

However, Genevieve reached for her straw hat. "Coming."

Luke, almost at the door, swung around and motioned to Vince. "Who got the honey?"

"Beg your pardon?"

"Who won the argument over the honey?"

Vince spoke slowly. "He did."

Luke stared and left the room.

They stepped into morning sunshine. The wind kicked up Genevieve's skirts. A blessed relief.

"Miss Norris," Luke began, "what I need to know is…why you two never married."

Miss Norris gasped.

"Let's not pretend," he said, "that nothing was going on between the two of you. Maybe not physically…"

Miss Norris moaned into her hankie.

Genevieve felt the heat rise to her neck. She didn't wish to be privy to such an intimate conversation, but was once again trapped by circumstance.

"…but there were certainly a lot of feelings involved. The judge, as I knew him, was a direct man. Did he ever ask for your hand in marriage?"

Miss Norris sobbed. "No."

"Why not?" asked Luke. "Any single man in his right mind would have."

"I kept asking myself that…" She repositioned herself at the tree. "I kept asking whether he didn't like the way I looked. I—I tried to do my hair the way he liked…I cooked his favorite meals…I was there whenever he called my name, whenever he wanted his jacket pressed or a private conversation to discuss his worries of the day."

"Did that come to grate on you after a while?"

"No." She was quick to respond. "Never. I…I loved Fergus. I felt it was only a matter of time before he asked."

"Did you know he frequented the casino in the evenings?"

"Yes, of course." Her shoulders rose a notch, as though insulted by the question. "We lived under the same roof."

"That's all. Thank you."

Miss Norris, pale and shaken, sobbed into her hankie, spun on her heel and left for the barracks.

"I suppose I'm next," said Genevieve, bracing herself. "You've offended just about everyone this morning. I guess it's my turn."

He looked at her. "That won't be necessary."

"Why not?"

"Because based on the answers I got…and didn't get this morning…and the observations I made…I think I know who did it."

"Luke!" Penelope interrupted them with a shout from the barracks. "Take me for a walk!"

Before she had a chance to reach them, Luke whispered to Genevieve. "Please keep this information to yourself. It would hinder my investigation for others to know I suspect someone."

Genevieve stood there, shocked by his disclosure. Who on earth did he think it was?

Not her. Certainly, that was evident, for he hadn't asked her a single question this morning. But who? Had Miss

Norris poisoned the judge in a fit of anger or jealousy? Why would Miss Norris then poison Orman?

Or was the killer Mr. Kendall, motivated by greed? He'd wanted payment for his horse from the judge, and revenge on the crooked deal Orman had given him?

One of the Cliffton brothers?

If Luke knew who the killer was, then she was off the hook, first and foremost. She was safer, too, since Luke could now arrest the person.

His disclosure also meant something on a deeper level. Luke had trusted her enough to admit that he'd solved the crime.

She listened as he led Penelope away, wondering if he'd mention it to her, too, but Luke talked of everything but the crime.

"Did you enjoy breakfast?" he asked the other woman. And as they walked away, Penelope prompted him on her hair. "Certainly," he responded. "I like when you wear it down like that."

Where was he going? Wasn't he going to arrest someone? Did he have enough proof yet?

Luke glanced past his shoulder to have a look at Genevieve, but gone was the private moment where she could ask him more about his discovery.

Yet, between them, there lingered a new privacy, an intimacy of having disclosed something perhaps he shouldn't have, that he had to know she'd ask about later.

He'd solved the crime in six days. Lord, he was remarkable.

It was three nights later, on Monday close to midnight, when Genevieve saw Luke alone again. She couldn't sleep and was turning in her bed. When Nugget whimpered at her feet, Genevieve stumbled up, reached for her skirt and blouse, and threw them on to walk the dog. Wearing her night robe outside, in front of the Mounties, was tempting but would be improper. She swept her hair back with a clasp and drank a glass of water in the kitchen.

Constable Zucker kept his eye on her as she headed out the door. "The inspector's out there, too."

"He is?" She peered into the dim evening sky. "He can't sleep?"

"Suppose not, ma'am."

Genevieve spotted Luke leaning against the fence, staring off at the hills. Twilight engulfed him. The dark hair, intense profile, the sharp cut of his chin, sent her pulse soaring. Would she ever get enough of him? Would his proximity ever stop tormenting her?

She made her way to his side, pretending he didn't affect her. Nugget yawned behind her.

"I believe we haven't finished our conversation," she said.

He turned around. "I wondered who the footsteps belonged to. Too light to be Miss Norris. Too slow and easy to be Penelope's. But Nugget's yawn gave it away."

"Who is it, Luke? Tell me who it is."

He searched her face. "I can't do that. I shouldn't have said what I did."

"But you've told the other Mounties?"

When he turned his cheek, the light played along the curve of his jaw. "Those who need to know, know."

"So we're safe, then, the rest of us."

"We're still concerned about the measles."

"Yes, yes, the measles, but the crime—"

"Yoo-hoo!" shouted Penelope across the way. She

raised her silken handkerchief from the door of the barracks. "Are you going out for your calls, again, Luke? May I come along?"

Was the woman stalking Genevieve? They lived together in such confined quarters that Genevieve's rustling, or Nugget's whimpering, had likely woken her.

Luke sighed. "I hadn't planned on it, but since I'm up I thought I'd have another look at that filly."

Penelope glanced in Genevieve's direction with a dismissive nod. "Good night, Miss Summerville."

Luke drew her back with a firm arm. Genevieve quaked at his touch.

"Perhaps both of you ladies would like to join me. I've called for Weston, so now we'll need another person for the second canoe."

Genevieve hesitated. She wanted to see how the animals were doing. She wouldn't be able to fall asleep again for an hour or two even if she tried, and since there'd be four of them going, she could keep her distance from Luke and Penelope. And she would dearly love to taste the freedom again of getting off the compound.

In a swirl of pretty fabrics and ribbons, Penelope cleared her throat and looked over the fence. "Why don't you call another man, instead of Genevieve, to accompany Weston? Mr. Kendall, perhaps. Or Vince. Vince enjoys late nights."

But Luke's dark gaze never left Genevieve's face. What was happening between them? She felt the pull. She wanted to be with him, she couldn't deny it.

"I'd like to see how the filly's doing," she said.

"Good, then. Get your duster and we'll go."

They headed out, this time Genevieve paddling in front of Weston, and Luke and Penelope in the same canoe.

It hurt to see them together, thought Genevieve. It was a mistake to have come. But when she saw the animals and how much they'd improved, her spirits lifted. The filly was still weak, but was nursing better.

Penelope tried to step closer to the horse, bracing her hand on the stalls and anchoring herself next to Luke. He was patient with her, but his focus soon turned to the filly and he had to ignore her. She clicked her tongue in annoyance whenever he turned away.

On their way back to the barracks, the steamy river enveloped their canoes. A loon called. The ebb and flow of the current lulled Genevieve. She wondered what sort of man she'd married. She let her mind drift as Weston took control of the canoe, demanding very little from her other than the soft stroking she was doing.

What sort of husband would Luke make if they'd truly gotten married?

Would he be the attentive type, quick to see to her needs around the house? And perhaps the bedroom?

Would he be the jealous type, turning away any man who paid her the least bit of attention?

Or might he be the passionate type, who'd always want her in his arms and in his bed?

She flushed at the pleasant thought.

They docked their canoes. Luke helped Penelope to her feet, then turned to assist Genevieve. He held out his hand and she slid hers in. She recalled the tremulous kiss they'd shared in this very spot. He seemed subdued as well, his quiet attention turning to her lips.

Thank the Lord no one could read her racy thoughts.

Luke as a friend.

Luke as a husband.

Luke as a lover.

Pulling away, she walked behind him and Penelope toward the barracks, enjoying the cut of his shoulder blades, the way the muscles moved beneath his shirt, the sway of his lean hips, the angle of his holster.

And as they reached their door, she was still studying the steely profile of her husband and didn't immediately recognize the gentleman standing with Constable Morgan at the far end of the trees.

The gentleman stepped out of the shadows to greet her. "Good evening, Genevieve. It's good to see you."

Joshua.

Chapter Twelve

Luke's breath quickened at the sight of the familiar face. A sense of unexplained disappointment quivered in his gut. He tried to summon enthusiasm. "Joshua, by God, how are you?"

But Joshua was too enthralled with Genevieve to answer. Ten yards away, he was smiling and politely holding his hat. His dark hair was ruffled above his ears. He needed a haircut, but had managed a shave. It was the middle of the night, thought Luke, but Joshua couldn't wait to see her.

"Don't step any closer," Luke told him. "We're under quarantine. You shouldn't be here."

Joshua glared at him as though restraining the true force of his emotions. His jaw tightened, his shoulders straightened. "*I* shouldn't be here?" He took a step closer to Luke. "*Me?*"

Unsettled, Luke turned to the others. Genevieve had paled. She was stiff and silent, and Luke's heart stirred with sympathy. And guilt. And goddamn jealousy. "Weston, do you mind taking Miss Wick indoors? There's no reason for her to hear this."

With great ceremony, Penelope lifted her skirts, kissed Luke on the cheek and flounced inside the barracks. Weston followed her inside. This left Luke and Genevieve on one side, and Joshua and a constable in the distance.

"I know how you must feel." Luke fumbled for words. "But I've got a duty here. My duty is to keep everyone out of harm's way. We don't want you exposed to measles." Luke turned to Constable Morgan, who'd been patrolling the perimeter of the property. "Did you let him go inside the barracks?"

"No, sir. He surprised me by comin' in so late, but going inside was totally out of the question."

"You've got to leave right now," Luke told Joshua.

But Joshua took two steps forward.

Luke riveted on the man. "Don't come any closer, McFadden."

Joshua stopped. "I'd like to speak to my…Genevieve." He turned to her again, leaning forward as if he wanted to sweep her up on the spot. "The woman who's supposed to be *my* wife."

Luke groaned. So he'd heard the news. "I'm sorry, Joshua."

The man shot him a hostile glare. "Sorry doesn't even *begin* to cover what you've done."

Genevieve, waiting in silence up till this point, ran her hand down her skirt and peered uneasily at Joshua. "How are you, Joshua? How was your trip?"

"Terrible."

Luke grumbled. Obviously, Joshua hadn't found any gold.

"Even worse when I got home to this. I went straight to my house, Genevieve, hoping to find you there. In our new marriage bed."

Genevieve looked down at her boots. From the barracks,

the curtains rustled at the open windows and Luke realized folks were listening.

The heat of a dozen emotions crept up his neck. It was so much harder to face this man than Luke had imagined. How could he look his friend in the eye and tell him that he, Luke, had failed miserably to look after the bride? That not only was she married to the wrong man, but she'd been exposed to a deadly illness, and was vulnerable to a murderer who'd already poisoned two people. The quiet interludes Luke had spent with Genevieve...the kiss on the mouth...the throat...burned vividly on his lips and on his conscience.

And yet he wanted more.

Joshua shoved his fists into the pockets of his wool coat. "Hunter, how could you be so clueless as to let the judge write down the wrong name?"

Luke didn't reply. Maybe he deserved it.

"You're not the trusted friend I thought you were."

"Joshua, please." Genevieve shoved her hands into her skirt pockets.

Joshua roared at Luke. "You're an ass—"

"Joshua, *please,*" she pleaded. "This isn't helping."

In his mind, Luke had called himself worse.

But Joshua's voice got louder. "What excuse, what excuse do you have?"

"The only excuse I have is that the judge was ill. He was in a fever. Not thinking straight when he wrote our names."

"Fever?" said Joshua. "And what sort of fever were *you* in?"

Luke moaned at his own shortcomings. "None whatsoever. I was getting him a glass of water."

Joshua kicked the dirt. "Then maybe you planned this."

"*What?*" Genevieve held her hands. "Don't be *ridiculous.*"

"It's possible," said Joshua evenly, facing his rightful bride.

Appalled at the suggestion, Luke dropped his veterinary bag to the ground. He'd forgotten he was even holding it. "Why would I plan this?"

Joshua shoved his fists deeper into his coat pocket. "Because after you met her, you liked the looks of her."

"I consider that an insult," Luke said through gritted teeth.

"So do I," said Genevieve.

Joshua swore beneath his breath. "No one has been more insulted by this than *me.*"

"And me," called Penelope from inside. The curtains at the window moved again, but she was invisible.

Luke exhaled. Penelope was also caught in this mess.

"Who's she?" asked Joshua. "Are you courting Penelope Wick, too?"

Luke groaned.

Joshua sneered. "Another one of your women."

Luke leaped forward, trying hard to restrain himself from stepping any closer than ten yards. Insulting *him* was one thing. Insulting Genevieve or Penelope was another. "McFadden, you're hovering on the precipice of a dangerous cliff."

Luke motioned Genevieve to move toward the shack. When she did, he followed her past Joshua. "We're tired. You're tired. We're going to bed. Next time, write a note before you come."

"You're going to bed with *two* women, and I don't even have one?"

Genevieve whipped around so fast her skirts snapped the air. "Joshua!"

"And I can't even get a kiss?"

Luke's temper snapped. "Have you been drinking?"

"None of your goddamn business."

"For your own safety, move out of our way. Or I'll have Morgan and Enscott—"

With a howl of anger, Joshua lunged for Luke. He swung hard and cracked a fist into Luke's jaw.

"Joshua!" Genevieve screamed.

Luke turned and swung back harder, hitting the son of a bitch right in the mouth, where he deserved it.

"Luke, stop," she shouted. "Every time you get involved in my life, you make things worse!"

Genevieve shrieked as she tried to break up the two men. She wedged her hand into Joshua's elbow and yanked hard but couldn't restrain him. He didn't give. Instead, he punched Luke in the eye.

"Stop it!" She whirled around, eyes pleading to the two Mountie guards who'd jumped back to allow the fighting men more space. "Can't you stop them?"

"I don't think so, ma'am," said the fair-haired Enscott. "You'd best step aside. They're not through yet."

Genevieve yelped as the brawling men came hurling in her direction. When Joshua raised his arm to swing again, Luke blocked him and punched Joshua in the stomach.

Joshua hit the ground.

Luke panted above him. "I didn't start this, but I say it's finished."

Joshua clutched his gut. "You did start this. If it weren't for you...if it weren't for you...I'd be *sleeping* with her tonight."

Genevieve said nothing, but the pain of his words settled

around her heart. How could he be so crass to talk like this in front of these men? She smelled whiskey and wondered how many drinks he'd needed to loosen his tongue.

She couldn't blame him. She'd been caught off guard by the accidental wedding just as sharply as he had. But she'd chosen to suffer silently rather than display her anger in physical form.

This is how men dealt with their pain. They fought for what was theirs. They protected their women and children with their muscles as well as their words.

Joshua had been terribly hurt. It must have come as a horrific surprise—enough to make him drink, because he'd never been a drinker when she knew him in Montana.

She looked at the crumpled man lying on the ground. He was heavier, more muscled, than he'd been seven years ago. His dark hair was a bit longer than she'd expected, grazing the top of his shoulders. His dark eyes seemed cooler than she recalled, perhaps from maturity, from seeing a tougher side of the world here in the wilderness.

She stood ten feet away, but wasn't quite sure whether she could go to him, lest she potentially pass him measles. So she stood, watching Luke, waiting for someone to do something.

"There's no block of ice in the barracks," said Luke. "But, Morgan, why don't you haul us a bucket of that cold water from the well?"

The constable grabbed a bucket by the door and raced toward the well on top of the hill.

"Yes, yes," said Genevieve, eager to set things right with Joshua. "You'll need a compress. Your lip's bleeding."

Penelope called from the door, pulling her shawl tightly over her shoulders. "Luke's eye could use one, too."

Genevieve noticed Mr. Kendall easing in beside Penelope.

Luke blinked at them, his left eye puffy, the scar beneath it more pronounced and red from the hits. When he winced, Genevieve winced with him.

Looking at the two men, she thought there was something extremely sad about the whole situation.

Joshua's pride had been hurt and, more directly, his dreams for an immediate future with her. But Luke was suffering, too. He'd stepped in as proxy groom to help a friend, and his life had been turned inside out.

Luke didn't wish to be married to her any more than she to him. It had been a horrid wedding day. Followed by another murder and Lord knows what else might come.

And yet, of all the men she might have been stuck with here in the Klondike, she couldn't think of anyone more capable of investigating these crimes; of keeping a calm head on his shoulders about the wedding fiasco; of tending to the precious animals that needed care, of trying to walk away when Joshua had provoked him.

If she'd had a say in that fateful day, if she had to choose her own replacement groom, she would have picked Dr. Luke Hunter.

She would've picked Luke. *Luke.*

The realization struck her dumb.

Lord, she was in trouble. She was feeling things she shouldn't be feeling, for a man who had no right to stare back at her with those glistening brown eyes that saw too much around him, who understood her and her life perhaps more than she would have thought possible in such a short time.

When Joshua groaned, she kneeled at his side. "Sit up slowly. Take it nice and slow."

It took ten minutes to get the cold compresses on the men. Genevieve concentrated on easing Joshua's discomfort, and tried not to let it bother her that Luke had to tend to his own aid. Why didn't Penelope help him?

She was busy being comforted by Mr. Kendall.

Everyone in the barracks was up and gawking from the doorway at them, standing at a distance, buzzing with their whispered comments.

"They heard us," murmured Joshua.

Genevieve lifted the compress off his lip and dabbed at the fresh blood. "They don't matter. You do."

Uncle Theodore came to the door. "Good to see you, son. Wish it was under better circumstances."

Aunt Abigail curled her round frame around his skinny one. "It'll be sorted out in no time. You just have to be patient."

Joshua nodded, smiling weakly at the older couple, but soon turned back to Genevieve. "God, you look good."

Her heart leaped. After all these years, she still had such warm feelings for Joshua. "I'm glad we're finally together."

He smiled, but the movement must have stretched his lip, for he groaned again.

"Stop smiling and try not to enjoy this so much," she whispered as she dabbed his lip again.

He didn't find her attempt at humor amusing. His face remained solemn. She smelled liquor.

"How did you find out?" She rinsed the washcloth in the tin bowl someone had brought her.

"Got in around ten last night. The rest of my gang split up to go to our various homes. I went straight to the house but you weren't there. I tried the Thornbottoms'. No one there, either. Finally went to the casino and heard it at the bar."

"I'm sorry," she whispered with shame. "But I wrote a note where you could find me, and had it delivered to your letter box. Didn't you see it?"

"I didn't check the letter box."

"I'm sorry."

Roughly, he reached for her hand. "You keep saying that, but it doesn't change things. Where were you when this mix-up happened? Couldn't you see the judge writing down the wrong names?"

She blushed profusely. "Nugget was distracting me—"

"Nugget?"

"A puppy given to me on the journey." Who at this very moment was likely sleeping in her basket in the shack, missing the whole ordeal.

Joshua squeezed her hand. She tried to enjoy how warm it felt around her own. "How long do we have to wait for a new judge to arrive? I heard about our options at the casino."

"I'm so sorry, Joshua," she repeated. "That's an awful way to hear about your life."

"I...I heard there's a judge supposedly on his way. Any word on him?"

"None."

Several yards away, Luke finally rose to his feet. "I think it's time we all got some rest."

Joshua followed suit, rising with the help of Genevieve, who was dabbing the compress to his lips. The bleeding had stopped.

"All right, then," Joshua said softly. "Let's go." He grabbed Genevieve by the arm, pulling her away from the others, attempting to take her with him to town.

Luke blocked his path, determination etched in his expression. "I don't think so."

"Beg your pardon?" Joshua snarled.

"Would you men please stop?" said Genevieve. "It does no one any good." Exasperated, she turned to Joshua.

"Good night, Joshua. I'm staying here, but I rise early so don't be afraid to join me as soon as you can."

"Oh, he'll be here as soon as you get up," said Luke. "He's not going anywhere."

With mounting dread, Genevieve looked from Luke to Joshua. "What do you mean?"

"He's in quarantine with the rest of us now."

Genevieve moaned.

Joshua struggled for air.

Penelope murmured.

Everyone at the door of the barracks turned their way.

Nugget had finally risen and now shuffled between the human legs to peer outside.

"Furthermore," said Luke to a stunned audience, "if Joshua comes down with measles, we may have to extend our quarantine."

"That's absurd," said Joshua.

"That's not fair!" shouted Mr. Kendall from the door, squeezed in beside Penelope, his bare scalp such a contrast to her flowing mane. "I'm not staying an extra day of my original fourteen."

"I agree." Vince stepped forward. "McFadden doesn't have to stay with us. Sorry, Joshua, nothing personal, this is business. He can be quarantined with the others down the road."

Genevieve, too, had heard there were four others now quarantined in the old fish house. A bartender and card dealer from the casino. Two of Miss Norris's neighbors.

"It's too late," said Luke. "Joshua stepped into our zone. He's been in contact with me and Genevieve for the past half hour."

Joshua tensed. He clutched her around the waist. "I'll

tell you what. I'll take Genevieve with me tonight, and we'll quarantine ourselves. Alone in my house."

Aunt Abigail let out an exclamation at the door.

Genevieve recoiled from Joshua. Without being married? He wanted to…to live under the same roof with her and send the tongues wagging even more…without a proper wedding ceremony.

"*No.*" Luke's voice had a cold edge she'd never heard before.

Joshua spit on the ground. "Who the hell are you to say what I can and can't do?"

"I'm the police. We enforce the quarantines around here."

Joshua stared then tempered his tone. "We'll stick to ourselves in the house, we promise to abide by the quarantine."

"You've got to eat. You've got to shop for foodstuff."

"We'll ask for it to be hauled in, like what you do here."

"It's too difficult to set up more quarantines. There aren't enough Mounties to go around as it is. Besides, my men have better things to do than act as sitters."

"But I hear you've got a murderer among you."

The group stilled.

Joshua tried to regulate his heavy breathing as he looked through the trees at the rising sun. "The summer's awfully short around here. Before you know it, there'll be snow on the ground. My barn needs repair. I brought back some venison that needs to be smoked for the winter. And I was planning on going back to gold panning as quickly as I can."

Luke tossed the compress he'd been clutching into a bowl of water at his feet. It splashed. Genevieve knew by the deep rumble in his voice that he was livid. "You should have thought of that when you pulled the first punch, McFadden. *You stay.*"

Chapter Thirteen

⟪ornament⟫

The following morning as Genevieve strolled the grounds with Joshua, she was hopeful matters would turn civil, but was keenly disappointed when he dwelled on his bitterness.

Beyond his shoulders, the women were watering the gardens while the men were in and out of the stables, exercising the horses. Luke, his left eye bruised, picked up an ax and swung it over his broad back. Penelope strolled beside him; they were likely headed to the riverside to chop wood.

Why, whenever Genevieve caught sight of him did she feel that inexplicable flutter inside her stomach? How could she justify the strength of her reaction to Luke when Joshua was standing six inches from her hip?

Joshua followed her gaze. "Your new husband."

"I don't for one minute consider him my husband."

"Whether you consider it or not, it's a fact."

She shook her head. "It's a dreadful delusion. A mistake a judge will rectify the moment he hears the horrid circumstance."

Joshua nursed his silence till she couldn't bear it.

She tucked her arm inside his elbow, stroking the soft plaid sleeve, and forced herself to concentrate on the man who'd soon be her *true* husband.

"What shall we do today?" she asked.

Brown hair framed his temples and sunshine lit the hollow of his bruised chin and swollen lip. "I suppose I should make myself useful and do some chores."

She squinted against the sunlight. "You haven't told me about your trip. What's it like to pan for gold?"

He grumbled. "I've been a failure at it."

"But your claim from last year produced enough to build your beautiful home."

"That claim dried up. And I've still got furniture to buy and a future wife to look after."

"When I open my store, I'll save for furn—"

"You'll do no such thing. Any money you earn will be yours to spend as extra. *I'll* take care of our home."

"But I don't mind—"

"*I'll* take care of our home," he repeated louder.

She sank onto her heels. It had been the same between her mother and father. Her father had always insisted it was his duty to provide, and his wife's duty to say thank you.

"Thank you, Joshua."

He nodded. His big work boots skimmed the grass. "Now let's go down to the river and see what there is to chop."

Following Luke and Penelope? Genevieve panicked. "Perhaps later would be a better time."

"Nonsense. The sun's out and it's gearing up to be a great day for working." Joshua cupped her waist and nudged her toward the stables, toward the axes leaning against the side door where Luke had gotten his. She wished Joshua would let his hand linger on her waist, so she might enjoy the warmth of his touch as she had enjoyed the warmth of—

She rubbed her temple and stopped herself from thinking *his* name. "Maybe the inspector and Penelope wish to be alone. And we're all so tired after the late night—"

"Did you see the way he looked at me when he picked up the ax? Like he thought I was a fool? If he can chop, so can I."

They made their way. A handful of Mounties kept guard at various spots along the fences.

"No one would dare commit a crime under these watchful eyes," said Joshua.

"You see, it's not so bad. As a matter of fact, Luke is closing in on the suspect."

"He said that?"

"Yes." Luke had asked her to keep this quiet, but she didn't feel she was truly betraying his confidence, for Joshua would soon be her husband. Husbands and wives shared things.

"Who does he suspect?"

"In my opinion, it's between three people. Mr. Kendall for one. He lost out on some business dealings with the judge. Then there's Miss Norris."

Joshua patted her hand. "The housekeeper?"

"Afraid so. Luke thinks they had a—a torrid affair and something went wrong."

"An *affair?* Those two old folks?"

She nodded. She didn't consider them that old.

"Who else?"

"Vince Cliffton."

"What would motivate him? With his casino, he's one of the richest men in town."

"He and Mr. Orman were former business partners who broke up on bad terms."

Joshua led her down the grassy path to the river, absorbing what she'd said.

"Need some help?" He hollered to the other couple when they reached the rushing waters.

Luke swiveled from his spot by a stack of fallen trees. Birch, pine and spruce lay strewn for yards into the woods. Obviously, other Mounties had already started on the firewood.

A purple ring circled Luke's eye. Genevieve grimaced at the sight. She turned and murmured hello to Penelope, who was wearing a pretty white velvet blouse. A flounce went partway up her bosom, and pearl buttons decorated the open neckline. Even Joshua was staring, to Genevieve's annoyance.

Luke cleared his throat, still vexed from last night's punch. Genevieve didn't blame either man for the scuffle; she only wished it over.

"When you stack it," said Luke, "separate the softwood from the hardwood."

The men rolled up their sleeves and began to chop.

This left Penelope and Genevieve to find spots to sit. They maintained their distance, lingering close to their hardworking men.

The top half of Penelope's hair was clasped at the back of her head, but the bottom hung freely. Next to her, Genevieve felt like a poor relation. The seams at the side of her creamy cotton blouse had worn through twice already, so Genevieve had sewn an extra band of cotton into the stitching. A person could see the mending, if they peered as closely as Penelope was now doing.

Genevieve jabbed her arms into her sides to obstruct the view. Her braided hair wasn't as stylish as Penelope's, but was comfortable and easy to maintain.

Genevieve realized the men were competing with each other perhaps even before they did. Sounds gave it away. The rhythmic thwacking of their blades, heavy panting, logs clunking against each other as each man steadily increased his pace.

Not thirty minutes into it and Joshua's shirt was drenched with perspiration. What was it with these big brutes that they needed to prove themselves in this manner?

"Perhaps you should slow down," said Genevieve, trying to sway Joshua. "Or there won't be anything for you to do tomorrow."

But he merely glanced her way, nodded through the drips of perspiration funneling off his brow, lifted his ax and split another spruce.

Luke sprung forward to collect his blocks of hardwood. The piles were about even, but he was chopping through denser, more difficult wood.

"Would you like to take five minutes and stroll with me to the river?" Penelope hollered to him, trying to end the competition, too.

"Later," he muttered, cracking through another branch.

Another twenty minutes passed as the piles climbed, the men raced, and the breathing got louder.

Genevieve couldn't take the sitting any longer. She jumped off her cluster of logs and eyed the forest floor for kindling. She collected a bundle.

Penelope noticed what she was doing and slid off her behind, too.

This was ridiculous, thought Genevieve, realizing that she and Penelope were now competing.

Penelope glanced at Genevieve's larger pile, clicked her tongue and ran into the forest for more. Her skirts flew behind her and the velvet flounce on her blouse vibrated against her bosom.

Genevieve ripped up sticks and bark while Penelope used her skirts—*velvet* skirts—to carry her wood.

After a long time of bending, scooping and running, Genevieve straightened. Sunshine struck her square on the face. They'd been at it for two or three hours, she imagined. She tried to stretch out the ache in her shoulders and upper arms. Then, pulling out a handkerchief from her pocket, she soaked up the moisture drizzling down her neck.

Luke glanced her way, caught and held her eye. His dark and raunchy gaze drifted to her throat...the throat he'd once kissed...and she felt that tightening in her chest again, the ache beneath her ribs.

What sensual gifts did he bring out in her?

Why did she *feel* so much around this man?

Did the others notice? Genevieve broke from his steamy regard to glance at Joshua, head down as he pounded at his wood, and then Penelope, skirts flying above her glossy leather boots with their pointed toes and high heels that were made for dancing, not work.

The humor of the situation tugged at Genevieve's sensibilities. She fought a smile, but it erupted at the corner of her lips and threatened to overtake her.

When she glanced back at Luke, he, too, was surveying the other two. The side of his mouth lifted.

Genevieve pointed to her eye, making an imaginary

circle, indicating how much like a raccoon he looked with his bruise, and he motioned to her beige skirt and the moss stains smeared on it from carrying wood.

There was an intimate spell between them. Private laughter and tenderness. Time slowed, her heart squeezed. His eyes penetrated through her as he lowered his ax.

She couldn't seem to stop whatever it was that was happening between them. It was as though he'd ambushed her heart.

"Genevieve," said Joshua.

"Genevieve," he said again.

When she looked at her about-to-be-husband, she realized he'd been calling her name for some seconds already.

"Oh, yes, yes, I'm sorry." She dashed to the wood beside his boot. "I see the kindling there."

"I've had enough." Joshua looked from her to Luke.

Penelope flung the kindling from her skirts, adding it to her pile. "I have, too."

But Genevieve knew Joshua was referring to something else as he stared between her and Luke.

"Tell me, Luke," said Joshua, swinging his ax to his side and rubbing his sweaty brow with his sleeve. "If you know who poisoned them, why don't you arrest someone?"

Luke's smile dissipated. The warmth in his eyes faded.

Heat from Genevieve's face drained to her boots.

She'd confided Luke's secret to Joshua. Perhaps it wasn't right after all.

Say something.

But Luke clutched the ax at his side without a word. The spell between them was gone. Smashed by Joshua.

Penelope looked from her to the other two, perhaps wondering what she'd missed.

"Because I need evidence." Luke spoke softly, but couldn't have accused Genevieve any louder if he had shouted.

She had betrayed him.

"You told her something you didn't tell me," Penelope whispered in Luke's ear.

"I didn't want to trouble you until I knew for certain." Luke shifted his weight on the bench, groaning at the painful aftereffects of chopping wood like a raving lunatic. His upper shoulders throbbed, the weeping blisters on both palms stung, and the small abrasions to his knuckles crackled with pain when he reached for another forkful of grilled salmon.

They were seated at the dinner table, engulfed by the clatter of forks and plates around them. The entire group was here, including the two constables.

Penelope flung her hair over her shoulder. Kendall, on her other side, passed her the oat bread and she smiled and took a slice.

"You can confide in me," she whispered to Luke. "I assure you, I've kept many secrets."

Luke raised a brow. How many secrets had she kept? And what sort?

Kendall commented on her pretty rings and Luke's irritation grew. What on earth was the man attempting to do? Steal Penelope right behind Luke's nose?

And what the hell sort of behavior was Penelope displaying? She preened at every compliment.

Luke took a forkful of his salmon and dreamed of better times when every muscle didn't ache, when his pride staring at Genevieve across the table didn't hurt as much, when his frustration at not being able to collect the evidence against Miss Norris didn't weigh so heavy on his mind.

Miss Norris had done it. He was quite certain as he peered down the table and watched her nibble on her dry biscuit. She'd made the judge's breakfast that morning. She'd gotten up to make herself tea in the middle of the night when Orman had been poisoned.

It was easy to surmise her motivation in killing Fergus. A lover's quarrel deeper than any she'd experienced, she perhaps pushing hard for a wedding ceremony and he resisting. For Luke had discovered an important letter with the boxful of papers brought to him within the first couple of days. Many in the group had seen it—a letter from Fergus Donahue's wife—but no one had paid attention to the date. It wasn't a cherished keepsake the judge had held on to from ten years ago when she'd supposedly passed on. It was dated last year. Which meant Fergus Donahue was still married to his first wife.

That's why he couldn't marry Miss Norris.

Orman must have discovered something about her and the judge. Something she didn't want revealed to the rest of the world, something perhaps more than an impossible wedding. The connection between the two men was what Luke had yet to discover before having enough proof to arrest her.

Penelope nudged Luke and shuffled in tight against his shoulder. He moaned from the muscular ache, but she took it to mean he liked the contact and thus squeezed in harder.

He refused to meet Genevieve's eye. It was a combination of guilt and shame and lust so deep he couldn't see straight.

He lowered his head and continued with his meal, leaning in toward Penelope whenever she slid against him, whenever she stroked his hand on the table and murmured in his ear. He wanted desperately to enjoy her touch, but it did nothing for him tonight. Out of curiosity, he allowed the touching to continue, hoping he'd snap out of his surly mood.

Hoping he'd become the same carefree man he'd always been with women.

Genevieve, to his confusion, was not allowing the same thing across the table. When Joshua leaned in toward her, she stiffened. Next he tried to gain her attention by commenting on her meal, but she glared instead at Luke without a smile.

He reminded himself that *she* had betrayed *him*. Not the other way around.

And why the hell was he more interested in her reactions than the gorgeous woman sitting next to him? Why couldn't Penelope hold his sexual interest this evening?

Why didn't her proximity thrill him?

And the manner she chose to flirt with Kendall was insulting. More than that, perhaps the flirting was a reflection of Luke. Was he the male equivalent of Penelope?

He'd been flirting with every pretty woman in saloons and businesses since puberty. Was he looking at his own shortcomings when he looked at Penelope?

Well, then, he couldn't stomach himself.

And frankly, he'd had it with Penelope. They were through before they'd even started.

He lowered his head over his slice of pecan pie while Penelope whisked away to get herself a cup of tea. When she brushed by him from the back, she seemed to slip and he reached out to steady her.

The yelp surprised him.

The clatter in the room stopped.

He turned.

Genevieve gaped at him, stunned. It was her behind he had his hand on.

* * *

Genevieve felt mortified.

"I beg your pardon." Luke dropped his warm fingers from her backside and stood up from the table. "Please, forgive me."

So sore from this morning's work, she craned her neck at him, shoulder muscles straining, her thighs quivering beneath her skirts. "Do you know what it's like to have a hand come up from behind…and…and…well, I hope you never do!"

Unable to get past the disturbing thought of his hand on her backside, and the impropriety of what these folks had witnessed, she couldn't move.

Apologetically, Luke stepped closer, then moaned and clutched his back. She hoped he was suffering from his toes to his head.

Penelope sauntered back with her tea, moving slowly from the far counter, gussied up with fresh paint on her lips, her change of clothes from this morning tidied up with an out-of-place bodice and skirt with so much beadwork on it, Genevieve could have trimmed twenty hats.

"What did I just see?" Penelope railed at Luke. "Luke?"

Joshua, stricken white at the other side of the table, rose slowly to his feet. He moved stiffly, also suffering from the idiotic race earlier. "I have had…enough of you."

"Joshua, don't," said Genevieve.

"It was an accident," Luke told him.

"Why do your accidents always happen to my fiancée?"

Luke tried to explain. "I thought Genevieve slipped on her feet…I thought she was…" He sounded like an idiot. "I apologize sincerely to both you and Genevieve."

"It's not enough." Joshua's mouth thinned into a blade. Genevieve's stomach twisted with impending doom.

Luke nodded slowly and stepped away toward the door. "I'm going for a walk."

To her exasperation, Joshua barreled after him, fists clenched. She followed outdoors with Penelope.

Luke stomped toward the hills. God only knew where he was headed, but Joshua wouldn't drop it.

"I don't know what happened to you, Hunter," Joshua shouted, "but you make me sick!"

Luke swung around. "You don't know what happened to *me?* Ever since you started on your quest for gold, you've been a changed man."

"You're crazy."

"Am I? Ask the Thornbottoms the last time they heard you say something positive about your life."

Aunt Abigail and Uncle Theodore had spilled out into the open fields with the others. They averted their eyes when Joshua turned their way.

Luke stepped right up to Joshua. "And then ask yourself this. What the hell difference does it make if you do or don't strike gold? You've got a beautiful woman waiting for you here, yet you raced off, knowing she'd arrive any day, to search for that goddamn yellow rock."

"You only say that because of what happened to your father."

"So what?"

"Not everyone winds up with a bullet in their back."

"Even one bullet is one too many."

They growled in each other's faces. Genevieve wanted to scream at them to come inside, to make things right, but she stood rooted.

"I hate that you married *my* bride. I hate that you just touched her. I hate that you even look at her."

She moaned and cradled her face with her hands, wishing it would end.

Luke turned his back and started walking toward the hills again. "That's an awful lot of hate for one man."

Joshua lunged toward him, but this time Luke was ready. He swung around, caught the punch and yanked Joshua's arm behind his back. Joshua groaned, Genevieve winced, and Luke shoved him a good three yards to set him free.

"You're not worth it anymore, McFadden," said Luke.

Joshua shouted after him. "I'm taking her right now and we're leaving." He nodded at Genevieve, signaling her to go.

"What?" she murmured.

Luke wheeled around. He scanned the crowd as though looking for someone. His gaze settled on Franks in the far corner, then Zucker by the trees.

"Get your things," Joshua told her. "We're leaving."

"But the quarantine, Joshua."

"I don't give a rat's—" He stopped himself. "Grab your stuff. We're going to my house."

"You'll stay put," said Luke, his voice strangely low.

"Says who?" Joshua swung around, then gave her another impatient look. "Hurry, hurry," he said, dismissing her with his hand.

"I give the orders here. If you leave, you're putting a lot of folks in danger."

"We won't get the measles. We're both feeling fine."

"I hope that's the case. But I'm not willing to take that chance."

"We're more in danger here, left in the hands of some…some murderer."

The crowd glared at him with disbelieving faces—the

Cliffton brothers, Mr. Kendall, the Thornbottoms and Miss Norris.

Joshua looked up at Genevieve, standing on the threshold of the door. "What are you waiting for? Go. Go. Get your things!"

She couldn't budge for the disappointment spiraling through her. "Joshua, measles killed one of my distant neighbors in Montana. I can't put anyone in that kind of danger."

Joshua fingered the gun in his holster. Slowly, he looked around, as if contemplating his next move. A chill prickled Genevieve's skin. His rage had been escalating for twenty-four hours, and she feared what he might do next. He reached for his gun.

Ever so slightly, Luke nodded at Franks, standing behind and to the right of Joshua. Before anyone could blink, the constable removed his handcuffs from his holster and shackled Joshua.

Gripping her face, Genevieve couldn't bear to watch.

"Let go!" Joshua stomped his foot. "I didn't do anything."

"You were about to," said Luke. "I can't take that risk."

Zucker raced to assist.

Luke's voice was filled with compassion. "Take him to the jailhouse. It's sitting empty. We'll start another quarantine there."

Chapter Fourteen

It was ten o'clock at night when Luke spoke to Genevieve again. In the never-ending sunlight, he sat down on the swing beside her, looking apologetic. She didn't care. Her logic understood what had made him toss Joshua into jail, but her heartache still blamed him for the misery.

"You haven't gone to see him yet," said Luke.

"I can't."

"He wants to see you."

She kicked at the grass beneath her boots. "I can't."

"Why not?"

"What am I supposed to say? Smile and pretend all is well? Thank him for trying to take me out of here? Thank him for trying to fight you? Or maybe I should tell him I didn't approve of how he behaved. How he didn't even listen to what I wanted."

"You might go with pecan pie and coffee. Simply bid him good night."

"I thought it would be so different here," she said.

Luke leaned back on the swing. She watched him try to fit his shoulders past the ropes.

"I thought he'd be here waiting for me when I arrived. I thought he'd never leave for gold mining again because his desire to see me would far outweigh it. I thought...I thought I mattered more than gold."

Luke peered out on the quiet horizon. Shadows loomed over the hills. "Perhaps I said some things about him I shouldn't have. I apologize. Joshua wants to strike gold so he can support you in fine style. You *must* matter more to him than any gold nugget."

She fingered the pocket of her skirt, wishing it were true.

"You don't believe me?"

"I'm disappointed it's you telling me. It should be him."

Luke turned to look at the mare in the corral behind the trees, softly ripping at the grass.

"Did your father die here?" she asked, curious about what Joshua had said in their argument.

Luke's voice grew hushed. The sounds of nature stilled around them. "It was another gold rush, a long time ago in California. I was seventeen, waiting for him at home in the East. My brother Colt was there, too, and our mother."

"Did your father return?"

"For an hour or so. I was the one who found him dead."

Her heart stirred. Air felt trapped in her throat. "That's awfully sad. I'm sorry to hear it."

Luke's mouth quivered. "I caught the man who did it. Unfortunately, the charge against him never stuck and he took off."

"Oh, Luke..."

"At least I put him through a good fight."

Her eyes widened on the wound snaking down his cheek. "Your scar."

When he shook his head, dark strands of hair tumbled at his forehead. "Yeah."

"How befitting that you became an officer of the law."

Luke shrugged. "I've seen worse things since then."

They sat for a couple of minutes, rocking in the light breeze. Solitude engulfed them and gave her some comfort.

"Your mother must've been devastated."

"I guess she was."

"Guess?"

"Every minute they ever spent together was spent in argument. They said the meanest, cruelest things to each other."

Her heart thudded in her chest. Their childhoods had been similar, then. "That is hard on a child's ear."

He nodded. "Yet, from the moment I told her he'd been killed, she never stopped weeping. She wept as though her heart was broken. I couldn't understand it. I always thought they hated each other."

Genevieve couldn't speak for the clamping of her throat.

He blinked several times, also moved.

"My folks," she admitted quietly, "used to argue so bad they'd throw things at each other. If I didn't duck in time…and sometimes I didn't…I'd get a pot in the head." She shuffled on her swing, embarrassed at her sudden disclosure. Her complaints sounded silly to her own ears. "That could be rather funny, I suppose."

Luke touched her hand. "It's not funny at all. Especially to a child."

There was a tenderness to Luke tonight that was magnetic.

"But after witnessing all of that," he said gently, "you still believe in the sanctity of marriage?"

She gripped the ropes. "Just because they did it

wrong…it's still a union worth honoring. I'm going to prove…that marriage can be calm and loving."

He whispered. "I've seen how it can ruin lives."

Turmoil deepened in his eyes. There was a tremor to his lips and anguish when he spoke.

Composing himself quickly, he rose abruptly from the swing. "I think you should pay Joshua a visit."

When he turned and walked away, a gentle sob burst from Genevieve. If she married Joshua, her marriage might be just like her mother and father's…arguing about money and material goods. In the case of Joshua, about gold.

The very thing that had once attracted her to Joshua now repelled her. He'd always been a driven man, high in accomplishments and ambition. But in Dawson, he hadn't found his pot of gold, and this had caused such deep disappointment in him that his character had changed.

With a painful realization, she knew what was keeping her away tonight. She wanted to avoid telling Joshua how she truly felt about their future.

"Brought you something." The following evening, balancing a small tray of refreshments and determined to speak frankly, Genevieve marched into the jailhouse where Joshua was seated behind bars.

On her way inside, she'd said hello to a new Mountie guard, ten yards down the hill. It was as close to the jailhouse as Luke would allow a constable who'd never had measles. Franks and Zucker were needed inside the barracks and couldn't guard Joshua as well. Since he was locked up, he wasn't going anywhere. Franks had escorted her partway to ensure she got here safely. Besides, she didn't wish to visit Joshua in a party of three. What she had to say was private.

At the sight of her, Joshua dropped what he was reading, a three-month-old copy of the *London Times*.

Not quite as confident now that she was here, Genevieve placed the tray on a stool and took a sideways glance at him. He eyed the pecan pie and coffee she'd brought.

She flattened her trembling hand against the waistband of her skirt. "Extra milk, how you like it."

"Is that how Hunter takes it?"

Frustrated by his bullish attitude, Genevieve groaned. "It would serve you well to think of your own predicament and not his."

Joshua kicked back on his cot. "I'd ask you in, but the cell is not fit for company."

She didn't smile at his poor joke. They'd have to make do, talking through the locked cell, for no one had any intention of allowing Joshua the freedom to escape. He'd threatened to do so twice already.

He was better off here for the protection of others in town he might endanger, but she still found it difficult to take Luke's side.

"I'll…I'll help myself to a seat." She lifted the hard wooden chair from the corner, brought it closer and sat down.

Despite her good intentions of trying to act as though nothing was amiss, a flush of embarrassment washed through her. The man she was supposed to marry was behind bars.

"Here, take the pie." It was stacked on two small plates. Luke had insisted she take an extra one, but she hadn't realized why until this moment. There was no way to get the pie through the bars unless she clamped it between two plates and tipped it sideways.

"Nice trick," Joshua said sarcastically.

Her cheeks heated. Next came the coffee. Luke had insisted she bring the entire coffeepot. She saw now that her tin cup wouldn't fit through the bars, but Joshua already had one, so all she had to do was stick the spout through the bars and pour.

"I made you a fresh pot."

"Big of you."

She smacked the pot onto her tray with a loud jarring noise. "Aren't you glad to see me, Joshua?"

"Of course." He brought his coffee cup closer for her to add the milk.

She did and then leaned back onto the hard seat. "You're not treating me very well."

"Sorry." He sipped. "You make a good cup of coffee."

Watching him bite into the pie, she nervously wove her fingers together. When would be the best time to say what she had to say? She tapped her toes on the floorboards. Up and down. Up and down.

"Uncle Theodore and Aunt Abigail will be here shortly. Uncle Theodore is bringing his cards. Says he knows how much you like to play."

Joshua nodded, but there was no sheen of interest in his eyes. "You think Hunter will keep me here the entire time?"

"I'm afraid so."

"You asked him?"

"Yes."

"Maybe if you asked a bit nicer…"

"What is that supposed to mean?"

"Nothing. I'm just…thinking aloud." He smiled a little. "Thank you for the pie, Genevieve. It tastes as good as the one you baked me the first time I came home to meet your folks."

She felt as though she'd been slugged in the stomach. "Joshua...before you say any more...there's something I've come to discuss with you."

He set down the plate and looked at her with a tough expression. Where was the kinder Joshua she'd known years ago?

"Discuss anything you'd like. We're going to be man and wife soon." So matter-of-fact. Taking her for granted.

Nonetheless, she felt nauseated at what she was about to say. "Precisely, Joshua. And the thing is...the thing is..."

The color drained from his face and she knew in her gut he understood.

"No," he said curtly. "No."

"It pains me to say it."

He scoffed. "Then don't."

"I don't think you and I...I don't see any common ground for us to build...it's upsetting, the way you treat me."

"I'll treat you better. I'll strike gold, I swear."

"It's not the gold."

"I'll be a rich man one day, I promise."

"It's *not* the gold. It's how you act *about* the gold. It's how you dismiss my words before they've even come out of my mouth."

He was voiceless.

"I used to accept it when I was younger. In fact, I never noticed much. But I'm an adult. When you returned and started speaking to me in that same thoughtless manner, it's come back to me how belittled you can make me feel."

"You wouldn't be talking to me like this if I were a rich man."

"That's not true."

"You do want the riches. Stop pretending you don't."

She colored fiercely.

"I see the clothes you wear. I know where you came from. I saw the hovel you grew up in."

She shrank in her chair, squeezing herself tighter to hide the shame of wearing such a ragged skirt. "I don't want the kind of marriage my parents had."

"What has that got to do with *anything?*"

"Everything."

"You speak in riddles. You scoff at money as though it doesn't mean a thing. Who's going to support you here? How would you live without me? Who's going to buy you a brand-new blouse to replace that—that *thing* you're wearing?"

He was playing on her weakness. He knew she was terrified of how she'd survive on her own without a man.

But she was more terrified of how she'd survive *with* him.

She'd already given it hours of thought, of how she might earn a living. Lord, it was all she'd been thinking about. She'd sew clothes, she'd put up a sign to become a tailor as well as a milliner. For men and women. She'd mentioned it to Miss Norris and Penelope not an hour ago, and hadn't both women replied that everyone in town would be interested? Hadn't Luke even paid attention to Genevieve's declaration?

In the breaking light from the window, where the sun came out from beneath a passing cloud, Genevieve drew up her shoulders. She swung to her feet full force, stepped closer to the bars and looked him square in the eyes. It was rude of him to play upon her weaknesses. Unkind to say the least. A husband and wife should be supportive, not destructive.

"I no longer wish to marry you." Genevieve removed her wedding band from her pocket and placed it inside the bars.

Joshua lowered his fork. It clattered to his plate. He stared at her for what seemed a lifetime.

"I do declare," said Aunt Abigail in the stunned silence.

Genevieve whirled around to face her aunt and uncle. She was expecting them, but they startled her nonetheless.

"I beg you to reconsider," said Uncle Theodore, gripping a deck of cards. "Joshua is a hardworking man."

"He's going to be rich one day," said her aunt. "The woman who's lucky enough to be his wife will live in wealth."

"It won't be me," said Genevieve.

Trying to stop a flow of tears that welled so close to the brink it blurred her vision, Genevieve nodded one last time at Joshua. She pushed back the chair and scrambled out of the jailhouse so quickly she never saw the dark figure coming from the trees until she crashed into him.

Luke steadied her in his arms and waited as she mopped tears with her cuffs.

"Sorry," she sobbed, "I didn't see you coming." She tried to scoot around him, but he caught her.

"What the devil is going on?"

She peered to the shadowy hills, past his boxy shoulders, unable to meet his eyes. "Nothing…I…I've had a chat with my aunt and uncle and they seem to be—"

"And Joshua? You had a chat with Joshua?"

Her sobs quieted. She looked past her lashes, clumped together with tears. "I spoke with him."

"What's gotten you this upset?"

"I can't say. I'm not proud of it."

He loosened his grip, fingers sliding down her sleeves. His touch was unbearable. Such a threat to the balance in her life.

"Genevieve…" He whispered her name. "Genevieve…I didn't expect you to turn him away tonight…"

"How do you know what I have and haven't done?"

"Because I saw your face at that crushing moment...when he ordered you to hurry and pack your things."

She ripped herself from his fingers, letting him know she didn't need his opinions or his comfort. "What makes you the judge of everyone? What makes you think your view of the world is the right one?"

The next day, for reasons Genevieve was still trying to fathom, she avoided visiting Joshua in jail but was fuming at Luke.

Joshua had treated her as though her opinions meant less than his; Luke had shown her nothing but respect for her time. Joshua kept mentioning the value of gold; Luke said it was meaningless. Joshua openly declared he wanted to spend the night with her; Luke couldn't wait for a new judge to arrive to dissolve their hasty union.

And most confusing of all...Joshua wanted to make her his wife, while Luke was courting another woman.

Sunlight danced through the windows, such a stark contrast to the desperation Genevieve felt about her future. She leaned back in her rocking chair and stitched the inner lining of a lady's snow hat. Black linen sat crisp and solid inside the black felt, with its turned-up brim and rosebud made of apricot-colored wool.

Others in the barracks were preparing to eat lunch. When the cook delivered the food, Miss Norris shouted to the men outside. Penelope was in her room, freshening up, and Milly played with Nugget on the Persian carpet.

Genevieve placed the finished hat into her trunk, filled with two other hats she'd made yesterday, and a dozen that had come before. Selling the few here wouldn't be enough to support her for long. It would also take a few weeks before customers came to her for tailor-made clothes, and so she burned with the question of how to earn her keep.

She'd have to sell her wedding dress.

The dress had symbolized so much hope and joy on her journey here. Selling it meant what? That she'd been a failure?

Above her on the fireplace, her wedding bouquet had nearly dried. The aroma of roses and lily of the valley scented the air, reminding her of everything gone wrong.

In time, she'd find another husband, she told herself. The town was filled with decent, working men. Surely there was one here who would treat her in the considerate way she wanted to be treated. One who would allow her to prove she could make a marriage work, despite the odds her parents had faced.

Luke was not among her choices.

"Joshua wants to see you," said Uncle Theodore, coming through the front door.

"Thank you for the message." She anchored a leather band to a man's straw hat and sank in her needle. She had no intention of visiting Joshua while her feelings were still raw.

Her uncle marched off, shaking his head at her aunt, who showed equal disappointment as she turned to make coffee and clicked her tongue.

"Would you like to sit by me?" the saloon keeper asked Genevieve.

"I've made a spot for her here." For some reason, Vince was spiffed up in his satin vest and cravat.

"Nonsense." Ripley patted the bench beside him, newly shaven. "I've poured her a glass of water right here."

Then she realized. The word was out that she'd broken off her engagement and would soon be available.

But none of these men made her heart leap. Avoiding

them all, she took a seat beside Milly, who was now reading the paper. Genevieve told herself she didn't care where Luke was, nor that his place at the table had sat empty for the third meal in a row.

It was after dinner when he finally came to her.

Looming tall above her rocking chair as she added feathers and sequins and cross-stitching to several stylish bonnets, Luke presented her with a wooden crate.

Penelope looked up from the newspaper she was reading. Miss Norris looked over from her ironing. Aunt Abigail and Uncle Theodore, their fingers knuckle-deep in rolling out the crust for three berry pies, stared from the kitchen table.

"What's this?" Genevieve asked.

"Open it."

She set down her trims and yanked on the crate to reveal stacks of red wool gabardine. "I don't understand."

"Fabric has arrived for new uniforms. We've got two other tailors in town, but they won't be available for another week. Are you up to the job?"

With a crush of excitement, Genevieve raced through the box. There was enough here for ten tunics and ten pairs of dark breeches.

Luke tapped on the box. "I know you said hats are faster to make, but you'd get a contract for these. If you did a good job, I'm sure the commissioner would send more work your way."

Was Luke doing this because he knew how terrified she was, a woman on her own with no man to support her? He was offering her work with the government. Sure money.

"Are you interested?" he asked again.

Penelope eyed her. Genevieve tried not to acknowledge the wave of heat and gratitude blasting up her neck.

Luke stood like a rock in front of her, studying her face. If she agreed, she'd be beholden to the very man who'd turned her life upside down. A man she craved, who seemed to feel nothing toward her but pity, perhaps.

"Yes, thank you."

Chapter Fifteen

"Penelope, may I speak with you?" Luke touched her shoulder blade as they exited the barracks into afternoon sunshine. It was Friday already. One day left in quarantine.

Telling her what was on his mind wouldn't be easy, he thought, taking her elbow and leading her through the breezy trees. Dealing with heated emotions was always more difficult than dealing with police investigations.

For the past few days, he'd been desperately trying to find some way to secure evidence against Miss Norris. Maybe she realized what he was up to, for she sidestepped all questions with vague answers. He didn't allow himself to think she was the only suspect, for he was still observing everyone. In his confidential investigation, beyond the confines of the barracks where he'd been discussing clues with his brother, Colt, and the commissioner, the paper trail had ceased. There were no further leads, no homes to search or deeds he could order his men to retrieve.

Many times when a crime was committed, it was the

most obvious person. Miss Norris was still by far the most logical suspect.

"Such a lovely day." Penelope adjusted her white velvet blouse. The frilly fabric at the front quivered down her bosom.

"Genevieve, we've—"

"It's Penelope."

"Oh? Oh, I'm sorry. Did I call you…?"

"You called me Genevieve."

"I apologize." Yet the embarrassment washed over his face like an ocean tide.

Penelope ran her tongue along the inside of her mouth and sat down on a stack of logs. "Luke, there's something I need to say." She peered out beyond the corral and settled her gaze on Kendall, who was walking a stallion. The man noticed her attention and tipped his hat.

Her corresponding smile was full of charm, and Luke once again saw himself reflected in her. He knew what she was about to say, for he understood her.

"Luke, there comes a time in a courtship when a woman has to make a choice. We've been together for almost two weeks and you've never once kissed me."

"Oh?"

"I mean, there've been pecks on the cheek…and pleasant times we've shared coffee…but a woman needs more. I need more."

"Hmm." He realized her intent and, in fact, applauded her for speaking her mind and being so forthright.

"Mr. Kendall is offering me a home. He's offering me a lifestyle that may not be as extravagant as I once antic-ipated, but what he's offering…is so much more than you're willing…"

Although he understood her, the heat of embarrassment

still crept up his neck. Now why was that? She was going for the sure thing. She wanted security and a means of survival; she wanted promises. Things he'd never considered. Things he'd never provided to anyone.

"Absolutely, Penelope. I understand."

"You do?"

"Yes, of course. I've noticed how attentive Kendall is toward you."

She flushed and smiled. "He spoils me."

Luke grinned. "And you like that."

"I do."

A squirrel raced along a fallen aspen behind her. He looked down into clear hazel eyes and clear peach skin. Leaning forward, he kissed her lightly on the cheek as a goodbye. "I understand."

"Now what was it you wished to discuss?"

"Only the matter of quarantine." There was no use broaching anything else. He wished to end their courtship, too, but allowed her the dignity of believing it was her choice. "We'll be out tomorrow and we need to arrange how to get your trunks back to your home."

Being released from Penelope didn't make him feel any better. He thought he'd feel a great relief, but as his thoughts turned to Genevieve, all he felt was a great disquiet. What did *he* want from life? Why couldn't *he* see himself sharing the rest of it with a woman at his side?

Why the hell did he feel so inadequate?

Quarantine was over. Laughter filled the barracks on Saturday evening as folks packed to leave.

Luke was staying behind because the barracks were still his sleeping quarters. Although he was pleased on everyone else's behalf that they were escaping, he was dissatisfied at his lack of progress in the investigation.

Sometimes, though, letting the suspects go about their natural course of business proved to be the best way to nab them. Sooner or later they tripped up in their alibis, or were apprehended trying to get rid of other evidence the police didn't know about.

Thankfully, no one new had contracted measles at the barracks or the fish house. And it was a blessed relief no more had died from the disease.

"Joshua's asking for you," Abigail spoke softly to Genevieve as the older woman heaved her suitcases from her bedroom to the parlor. "They've released him. He's going home."

As much as Luke tried not to get caught up with Genevieve, every move she made seemed to affect him. Even now, he waited for her response.

"Tell Joshua to come by the house tomorrow," said Genevieve. "I'll...I'll be more myself then and maybe... we might share a cup of coffee."

She hadn't seen the man since he'd been jailed. It was her business, Luke told himself, although he couldn't help but wonder how that meeting might go tomorrow.

A breeze curled in from the propped door. It had rained earlier in the day and a mist hovered above the mountains.

"Bye, everyone," the Cliffton brothers shouted and waved. Vince bounded out the door, dressed in his vest and headed to his casino, followed by Ripley, leaping to his home in the opposite direction, and Burt dashing toward his saloon.

"Night, all." Kendall heaved his duffel bag past the table, scooped the giggling Penelope in his other large arm, and they were gone.

With a flustered glance, Genevieve looked from Penelope's receding skirts to Luke.

He shrugged at Genevieve's look of dismay.

Yes, he'd lost Penelope to Kendall. It seemed to affect Genevieve more than Luke. She stopped for a moment to watch the couple hoist their baggage to a wagon. The soft curve of Genevieve's cheek dimpled, the corners of her mouth tightened with emotion, and she heaved in a breath to steady herself. What was she thinking?

The same as he?

How much things had changed in two short weeks. Turning away, Luke helped the others.

Weston left to report to the commissioner. The Thornbottoms packed their bags on a wheeled tram that Zucker and Franks were hauling home for them. Enscott and Morgan went to town for dinner. This left Genevieve dashing to move her clothing from the armoire into her luggage while Luke was packing his veterinary bag.

"I'm sorry," Genevieve told him. "I'm the last one to go because I've got so much to pack. Look at all these fabrics and notions."

She'd been busy for two days basting Mountie uniforms from the patterns she'd made from their old ones. Luke's was the first one she'd basted. She had requested a fitting from him, but had done all the other men first. Was she avoiding his?

"Coming, Genevieve?" Abigail hollered from outside.

Behind her by the trees, Milly, in matching calico skirt and bonnet, brown hair braided in two, picked up the energetic little pup.

"I've still got one quick fitting to do," Genevieve hollered back. "Perhaps you should go without me."

"Nonsense. You finish the fitting with Luke, and come get us in the stables when you're done. We've left a spot on the tram for your bags."

The room got suddenly still. Genevieve turned around to face him.

"I haven't seen it this empty for a long time," Luke said with an echo.

Genevieve rubbed her palms against her skirt and took his newly created tunic from a wing chair. "It's pinned and ready to go, if you don't mind."

"All right."

She was a tailor, and although he felt awkward unbuttoning his shirt in front of her, he did so matter-of-factly and tossed it over the chair.

She brushed by him to stand in front of the fire, but couldn't hide the nervous flicker of her mouth and twitch of her shoulders.

In his sleeveless undershirt, Luke picked up his tunic and pulled his arms through.

"Ow," he said when a pin jabbed him.

"Careful." She was at his side in a flash, a measuring tape draped around her neck, pulling and tugging at his sleeves and kneeling to baste something at his pocket.

He listened to the swish of her petticoat, enjoyed the warm touch of her fingers at his palms, inhaled the scent of her newly washed hair as she leaned at his thighs.

"I think we'll need to let it out an inch here." She pressed against the underside of his sleeve where it met with his chest. "It'll allow more movement of your arms. And when you rest your gun here—" she tapped his waist "—the fabric won't pull."

"Hmm."

She smelled heavenly. She moved with the drama of an actress, self-assured as she pinched and pressed her fingers around his collar. When she was standing but an inch away, he looked straight down into her face. Her lashes flashed up.

He wanted to kiss her. Just once, just softly grazing the cheek that seemed so hardened against him.

Her eyes flicked with something unreadable, her lips tugged, and when she maneuvered around him, her bosom grazed his chest.

"Come with me tonight, Genevieve. On the river, one last time to do my rounds. Meet me tonight at nine at the wharf. The wind's calmed down. We'll take my raft."

At first, she didn't reply. Her fingers flew over his lapel and she stepped back in such a professional manner, he thought he might have insulted her by the mere question.

She hurried with the last few things, leaving the items of her wedding behind to pick up later—the wedding dress, bouquet, the marriage license on the table—and finally responded.

"I'm not sure, Luke," she said softly. "I'm not sure."

He packed her bags on the tram, waved goodbye to the Thornbottoms, and as he stood at the door of the barracks he felt desperately alone. Wasn't it obvious? How obtuse could he be? She wouldn't bother to show up, he predicted. She wanted nothing more to do with him.

Genevieve walked toward him beneath the trees by the river, and Luke stood enthralled by the way she moved.

She'd come. She'd come of her own free will.

The night was like a dream, and he refused to break the

spell by giving it deeper meaning. They would be together one last time.

The breezy evening brought with it the scent of wild grasses, the hum of the current passing ten feet to his right, the taste of dew on his lips. This warm summer wind snatched at the hemline of her skirts, playing hide-and-seek between his searching gaze and the turn of her ankles in polished, high-heeled boots.

From head to toe, she wore wine-colored burgundy. The clothing, new to him, dazzled against the brilliant black sheen of her loose hair. A velvet choker adorned her neck, and its cameo brooch, the same rich apricot as her skin, pressed at the hollow of her throat. Draped over her shoulders, a loose silky shawl dangled at a tantalizing angle over her breasts, long fringes sliding across the taut fabric where buttons met with corset. He swallowed hard, imagining the sight of Genevieve in corset alone, searching for the telltale outline of her straps and the rigid whalebone that pressed against her blouse just above the swell of where he envisioned her nipples. He found the ripple of her straps and savored the view.

Her gaze skimmed over him. He was dressed in a fresh cotton shirt, denim jeans and the cowboy boots with shiny metal tips. He wore no hat, but his holster and guns were firmly planted on his hips.

"Hi." She smiled warmly and his pulse flared.

"Hi."

They wove their way along the path toward the dock. "Luke. Why did you invite me?"

"Our last night on the river… It seems like a fitting tribute to the two weeks we spent together as man and wife."

His mind took a runaway leap at the possibilities, and

heaven help him for thinking it but they *were* married, weren't they, and wouldn't he be allowed to do whatever he wished with his wife?

Perhaps she saw the want in his eyes, for her green eyes misted and she fanned her cheeks with a hand. "Well, then...shall we get on with it?"

With what? he begged to ask. With a very improper kiss on those very proper lips? Or perhaps lower...to her rib cage...and the smooth contours of her belly.

"Why do you look at me like that?" she murmured.

"Am I not allowed to gaze upon my wife?"

"Your wife?" She smiled again, realizing he was teasing. "Shall we be husband and wife, then, on this last tour of the river?"

"If that's the game you'd enjoy, then I'll play along."

She laughed deeply as he led her to the awaiting raft, which he'd already equipped with two long oars, his veterinary bag, and blankets and fur jackets for the later chill.

"It's a dangerous game," he whispered in her ear as he took her by the hand and eased her onto the rocking craft. "Your reputation's at stake."

Her smile dampened. "My reputation seems to have run amok in the last two weeks."

"It needn't be. It'll settle down once the judge gets here."

"Any word on him?"

"I understand he left Skagway a month ago. Which would place him here very soon."

She knelt onto the sheepskin pile. "That is such wonderful news. Such a beam of hope in this entire mess."

She was only being truthful, but the words cut open a raw wound.

Would it be so bad to be married to him?

Thus far, he'd been thinking mostly of himself and how the accidental wedding had disrupted his life, but what of hers? She obviously felt the same, but it didn't sit well to hear her say aloud how awful it was.

What would it be like to be married to her, in true terms?

He contemplated the thought as he navigated them down the river, pushing on his long oar while she sat beside and in front of him, smiling lightly in the breeze, turning her head to the bend in the shoreline to watch the turtles swimming by, and a loon calling through the trees that swept the river.

At quiet moments like this, being married to Genevieve would be…he admitted softly to himself…quite remarkable.

Satiating. Exhilarating. Filling his senses with the raw materials of life, the wonder of a beautiful woman kneeling two feet past his knees, her mouth made for kisses and her body made for love.

She tilted her face up at him. Shadows dipped along her throat and beams of sunlight lit one side of her—the silhouette of her pretty mouth and the shape of her bust. He was struck by the urge to press his lips against her cheek. Above them, the fading sun slid behind a cloud and covered them in a shade of darkness they wouldn't normally have for a summer night.

"Can I help with the rowing?" she asked softly, as though attempting to gain hold of her emotions.

"There's no need. The current's with us. Maybe on the way back you can lend a hand."

This *was* a dangerous game, he told himself. He'd asked for her time in a moment of weakness, when their quarantine was over and he knew their separation was imminent. But what did he mean to prove by this?

That he could handle Genevieve at close proximity, that

they'd perhaps gained a friendship from all of this, that he could get close to the flame without being singed?

And now, pretending to be husband and wife...was she thinking it, too? How easily they could slip into that role for one beautiful night?

His fingers ached to touch her. His mind raced at the memory of holding her breast, at the gentle pull of her budding nipple and how it had pressed against his palm.

Was she a virgin?

Most certainly.

Did he wish to take her?

With a groan, he pushed the question from his mind and heaved his oar, sinking it into the soft bank of the river and steering them onto their first property.

Henry Solbaucher greeted them, this time with no rifle and able to get close enough to shake Luke's hand when they approached his cabin.

"Right this way," said Solbaucher, leading them toward the small barn and the cows inside. "Glad to see you folks are back to normal and outta quarantine."

"How's she doing?" Once inside, Luke squatted to the cow's hind leg and had a look.

"Doesn't seem to be touchy," said Solbaucher.

"Much better," said Luke, looking at the soft muscles.

"If cows could smile," said Solbaucher, "she'd be smilin'."

Genevieve laughed softly and met Luke's quiet gaze.

It didn't take them long to finish and paddle up the river to their next stop in the middle of nowhere.

"Ahoy!" Luke shouted to Otis Rutledge, who was surprised to see them.

"What the hell are you doin' here?" asked Rutledge. "Is the quarantine over?"

"Yes, sir."

Rutledge nodded. "Son of a gun." He removed his rumpled hat, slapped it on his thigh and held out his hand to Genevieve. "Nice to see you again, ma'am. Or should I say Mrs. Hunter?"

With an awkward pause, she struggled to explain. "It's not really Mrs. Hunter…the marriage was a misunderstanding."

"So the story's true." The man chuckled.

"It was my fault," said Luke. "I should've been more careful when Judge Donahue was signing the papers."

Rutledge rubbed his unshaven jaw. "And the other story… Hell, Luke, do you still think both men were poisoned?"

"Afraid so."

"Arrest anyone yet?"

"Not yet."

"How could you let 'em all go?" He looked pointedly at Genevieve. "I'm not implyin' you, ma'am. Obviously, the doc here has faith in your character."

Genevieve lowered her eyes to the grass. "Right."

Luke pressed on. "I let them go because I couldn't arrest anyone. Now…how's the filly?"

"Eatin' like a horse." Rutledge laughed at his own joke. "Come see for yourself."

He led and they followed.

The foal had gained some weight. Her ribs weren't showing through anymore, and she nuzzled him with energy. "Good to see you, too," he murmured, then noticed Genevieve watching him.

The broodmare was also heavier than when he'd last seen her about a week and a half ago. Her coat was the color of deep gold, and its sheen had returned. Her eyes, once sunken, now looked at him with a keenness, and the mucous membranes lining her mouth pulsed a healthy pink.

Luke patted her side. "Good girl. You're doing a fine job with that filly of yours. Keep up the good work."

Genevieve stroked the mare's mane.

"Thank you for all you've done to help," he said, elated that the horses were well and he was sharing this moment with Genevieve.

She gave him a smile that roused his senses. As they made their way back to the river, shouting goodbye to Rutledge and his brother, Luke bounded through the moist warm air of the Yukon, pressed his boots against the raft to send them off, and slid his hand along her waist to guide her to the blankets.

Neither spoke, as if content to let harmony flow between them. She took a paddle and stroked through the current, a gentle tug of water as it lapped against the boards.

Did he wish to take her?

He tried to push the question from his mind, but it hovered near the surface at every stroke, every sound of the night, every rustle in the trees.

Even the weight of the air seemed heavier in his lungs as he tried not to watch her. Genevieve, with her back turned, sitting on her knees, made a lovely picture from behind. Her burgundy blouse stretched across her back with each stroke, fabric tugged at the slender waistline, her skirts ballooned around her hips. When they paddled around a bend and he turned and pressed closer, he enjoyed the view of shapely cotton molded to her breasts.

Did he wish to take her?

"There," he said, pointing to a half-built bridge in the distance, hoping to tame the lust coursing through his blood. "There's the new bridge I haven't seen in two weeks."

Its wooden trusses spanned the air and stopped midway. There was beauty to its puzzle.

Their raft drifted to the bank and stopped. He was about to push off with his ten-foot oar again when she turned.

"Can we stop and have a look?" she asked. "I've never seen a partially built bridge."

"All right."

Thankful for something else to occupy his mind, Luke anchored them in the mud, leaped off the raft and held out his hand.

Laughter escaped her as she stood up and balanced her way along the logs. "You make this look so easy, but I can't seem to stay on my feet."

With a smile, she took a flying leap toward him, sinking inches from his right.

He grabbed her by the waist to help and when she straightened, her skin was flushed with laughter.

The night, dimly lit due to the clouds above, stilled around them. An owl's hoot ceased, rustling of the leaves stopped, the lapping of the river faded from his ears. He caught his breath at the fine line of her jaw and the clarity of her skin.

Her laughter softened to a light moan of apprehension as she pierced his heart with her gaze.

Heat and power pounded through him.

Did he wish to take her?

Chapter Sixteen

Genevieve tried but couldn't will herself to look away from Luke. The air between them seemed to crackle with life. Without even touching, she connected with him fiercely, senses heightened, the sound of his breathing in time with her own, the scent of soap from his neck drifting down toward her, filling her lungs with Luke.

He leaned down and kissed her, sampling her lips lightly. Every hair on her flesh stood aroused. He nibbled on the corner of her lips.

How could she deny it? How could she fight what she'd wanted perhaps from the moment she set eyes on him in polished uniform? Standing proudly at her side at the wedding ceremony, the epitome of politeness, mixed with a dash of danger and wickedness he exuded from deep, dark eyes.

"Genevieve," he whispered at the side of her mouth, making her heart hammer. "When are you going to kiss me?"

Her limbs ached with the need of Luke. She met his eyes as his fingertips grazed the back of her neck, stroking the sensitive skin at her velvet choker.

"You're my wife," he coaxed.

"You make it difficult to resist."

"Don't resist."

"Why not?"

"Because…" He cupped the back of her neck and she pressed into his palm, reveling in his touch. "Because you want me and I want you…and we're alone and we have all night."

She was lost. She'd never felt this urgency with a man before, the total need to be held and to hold. She succumbed, sliding one hand and then the other up along his firm chest, feeling the quiver of his muscles when she touched him, knowing she affected him as much as he did her.

Stretching up on tiptoe, she reached for his mouth—what he wanted—and just before she pressed her lips to his, he twitched with an ever-so-slight smile of pleasure. *She* was kissing *him*.

His mouth was warm and responsive, following her lead of softness and restraint, a gentle exploration of who this husband of hers was, and what he had to offer.

A tremor of delicious excitement raced through her. She smiled into his lips. "Is this what you wished?"

"Oh, yes…"

"And this?" She raced her lips along his cheek, down along his newly shaven jaw to the soft flesh of his throat.

"…yes…"

"Perhaps this?" She wrapped her arms tighter along his waistline, stepping closer until they were pressed into each other and she could feel the firmness of his body and his response to her. Overwhelmed by the size of him and what to expect on this night when she'd never been with a man before, she moved by instinct and the power of her own sensuality. In all likelihood, she told herself, willing her nerves to disappear, no matter what she did he would adore it.

"...you've got it right..."

And then he grabbed her, pulling her tighter, ravaging her throat, kissing her in strokes so fine she could barely feel them, then kneading her shoulder with his firm hands and finally, finally, slipping lower to circle her waist and the swell of her aching breasts.

"Genevieve...hmm...Genevieve...is this your first time?" He kissed the tip of one breast through the cloth and the feeling shuddered through her body right to the center of her thighs.

She moaned at the fever in his words. "Yes."

He pulled himself away, panting, catching his breath, as if trying to withhold himself. "Then maybe...maybe this isn't the right way or the right place."

"Touch me," she whispered. "Take me."

And it was all he needed.

"I wanted you from the minute we shook hands," Luke murmured into her hair, basking in the wondrous feel of her skin and her scent. "From the moment I touched you."

She pulled her head away with a slow sweep. Her black lashes accentuated the depth of her green eyes. "At the ceremony?"

"Mmm-hmm."

Genevieve relaxed in his arms. "I don't have the strength to fight you anymore."

"I can think of something better than fighting."

He kissed her again and the sensation surged through his veins. The feel of her heavy breasts beneath her burgundy blouse drew him closer. His skin tingled where her silky fingers raked the back of his neck.

"Mmm…" He allowed himself the pleasure of one more kiss, soaking in the heat and power of her touch.

"What are you doing to me, Luke?"

"Everything…I want to do *everything*."

She uttered a groan and smiled in a lazy, heady way that made him want more.

Parting from her, he grasped her hand, wove his long fingers into hers and pulled her toward the dimly lit river.

Her shapely black eyebrows lifted. "Where are we going?"

"To the raft. Around the bend. It's private."

"Is it safe? Do you think anyone could stumble upon us?"

"Very safe. We haven't seen a soul for hours. It must be somewhere close to midnight."

Reeds swayed. Grasses crunched beneath their feet as a ruffle of wind caught his sleeve and plastered it to his arm.

"I like holding your hand."

She smiled in response, lifted their woven hands and kissed his knuckle.

They approached the raft, ensuring it was tied securely to a clump of pines, then anchored it into the soft mud of the river. The other side bordered deeper water. He stepped onto the dry planks, luring her behind him, setting her down on a spread of sheepskin and blankets.

"So that's what these are for," she said, teasing, indicating the blankets.

"Not what I intended, but we'll certainly put them to good use."

She became suddenly shy again, as though she might be changing her mind.

He wouldn't allow it. With a swoop, he pulled her close, angled his mouth over hers and gave her an ardent kiss. They wove together, enjoying a tighter, warmer fit. He lowered his hands along her back, cupping her behind and rocking her hips into his. She made a pleasuring sound and it heightened everything he felt—the moistness of her tongue, the heat of her fingers curled into his waist so hard it nearly hurt, the tantalizing scent of her skin mingling with the dampness of the river.

Looking up at him with wonder in her eyes, she leaned back onto the pile, framed in sheepskin. She'd be warm, he thought, in the nest he'd built for them.

He knelt above her and ran his index finger over her lips, down her chin, the valley of her throat and lower to the buttons of her blouse. With a deft hand, he unbuttoned the wine-colored cotton, tugging it out of her skirt to display, in full frame, the beauty of her body in a black lace corset.

Fading sunlight glistened along the water and caught the swell of her upturned breasts and the tiny pearls sewn beneath her cups. Her cleavage drew his eyes. Cream-colored skin, brushed with the strokes of shade and shadow, rose and fell with her breathing. Whalebone straps sewn into the seams along her ribs accentuated her slender waistline. Laces crisscrossed the corset at the front, tying her together. He unfastened the button that held up her skirt and tugged it down to reveal the curve of her hips.

"You're stunning," he whispered, lowering his lips to her cleavage.

He kissed her lightly along the top ridge of her corset, flicking his tongue along the soft down of her skin, bringing one hand up to the corset's laces and tugging her free.

"That's very naughty," she said, caressing his head, running her fingers along his temples and causing his pulse to race. And yet she arched slightly on the fur to acknowledge his hand.

"Indeed…"

With his hard yank on her laces, she spilled out into his hands. Budding, perky nipples, almost pointed, drew his attention to the tips of lush breasts. The size of her areolae were larger than gold coins, flat and smooth and faintly colored. And, oh, so needing of attention.

He kissed one, softly, then lowered his head to the other. Genevieve responded with a twisting of her body, feeding a breast up into his mouth. He filled his mouth and she squeezed her breasts together, begging for his lips on the other side. He complied, as eager to taste her body as she was to give it.

With a firm hand, he reached beneath her legs and tugged her skirt down to her feet. She kicked it off, and the movement made the raft rock to and fro. Water lapped at the edges of their makeshift bed, bringing the scent of dry summer weeds and rich damp earth.

He inhaled the air around her. Sitting up on his knees, he took in the view. Topless, her black corset shimmering against her apricot flesh, her breasts heaving as she inhaled a lungful of air, she wore black bloomers and thigh-high stockings. He ripped them off her and she struggled to sit up.

When she was totally nude, he held her at arm's length to rake in her beauty.

Her skin was olive-colored, smooth and clear from the Yukon air. Long black hair tumbled around her shoulders. Lips were parted, swollen and red from the force of his kisses. Her rib cage pushed up against the large round shape of her breasts, those pointed nipples of such beautiful proportion driving him insane. He followed the soft swell of her belly down to the triangle of glossy black curls.

Speechless, he watched her glide forward to unbutton

his shirt. She peeled it off, running her soft hands along his firm biceps and shoulders, so much bigger than hers.

Eagerly, he raced to undo his belt buckle and tug off his jeans, until he, too, was naked.

A duck called somewhere over the river and she turned, a silhouetted form against the black water. She dipped her fingers into the water.

It was heaven, he silently nodded and agreed, to be surrounded by an ice-cold river, yet perfectly warm in each other's arms and roasting among the blankets.

She trailed his flesh in silence, her fingers digging into his muscles as he cupped her face. He watched her glorious expression while she explored his body.

"I've never seen anyone—" she whispered "—so handsome."

They kissed and then he gently rolled her over.

"What's this?" she asked, tilting her face past her shoulder toward him.

"It'll be more comfortable for you like this...the first time."

She allowed him to lead. He caressed her shapely backside, yearning to place himself inside, but restraining himself in order to please her first.

"Turn to your side," he coaxed, easing himself onto the blankets behind her. Gently, he slid his hand down between her thighs and parted her hot center. With a burning ache, he slid his fingers along her lips there, careful to press lightly. She bucked against him, understanding what he meant, riding his hand first slowly, then with greater urgency.

He kissed the crook of her neck, lightly grazing her shoulders, and when she lifted her arm to expose one dangling breast, he kissed the side of the round swell.

When she was feverish and hot and wetter than he thought possible, he slid in another finger and then another, till she was riding four. When she burst into ecstasy, he suckled the skin at the side of her breast and marveled at her waves of contractions on his fingers.

They lingered for several moments. Even though she'd never been with a man before, she was aware of her own body, and it thrilled him.

Relaxed and dampened with the dew of exhaustion, she gazed up at him. Slowly, he slid his erection inside of her from the back. It was tight, too tight, but he took his time, gently nibbling on her arm, cupping her breast now that his hands were free, skimming her belly and latching his grip to the bone of her hip till he finally broke through. He was fully inside of her.

She winced with the pain. He waited and although he could barely breathe how urgently he wanted her, he stopped for a moment till she relaxed again. Easing slowly, he began a rhythm that she responded to with a gentle rocking of her hips.

"Are you all right?" He caressed her arm. She was stiff with discomfort but his touch seemed to relax her.

"Mmm. Keep going, Luke…"

Surrounded in slippery heat, he pushed harder and faster, kissing her dampened temples, feeling a trickle of perspiration down his shoulder blades, the wisp of the cooling wind blowing gently on his naked spine.

With sheepskin cushioning their bodies, waves of water splashing at the edges of their raft, moose calling to each other and the span of the new bridge arcing above them, Luke, body and soul, united with the woman he called his wife.

* * *

Luke was her lover. The word was delicious and wanton and carefree. And totally, totally private. This moment would be held just between the two of them, and Genevieve would always try to remember its purity.

Totally satiated, she languished in his arms. Legs woven together, they were two nude figures half-buried in a sea of down duvets and sheepskin. They'd already rinsed the evidence of her first time from one of the blankets. Luke had been so tender about it. The raft rocked gently beneath them. He ran his warm hand along her arm and pressed his face against her ribs.

He was so solid.

She felt no shame for what he might think of her. This was how it felt to lose herself in a man, and it seemed natural. Peaceful. The deep connection between them was not simply physical. It was the emotional and spiritual awakening of two lovers bonded in trust.

He stilled, with his ear pressed to her rib cage. "I can hear your heart beat."

"You make it go so fast."

"Do I?" His laughter rumbled against her skin.

He rose on an elbow and ran his fingers in circles around her belly, arousing her again.

"Be careful, you've awakened a great appetite."

He laughed gently. "I take full responsibility."

Her sentiments deepened and she fought with her uncertainties. "Did you…what did you think of…I suppose you've always…"

"It was like nothing I've experienced before."

She sighed with great contentment.

"Did I hurt you so much?"

"You were worth the pain," she teased softly.

His eyes glistened in the twilight. "What sort of pain are we speaking about?"

Her heartache with Joshua? Her accidental marriage to Luke and all it had entailed thus far?

She didn't reply.

He kissed her upper arm. It tingled where his lips met her skin. His large hand cupped her cheek and held it. "Sometimes we plan and we plan and we plan... But then an unexpected event comes along—it's the one that truly matters."

She felt drugged by this man. He seemed to sense every need and doubt and was trying hard to assure her that no guilt or shame was needed here.

He kissed her hip and that familiar shiver of delight raced through her.

"We should get going," he murmured. "But I can't seem to stop."

"Don't then."

"You're my responsibility. Won't your aunt and uncle be wondering where you are?"

"They left for dinner at the casino when I left the house. They retire to bed early, and I told them I'd go with you on your visit to the animals."

She turned to face him directly, looping her arms up around his neck.

"No," he said, smiling as he tried to resist, then gave in and kissed along her waist. "We should put on our clothes and get back."

They heard voices calling from the river.

Genevieve stiffened with alarm and grabbed a blanket to cover her bosom. Luke froze at her side.

"Oh, no," she whispered, instantly cold. "Oh, no."

Luke shook his head, not saying a word, and slid the covers tighter around her. He snatched his jeans from the base of the raft and tugged them on.

Voices drew nearer. "There's the bridge," said an unknown voice.

At the sight of Luke madly clawing at his pant legs, Genevieve moaned and covered her head with sheepskin. He could face them alone. *Coward,* she told herself. Perhaps it was a combination of fear and utter embarrassment that made her giggle.

The raft pitched as Luke presumably dressed.

The voices called louder and quicker. Whoever they were, they were nearly around the bend and rapidly coming toward them.

Dead silence filled the air. Then someone called out, "Luke!"

Stricken with fright, Genevieve clutched the blankets.

"Yeah?" Luke hollered back.

"Have you seen Miss Summerville?"

"Why do you ask?"

"Her uncle sent us looking for her. Her aunt is worried sick."

Genevieve groaned.

"If I see her I'll let her know."

She heard nothing more for several seconds. Perhaps the men were satisfied and turning around their craft. Her fingers eased on the blankets, her shoulders fell.

And then came the stranger's words, close to her buried head. "Miss Summerville, we really must advise you to come home."

Chapter Seventeen

She woke up thinking about him.

Sunlight slanted through the bedroom window onto Genevieve's hand. She opened her eyes, squinting in the brightness, rolled onto her side and stared at her knuckles. Golden rays illuminated the tiny hairs on her wrist, warmed her cheek and fell upon her naked shoulders.

Luke.

Genevieve rolled her hip toward the heat, realizing the loose buttons down the front of her nightgown had come undone again, exposing her body to the sun and allowing its rays to touch her breasts and belly. When she moved her legs, she throbbed down below, still sore from last night.

She smiled into her pillow. They'd spent hours making love.

Did the passion always make a person's heart swell the way it did hers? Did it always take a person to such extreme heights of joy?

She was torn by what she felt, the fever of a new love battling with the concern of who this man was and what he stood for. In his work, he garnered everyone's respect, but his personal life was awash with whispered rumors.

Would *she* turn out to be another rumored whisper in his life?

She rolled back to the other side of her pillow and stared up at the sunny rafters. The men who'd caught them were neighbors of her aunt and uncle's—Toby and Adam Langstaff. Genevieve didn't really know the brothers, had met them once in passing. The look they'd given her as she and Luke made their way home had been enough to condemn her in her uncle's eyes, as well, when she walked to the front porch and the men exchanged glances.

Her aunt Abigail hadn't seemed to notice the relationship had gotten as far as it had, but one look at Uncle Theodore's knowing expression, the solemn turn of his lips, the slight lowering of his head as he'd shook it in disappointment, told Genevieve he'd surmised what had occurred.

No words were said between them. Aunt Abigail had kissed her good-night and gone to bed, joining Milly, who'd already gone hours earlier. Luke had apologized to Uncle Theodore for keeping her out so late, but defiantly refused to mention anything more.

And as for the neighbors, Toby and Adam, they'd disappeared as silently as they'd come.

Which still left Genevieve with her feelings about Luke. How could she run so quickly from Joshua's arms to his? What did that make her?

Getting caught red-handed last night by total strangers accentuated her own confusion. How quickly she'd strayed from her own path. She'd come to Dawson hoping to marry a man she'd known for years, trying to prove she could make a marriage work despite the troubled one she'd witnessed between her parents, and here she was alone, counting nail heads in the ceiling, going to bed with a man she'd known for little more than two weeks.

With not a promise to her name.

A bird pecked at the windowsill, scratching its claws along the wood. Nugget, who'd been sleeping in the basket at the foot of the bed, came to a slow awakening. Her ears pricked at the window. The movement of the bird's feathers flicked shadows into the room. Genevieve's heart squeezed with the blossoming sentiment of perhaps being no further ahead today than she'd been yesterday, with the man she was growing to feel so much for, when she wasn't sure what on earth he felt in return.

He woke up thinking about her.

Sunshine poured into the solitary barracks, onto the bed where Luke lay naked, drizzling his torso with heat. With everyone else gone, he hadn't bothered with nightclothes, had simply stripped from the pair of jeans and shirt he'd worn with Genevieve and tumbled into bed, exhausted.

What was he going to do about Genevieve?

In the dream he was rousing from, he was still lying on the river with her. She was sitting above him, straddling him with broad creamy hips, her pointed breasts glistening with the heat of their contact, dangling inches away from his awaiting mouth. As he woke, he was so fully aroused he ached.

He swore softly beneath his breath because he'd been robbed in finishing his dream.

Blinking, he oriented himself to the room. Two windows on the far wall. An armoire. Three bunk beds and the full one where he slept.

The sun's summer rays pounded through the window and blasted his skin. Perspiration trickled down his temple. The muscles of his arms and chest rippled with curved shadows and lines. He kicked off the last of the sheets, totally naked, and propped a long leg up on the mattress.

His thigh glistened in the golden light, the muscles taut with tension and his lower body thrumming with the aftereffects of the dream. How could one woman rouse him to such height and firmness?

He sighed in a drugged stupor.

He was lost to her power like a bird to sunshine.

What was it he expected from her? Last night had been more intimate than any he'd ever shared with anyone.

He hadn't planned an evening of making love. He'd truly thought he might take her to see the horses, then deliver her safely to her aunt and uncle's door.

The Langstaffs were generally discreet men. The two brothers had struck gold last year, and were among the few who managed to keep a lid on their spending.

Dealing with her uncle was another matter.

And what of Genevieve? She had definitely enjoyed the pleasures of the evening. He had satiated her, and there was nothing more gratifying to him than to hear her moan beneath his caress.

Was it fair to expect more?

How much more did he want?

Why was he having such a problem coming to grips with Genevieve? Hadn't he always known what to say and how to let other women down gently, if their expectations exceeded his?

But in this case, they were married. It stuck in his throat. *Married.*

He hadn't willingly chosen marriage. It was thrust upon them both. And…she had just called it quits with Joshua. Wasn't it too soon for Luke to expect her loyalty?

It was selfish of him to expect it.

Or was that perhaps easier to deal with, to pretend she needed more time, than dealing with his own burden of feeling inadequate…not good enough to sustain a relationship for longer than a few months. Sooner or later, all women moved on from him. He used to be able to fool himself, thinking it was he who got bored and left them. But looking back at things now, weren't most of the women he'd courted just like Penelope? They'd realized he wasn't willing or able to make promises and so they'd moved on to men who could.

Men who were better suited to marriage and family and remaining steadfast in times of woe.

His head swirled with the questions, but he tried to focus on his duties. He had a lot to do today, his first day of investigation without the hindrance of quarantine.

Swinging his long legs over the bed, he hit the cool floor and walked to the armoire for fresh clothing. Totally naked, he passed by the window, enjoying the burn of the sun. He opened the armoire doors and his eyes settled on his uniform.

He reached in and took the hanger. He'd look as official as he could.

Ten minutes later, still thinking of Genevieve, he walked into the empty kitchen that he'd shared with total strangers for the past two weeks, and thought of the last time he'd seen her.

Saying goodbye on her aunt and uncle's small log porch.

Luke brewed himself a cup of coffee and passed by the fireplace. Her drying bouquet hung over the stone. She'd left it behind on purpose. She didn't want anything to remind her of Joshua.

Luke headed out the door, dressed in full uniform, his gun holstered in his leather harness across his shoulder, his boots pounding the soft earth.

He should stay away from Genevieve. The distance would give him clarity.

But he couldn't stop himself from thinking maybe Miss Norris would answer more questions this morning if he brought Genevieve with him.

"Genevieve, Joshua's here to see you."

With a whoosh to her stomach, Genevieve looked up from the kitchen table at Milly, who'd entered with the horrible news. Surrounded by feathers, buttons, colorful felts and homemade patterns cut from brown paper, Genevieve slid the velvet pin cushion from her wrist.

"Where is he?"

"Outside on the porch, talking to my pa." Milly rubbed her freckled nose.

Genevieve paused. "How did he seem?"

"In good spirits. Carrying an awfully big package."

"A package of what?"

Nugget barked at their feet and Milly, in a blue cotton blouse, bent down to pat the dog. The puppy licked her fingers. "I think it's a surprise for you, so I better not say."

Genevieve groaned. What did Joshua hope to accomplish? She'd asked him to drop by for a cup of coffee, but didn't want packages.

She untied her full-length apron, draped it over a chair and tucked the dangling ties away from Nugget's reach. She headed down the hall. "Thank you. I'll go say hello."

"Can I take Nugget for a walk?"

"She'd adore it."

The queasiness in Genevieve's stomach rolled upward through her chest when she spotted Joshua standing on the porch with a big bouquet of flowers.

Stabilizing herself, Genevieve opened the door and stepped out into bright morning sunshine to join Joshua and her uncle.

Joshua removed his cowboy hat and smiled. His dark brown hair, newly washed, glistened in the sun. "Morning, Genevieve. These are for you."

Genevieve hesitated for a moment. What would accepting them mean?

Her uncle, seated on a woven willow-branch chair, cleared his throat and nodded to the gift.

Genevieve reached out. "Thank you. They're beautiful."

The flowers were magnificent. She lowered her face to the daffodils, tulips and wild roses. "It's hard to believe such things of beauty can grow this far north."

"Denny Prinz takes pride in his work. Apparently in Holland, folks used to ride for miles to catch a glimpse of his gardens."

"I'll go put them in water while you two men finish your discussion."

She turned but Joshua stepped forward and touched her shoulder. "Genevieve…please…can we talk?"

"I'll brew some fresh coffee."

"Please?"

She didn't stir, but she heard her uncle clatter out of his chair. "I'll leave you two alone. Good day, Joshua. Nice to see you come around."

Genevieve looked down at the weathered floor planks

of the porch. The heat of shame crept up her neck. Her uncle Theodore, despite what he knew about her behavior with Luke last night, still thought she should talk things through with Joshua.

She no longer had her virginity, and Joshua hadn't been the one to take it. Even if…even if things turned around, which she knew they would not…how could Joshua possibly forgive her?

And she didn't wish to give him that option. They simply weren't suited. He behaved kindly toward her when things were going well, but poorly when things didn't go his way. And wasn't that the true test of character? How a person behaved in tough times, not good ones?

Her uncle's footsteps receded down the stairs and out the yard. Slowly, laden with the scent of summer blooms, Genevieve pivoted to face Joshua.

It was the first time she'd seen him in about a week, since the night in the jailhouse when she'd told him it was over.

He was clean shaven. His clothes hung neatly pressed.

"Give me another chance, Gen."

"Please don't make this harder than it has to be."

He scoffed. "Hard on you?"

"I was thinking of you, Joshua. I don't want to make this harder on you than it has to be."

"We could be married before the sun sets tonight."

"How?"

"The minister—"

"He thinks I'm married to Luke—"

"We'll force him to annul it."

"The minister won't do anything until the new judge evaluates whether Luke and I are legally married."

"Must every sentence contain his name?"

"No. No, it needn't. Because my situation with him is totally different than my situation with you."

With a soft bellow, Joshua thrust his arms in the air. "Stop this double-talk. We've been sidetracked by a chain of events, but we can get it back on track. Marry me, Genevieve. We could have a good life together. Remember what it was like at the country fair in Montana? Our first kiss?"

Their first kiss had been a light peck on the lips. No depth. No hunger. Nothing like the rocking sensuality of Luke's kisses.

Her eyes misted. She closed her lids briefly, wondering how she might get through to Joshua, but the sound of heavy boots raced up the stairs, cutting into her thoughts. When she opened her lids again, Luke was standing there beside Joshua.

Much taller and thicker than Joshua, Luke was dressed in full uniform. She hadn't seen him like this since their wedding day, and once again, the vision stole her breath.

The scarlet hue of his jacket contrasted with the sharp dark features of his face—the slash of black eyebrows that intensified the specks of brown and black in his eyes, the straight nose, the riveting, firm jaw. The scar beneath his eye, once the first thing she'd noticed about him, now faded to oblivion whenever she looked at him.

He pressed his lips together thoughtfully. There was sentiment in his eyes.

They'd made love last night, yet how could he look at her in public without acknowledging something? Had he rethought how he felt?

What did *she* feel?

So very much, but unable to express it all.

"Hello, Genevieve," Luke said gently. Her heart turned at the seductive sound of his voice.

"Good morning."

Joshua swiveled his shoulders toward the intruder and scowled. "What the hell are you doing here, Hunter?"

Luke cleared his throat and removed his broad Mountie Stetson. "Business."

There was a deeper significance, though, to the way Luke looked at her. Joshua seemed to sense it, too, for he stepped beside Genevieve and boldly pressed his hand to her waist. It was an act of possessiveness.

Luke stared at the hand, then the flowers.

She waited, heart beating in expectation.

"I need to speak to you about the quarantine."

"What about? Have you made an arrest?"

"Not yet. But with your help, I'm hoping to this morning."

A wave of relief, much greater than she'd even anticipated, washed over her. Their ordeal was soon to be over.

Joshua pulled her closer. "Can't you do your own work and leave my bride out of this?"

Uncomfortable at his embrace, Genevieve tried to tug away.

Luke blinked at them. His jaw clamped, he gripped his hat and stepped forward, but must have seen the silent pleading in her eyes to keep the peace, so turned instead to the muddy street and the passing pedestrians clomping their way along the boardwalk to the shops in town.

"This doesn't concern you, McFadden," said Luke. "It's got nothing to do with your personal situation, and everything to do with the quarantine. I'll step aside and wait for you down by the boardwalk, Genevieve, and I expect you, McFadden, to step aside and let me do my work."

With a deliberation that frightened her, Luke strode off the stairs, long legs in dark breeches, shoulder harness strapped across his broad chest, black hair shining in the sunlight.

"I forbid you to go with him anywhere." Joshua breathed the words more than he spoke them.

"Joshua, please. Don't make me choose like this."

"I forbid you," he said.

I'm sorry, she mouthed.

Aunt Abigail called from inside the house. "What's going on out here?" She opened the door and stuck her head out. "Joshua, so…so good of you to visit. Do sit a spell. Maybe you'll join us for lunch?"

With an apologetic look at her aunt, and a decision she knew she might regret later, Genevieve planted the bouquet in her aunt's arms. Not waiting to listen to the astonished reply, she stepped down the stairs and left Joshua, mouth gaping, on the porch.

On the boardwalk, standing in his irresistible uniform, Luke turned and watched her approach. She tried to suppress the nervous flutter inside of her, wondering if she'd have the strength to deal with whatever more was coming.

Chapter Eighteen

Luke's heart beat stronger as Genevieve drew closer, but he restrained himself, vowing to take things slow. Slower than he ever had with a woman, because this woman was like no other.

She moved toward him with grace, her legs hitting the underside of her skirts, hinting at the curves beneath. The lace at her throat parted, revealing the hollow of her neck and its soft shadows. The belt cinched around her waist drew attention to the beautiful shape of her breasts.

Her face melted into a smile when she reached him.

Luke pressed a hand to the back of her shoulder blades, drank in the comfort of touching her again, and resolved to give her time to sort through what was happening between them. When he'd seen her with McFadden on the porch, Luke had damned well desired her all the more.

Although he wanted to pull her into his arms, he was careful of who was watching, and so only touched her arm. "I can't get you out of mind."

She smiled again, and he was taken back to last night. The longing that had been building for fourteen days and nights.

"What are we going to do?" she asked.

"I think, as a gentleman, I have to step back and give you time to sort your feelings."

Nodding, she looked down at her hands and then out into the busy street. Men went about their business, walking into shops and hauling supplies down the rutted road. "It wasn't easy seeing Joshua. How is it with... Penelope gone?"

"I never would have been with you last night if I missed Penelope."

The honesty of his statement reflected as a flicker in her eyes. It was the truth, and that much he could admit both to her and to himself. He'd courted a lot of women but never at the same time.

Her hair tumbled down her back. He remembered how it had fallen across her naked breasts last night. The image made his body come alive. Alarmed by how affected he was getting, he dropped his hand from her back and tipped the brim of his hat toward the sun.

He led her down the boardwalk. "I'd like you to come with me to speak to Miss Norris."

Genevieve's eyes widened. Her voice was a hoarse whisper. "That's who you think did it?"

He nodded. "I need her to answer some questions she's refused to answer thus far. You've become fairly friendly with her. I thought she might open up more if we went to see her together."

"Why do you think she did it?"

"The torture of not being able to marry. Of being shunned, pushed into the background at every social occasion."

Her boots padded along the planks. "Am I missing something? Why couldn't they marry?"

"Because all the time he lived in the Klondike, he was married to another woman."

Genevieve gasped. "I thought he was widowed."

"That's what he wanted folks to believe. He'd separated from his wife, but didn't let anyone know."

"How did you find out?"

"Found a letter of hers in his things. It wasn't very friendly. Just a reminder to send money to their daughter, who'd delivered their first grandchild."

Genevieve made a face. "He pretended his first wife no longer existed."

"But he couldn't, of course, pretend enough in a court of law. He couldn't legally marry Miss Norris."

"I had no idea when we said our vows that the man officiating was such a…a scoundrel. Poor Miss Norris."

"*Poor?* She's the one who did him in."

"Well, yes, I suppose I'm being sympathetic to the wrong person. What she did in return was unforgivable." Genevieve looked over her shoulder and spotted the two constables thirty paces behind them. "Are we being followed?"

"An extra precaution. I don't believe Miss Norris has any plans to do away with anyone else, but if she feels cornered, we've got help."

Genevieve tilted her face away from the sun. "Why do you think she poisoned Mr. Orman?"

"I think blackmail is somehow involved."

The town of Dawson City sprawled before them as they crossed the street. They passed beneath storefront banners reading Cures of Scurvy, Waffle House, Imported Linens, Gold Outfits and Gold Pans. Luke kept his eyes trained on the activity in the street.

They passed a lineup of men standing at the entrance to

a place where gold nuggets were bought. They were chattering and laughing, dragging buckets filled with gold.

Luke shook his head as he always did when he passed this place. These men in greasy overalls, who hadn't shaved or bathed or brushed their teeth for weeks, were the Klondike's newest millionaires.

Plenty of them followed Genevieve's twirling skirts as Luke led her through the crowd.

"You'd have no problem finding another husband here," he teased softly. "Take your pick."

Genevieve raised her hand to shield her face from the strong light. "Luke, you know I don't want any of them. Not after…"

The night they'd shared.

With affection, he ran his hand up her back and pulled her closer.

Luke nodded to the two Mounties who were following. They moved past the livery stables, ducking through a team of horses. Several men pushed supply carts. There was no extra livestock to be had in Dawson to haul it for them.

They barreled past the BlackJack Casino. The posh building glistened in the sunlight, elegantly trimmed and painted, with white lettering stenciled on the window: The Casino Restaurant, Dawson's Finest. Business was slow and Luke knew it wouldn't pick up till the evening, around six or seven when Vince usually arrived.

Luke led Genevieve across another dirt street, dodging hordes of men pushing carts filled with supplies.

"A paddle wheeler must've just come in," he said.

Heaps of clothing passed before their eyes, miners' shirts and jeans and long winter coats lined with fur pelts.

Another wheelbarrow, laden with crockery and cooking

pots, rumbled by, followed by one loaded with fishing equipment, another with ledgers and quill pens, and then a mule pulling a cart of canned meats and vegetables. Behind the mule and the BlackJack Casino, a new café advertised French cuisine. Luke spotted Ripley Cliffton going in with another gentleman.

"That's odd," said Luke.

"What is?"

"Ripley Cliffton eating at the new place instead of his brother's casino."

"Maybe he's assessing the competition on behalf of his brother."

"True enough."

They turned the corner and there it was. The grand home of the late Judge Donahue. And who should be hoeing the front garden but Miss Norris herself. Something was different though. She didn't look well. Her skirt was wrinkled, not pressed in its usual form. Her linen blouse sat limply at her throat as if she'd forgotten to starch it. The housekeeper's hair, usually immaculate, was half-clasped and falling down her back.

Miss Norris turned, and instead of a smile when she saw Genevieve and Luke, she dropped her hoe and headed for the back door.

"Hold on there, Miss Norris," Luke shouted. "May we have a minute?"

"Are you here to take away my home?" When Miss Norris stared at Genevieve with tears in her eyes, Genevieve's throat constricted. So this was what the woman feared.

Sitting on a firm sofa in a parlor decorated with ruby-colored wallpaper and mahogany furniture, Genevieve lowered her coffee to a saucer on the side table. She avoided Luke's attention from the wing chair beside her, and tried to calm Miss Norris. Behind the frail woman, a large bay window, covered with silk organza drapes, let in a waterfall of light.

Genevieve leaned forward and pressed her hand onto the housekeeper's. "I'm not sure what the judge's last will and testament said about this house."

"I'm afraid, Miss Norris," Luke said softly, stroking the arm of his chair, "the news isn't good. Judge Donahue left this home to his family. To his wife and three surviving children."

Miss Norris puckered her mouth grimly. For a few moments, she didn't speak. When her initial shock faded, her posture strengthened and her resolve returned. "Then I suppose it'll need cleaning and scrubbing. They'll want to sell it."

Genevieve pondered how such a love could exist. The housekeeper still wished to clean and scrub for the old judge, despite the slap in the face? Was she acting? Pretending to be kind and helpful, when in truth, she'd poisoned the old gent in heated retaliation for a love she couldn't have?

Luke obviously believed so, and Genevieve knew he'd seen many unusual crimes, many more than she'd ever witnessed. Surely, then, he recognized a much deeper anger than Genevieve did in this woman.

Such a pitiful waste of life. And love.

And the judge's wife. Why weren't they together? Why did Judge Donahue feel the need to travel thousands of miles from the woman he'd once shared a life with?

"This is a very troubling time for you, no doubt," said Luke. "But may I ask you some questions about the night before the judge died?"

Miss Norris blinked with fright. Genevieve couldn't stop herself from reaching out and stroking the woman's clenched fingers.

"Just a few is all we need. Then it'll be all over, I promise."

The woman looked down at her lap and whispered, "He promised, too."

Genevieve squeezed Miss Norris's fingers and the woman looked up. "I was protecting him for no reason. He didn't even leave me his home. *Our* home." She cleared her throat and steeled her voice. "Yes, Inspector, go ahead. What do you wish to know you haven't asked already?"

"What did you cook for dinner the night before our wedding? The night before the judge died?"

"You've already asked me what I made for breakfast the day he died. Now you want to know what I made for dinner?"

"That's right."

"Corned beef, evaporated potatoes and gravy. It was his favorite meal and we always had it on Friday nights."

"I see. You wouldn't happen to have a sample of the tins you used, would you?"

"As a matter of fact, yes."

The housekeeper rose, straightened her back and showed them into the kitchen. She crouched over a cupboard draped with a cloth and pulled out two tins.

Luke read the labels. "Evaporated potatoes. Just add water. Evaporated gravy. Just add water."

"Did *you* eat some?"

She nodded.

Luke sighed, as if it wasn't what he'd expected. "Thank

you, Miss Norris, that's all I need for now. May I take these with me?"

"Certainly."

Luke led Genevieve back to the front door. She caught his eye and motioned to him. Wasn't he going to arrest the woman? Or ask her any more questions?

He discreetly indicated no.

"Thank you for your time," he said to the housekeeper. "I appreciate you letting me know about his last dinner."

Miss Norris fiddled with her limp collar. "Oh, that wasn't what *he* ate."

"Beg your pardon?"

"You asked me what I made for dinner. It was corned beef and gravy. But he didn't eat it."

"Why not?"

"He ate privately at the casino."

"Casino?"

"Oh, yes. I've kept his secret for two months, but now that he's gone with no regard for how he left me…" She played again with her collar, wrinkled fingers catching the light. She was grappling with something, Luke observed. Whether to say something or not.

"Well, you're a respectable man," she finally said, "and you're trying to do your duty. Fergus ate garlic soup, he told me that night in bed."

Miss Norris turned the color of canned beets, perhaps mortified at her disclosure that she and judge had slept together. She removed a handkerchief from her waistband and pressed it to her nose.

Luke carried on without a hint of recognition for the slip. "You're telling me he ate garlic soup at the casino?"

She nodded, hiding behind the handkerchief.

"Why, Miss Norris, is that a secret?"

"The soup is not a secret. His gambling was."

Luke looked at her, stunned.

"There are private rooms at the casino," she explained. "Fergus lost ten thousand dollars' worth of gold the night before he died. Gambled it away to Vince Cliffton."

Genevieve clutched her throat and stammered for air.

"And you might want to find out what the Cliffton brothers argued about last year. Something went very sour there. I didn't overhear much, but the row happened when Fergus transferred the title of the casino from Ripley to Vince."

"I've been looking at it all wrong."

With his pulse leaping, Luke hurried Genevieve down the boardwalk five minutes later, dashing toward the outpost to speak to Commissioner York. "I've been concentrating on my horse medicine as the poison. I was sifting through opium and licorice powders, but maybe the judge was poisoned by something he ate."

"But then how was Mr. Orman poisoned? More garlic soup?"

"I don't know. Listen…I've got a few hunches. I'm going to the casino at seven o'clock tonight, when Vince gets there."

"My aunt and uncle dined there last night. They said Vince invited them back this evening as his guests, and asked them to bring me along. Should I go and meet you there?"

There wouldn't be any real danger, Luke thought, for he didn't plan on confronting anyone. He'd ask a few questions and scout the premises. "If I change into street clothes, it won't look so much like I'm there on business. And dining with you instead of another officer won't trip off any alarms bells."

"All right," she joked, "but I'm not having the garlic soup."

"That's not funny. If we get to talking to Vince, don't eat anything. We'll make a big fuss about ordering from the menu but don't eat any of it when it arrives at our table."

"How am I supposed to avoid it?"

"Just follow my lead."

"And…if this doesn't pan out, Luke…what then?"

"Then I've got nothing and have to start from scratch again."

"You no longer believe Miss Norris did it?"

"When I saw her sitting in her parlor today, she didn't seem like a desperate killer."

"I still don't trust *anyone*."

"Good."

When they reached the Mountie outpost, Genevieve waited outside on the slopes. Luke disclosed everything he knew to the commissioner and asked for two men to follow them to the casino tonight.

"Commissioner, could you also send a man to the Land Claims Office? Have him go through every single person who was quarantined with us, and make note of who owns what property here in Dawson. The deceased, as well. That's a list of ten."

Commissioner York popped a peppermint candy into his mouth. "What about Miss Summerville?"

Luke blinked. He had to appear objective, even though there was nothing objective about the way his heart pounded around Genevieve. "Of course. A list of eleven. We don't want to leave anyone out."

But God help him if anything turned up on the woman he'd made love to last night.

Chapter Nineteen

Luke was so handsome in his uniform, thought Genevieve, he seemed untouchable. He finished speaking to the commissioner and joined Genevieve on the grassy slopes. Sunshine melted through the trees and poured over the rich red fabric of his shoulders. She imagined peeling off his jacket, wondering how he'd look dressed only in tight black breeches and naked torso. She wondered how the sunshine would enhance the muscles of his chest and glaze the hairs of his stomach.

"I'll walk you home, Genevieve."

The way he said her name and held her gaze made her stop. There had to be more between them. There had to be more to her life than what she'd been given already.

He wished to give her time to sort through her feelings. But how much more time did she need to recognize that every time Luke came near, her hopes and her heart soared?

Unrepentant for her private thoughts, Genevieve glanced to the barracks. "I forgot some of my things yesterday. Since I'm here, I should go get them."

Her wedding dress for one. If she planned on selling it,

she had to clean and press the train. She had no use for her bouquet, but Milly wanted to press the roses and Aunt Abigail wished to collect the dried petals in a bowl and scent the parlor. Her aunt had made it very clear how much the bouquet had cost them, and the least Genevieve could do to salvage their loss would be to bring the flowers home.

"I did notice you left a few things behind." Luke pressed his hand to her waist and her temperature rose a notch.

If she admitted how deeply she cared for him, would he send her away again? Would he tell her he wasn't ready to settle down with *anyone,* no matter how much time *he* was given?

And as he squired her up the hill and directed her down the path toward the barracks, she wondered if he, too, was thinking of their evening last night. How warm and good their bodies had felt together.

She listened to his breathing as they walked along the grass, her slender shoulders brushing his upper sleeve, causing a pounding sensation in her chest and a quivering of her stomach.

How much more did he want from her? Or anything at all?

Was one night of bliss enough for him? Surely, she hadn't been just another conquest in a series of many.

Suddenly feeling awkward and unattractive, sexless beside a man whose mere glance was saturated with sex, she stepped away as he swung open the door.

He turned around and nodded. "After you."

She craned her neck to look up at him as she moved inside. "Thank you."

The door clicked closed behind them.

The place was airy and lit by the sun, much tidier with the whole group gone. Only Luke's things remained in one bedroom, but there was little sign of him in the great room. The place had been swept and scrubbed by the staff. Shiny tin bowls sat stacked on the counter, utensils aligned beneath the cupboards, drinking glasses sparkled from the light shining through the windows.

"When are the other officers returning?"

"Tomorrow or the next day. Soon as they get a chance to break from their duties and pack."

She crossed from the door to the sitting area. The sound of her high-heeled boots clattered on the wooden planks and then grew muffled as they sank into a Persian rug.

It seemed so barren and cold without the others, but in another way, so heated with Luke standing beside her. The two of them were alone as they never had been in these quarters.

She looked above the fireplace mantel and spotted her bouquet dangling over the stone ledge where she'd left it.

"There it is." She reached forward on tiptoe but couldn't grasp its center. Last time she'd used a chair to stand on.

"Here, let me help you."

Luke rushed up from behind and grazed her hip.

Air rushed between them. He didn't move for the bouquet. She gulped, not knowing what to say, pressing her hands together.

"Genevieve…Genevieve, I'm sorry…I shouldn't have taken you out last night and let it get as far as it did."

"You probably shouldn't have, but you did…and we did…and Joshua's gone and I don't want him back."

"He wants you."

"It's not so much about what he wants anymore. You were right. You told me we weren't suited."

"If I hadn't come along…you and Joshua would be married."

"But you did come along and made me realize the truth about my life. The truth about what I was lacking, and what Joshua would never be able to give me."

"That's not what I had in mind. I don't want to be the one to break up anyone's marriage…"

"I'm not married to him, I'm married to you."

"Accidentally."

"However it came to be. It is."

"Two weeks is not enough time for you to decide."

"You mean it's not enough time for you."

The comment affected him. He glanced down at his boots, the wisp of guilt etching his mouth.

"Genevieve, I've had too many women…quick women…women who don't need much…and you're not one of those."

"I'm glad to hear you say it," she whispered.

"But two weeks is not enough—"

"Then maybe we should spend more time together, not less."

"Maybe. Maybe, maybe, maybe…" Frustrated, he ran a hand above his ear. "I don't know if we could go back. I don't know if we could pretend nothing happened between us…but we *can* go forward. Joshua still wants you as his wife. I don't want you to go to him. But I *do* want you to chose what's best."

She exhaled, heavy with the misery of being cast away from Luke. He reached high above her and brought down the bouquet. The scent of flowers drifted around them.

He pushed them toward her. "Take them."

She spoke in a strained voice. "You're telling me to go?"

"This morning when I saw Joshua standing on your porch, I knew it wasn't over. You were angry with him, yes, but you didn't have the heart to give him back his flowers. To tell him to leave you alone."

"I wanted to."

"But you didn't…and you've got to question why." He pleaded, "I don't want to be responsible for what I might do if you stay here for one more minute looking at me like that."

Her focus dropped to the gentle hand that held the flowers. She couldn't move.

"Do you think it's easy for me to resist?" he asked. "Do you think I don't want you? That I don't imagine you in my arms with nothing but the moon and the sun above us? I couldn't sleep last night for the images burning in my thoughts."

With a shaky hand, she reached out and took the flowers. She dipped her fingers down below the bunch, skimming his. At the flash of contact, her attention shot up. His mouth parted.

With a groan, he pulled her into his arms, taking her lips with his. She forgot about everything except this moment and the man who rocked against her, stealing her heart and her life and everything calm she'd ever known about herself.

Her lips fell open with his urgency. She raised her face and body to Luke. But along with the joy of his caress came the pain of not knowing how to proceed or what to say or how to say it.

The pain of perhaps never sharing this moment with him again, if he chose to leave.

The need, the drive to be with him superseded reason. She wanted Luke. She wanted this.

The bouquet crashed to the floor.

And suddenly the laughter started. She smiled into his mouth and he responded with a moan. He snared her with massive arms, pressing her soft hips into the crux of his till she felt needed and wanted and understood how deeply she moved him, too.

"Genevieve," he uttered into her throat, her ear, her skin.

He smelled of roses and leather.

"Genevieve, when it comes to you, I can't control myself…"

He scooped her up, his heart surely pounding as quickly as her own. With a firm step, he carried her to the front door, secured the lock and swept her to his bedroom.

Gently setting her down upon his bed, he stroked the fallen hair at her temples and kissed her lips.

"Here we are again," he whispered, in one seemingly last attempt to wrench himself free. "But this is so wrong. I'm influencing you and your choices in ways I shouldn't."

"It's not wrong if we both feel the same way."

He lowered his face to her bosom. He kissed the swell and kissed every pearl button on her worn-out cotton blouse, the one whose side seams she'd reinforced to keep from ripping open. But with Luke, she didn't feel her clothes mattered. He'd never made her feel that her looks or wardrobe were what drew him.

His warm breath grazed the front of her blouse. She curled herself upward with every stroke of his mouth.

"…I bet you could make love to me with only your mouth to guide you."

"That's precisely what I intend."

She gasped at the blazing thought. She'd only been teasing…didn't think it was possible…was it possible?

The heady sensation, the feeling of being so wanton, so fast, melted her, at the same time making her blood pound.

How low was he going to go with that mouth of his?

Surely not any lower than…than her breast…the side of her waist… When his hot mouth breathed against her belly, she flinched with delight. She closed her eyes and let the feeling take her. Heat throbbed within her, swirling through her body and centering between her thighs.

With a quick stroke, he slid his hand up her skirts, past the cotton stockings she'd mended twenty times over, above her bare knee and straight up her fleshy thigh. He moaned and gripped the high part of her leg where her hip met her center. With another swoop, his hand was inside her bloomers, his fingers silky smooth against the fine hairs and the feminine spot she had never allowed any other man to touch.

He yanked her skirts up and bloomers down, hungry with the desire to touch her. It was torture to be this close to Luke and not be pressed together as one, arching and straining and stroking.

Luke didn't wish to risk shocking Genevieve, but he was breathless with how much he yearned to please her.

Warm golden sunshine spilled down his uniformed shoulders and dipped along the side of her body. Her skin, tinged with a healthy glow, felt soft and raw beneath his kisses.

Helpless to control himself, he tore off her skirts and bloomers and slid down her stockings, cupping her feet, kissing her ankles and the inner part of her heel.

Hungrily unbuttoning her blouse, he smiled at the green in her eyes deepening, the curve of her cheek turned to the sun. When her blouse parted, he bore his weight down on one knee and lingered at the view. She filled her white lace corset to overflowing.

The gentle rise and fall of her breasts swelled above the ruffled neckline. With expert control, he tugged at the laces crossing her bosom, until the corset, too, parted and he was privy to the most extraordinary sight.

Golden breasts in the cascading sun. Golden nipples that pointed upward and begged for his mouth. How could he let such delicious skin pass him by? He met her eyes, felt the tug of a smile at the corner of his mouth, lowered his head and lightly kissed one tip.

She groaned, as if urging him to dare further. He cupped the other breast, kneading it like soft dough in his hand, tonguing the nipple lightly, ever so gently that she might not even suspect his mouth was upon it.

He ran his fingers along the side of each breast, pressed the mounds together and sucked one and then the other. She stirred beneath him, raising and parting her knees to greet him, and he was nearly gone.

"Take off your uniform, Luke. Let me see you."

He didn't rise from her breasts, simply undid one button and the next and the next until his tunic was off, revealing a cotton undershirt that molded to his chest.

At her insistence, he removed that, too, so he could press his naked chest to hers. He rocked her and she pushed him over so she could gaze at him for a moment. As her eyes roved over his naked body draped only in his breeches, she caught her breath.

"You are the most handsome man."

"Touch me, Genevieve. If you want me, touch me."

With exploring fingers, she reached up and slid her hand along his ribs. The sensation made him quiver.

She explored the length of his thighs above his breeches, then ran her fingers upward, teasing him with how close she came to his erection. Just when he thought he couldn't take it anymore, she continued her journey upward along his breeches and rubbed his shaft.

Exquisite torture.

Her movements caused her breasts to rise and fall, a beautiful view.

"You steal my breath."

Her rich round areolae, so faintly colored in the sun's rays, had little goose bumps along the edges. He lowered his head and tongued the soft flesh until one was a large button in his mouth. He went to the other and did the same, loving the feel of Genevieve.

Lowering his mouth while perched above her, he kissed her cleavage and worked his way down her ribs, the soft arch of her stomach, the gentle hairs that met his lips. He heard her gasp when he parted her lips there and kissed her center.

She tasted like morning dew. His Genevieve.

Her knees rose, as if giving him approval, and he concentrated on kissing and licking her, trying to be as gentle as he could, trying to allow her all the time it might take for her to savor this experience and let it culminate into the ultimate pleasure.

He stuck his tongue deeper and brought his fingers to her sensitive tip, dipping and pressing and stroking until he felt her body tense, her legs stiffen, her muscles contract.

Buried in a sea of soft blankets and pillows, she arched and moaned and made him feel as if he'd accomplished the moon.

When he felt her body relax, heard her moaning subside and a soft laugh escape her throat, he knew he'd done well.

"You do surprise me," she whispered.

Gently, he laughed into the soft flesh of her thigh, kissing away the moistness from his face. Still heated from her touch, still ready to come inside of her, he wasn't prepared for what she did next.

She slid down to his level, pulling him upward, tugging at his breeches. He readily gave in and removed his clothing till they were both exposed, he fully, and she wearing nothing but a soft cotton corset opened at the center and revealing gorgeous breasts.

Teasing him, she gave his chest a push till he was lying back on the bed. Very softly, she nibbled at his throat and worked her way downward.

Oh…was she about to do what he imagined? What glory was his to come…what wonder in paradise…?

She splayed her knees over him, sitting above him, her black hair traipsing down her body and sweeping across his. He knotted his hands in the soft strands, her skin beneath peeking through like golden honey.

Her mouth worked downward, lightly nibbling on his skin, down the trail of hair. He cupped her dangling breasts and thought he'd surely died and gone to heaven.

She flicked her tongue on the tip of his shaft, kissing down the side, then back up the center. He moaned in ecstasy, gripped her breasts and pressed them on either side of his erection. She tongued him as he did so, and he relished the feel of being so utterly enveloped by mouth and breasts.

Mimicking the in and out motion he'd done on her, she fondled and licked and drove him to a frenzy.

Unable to bear one more second, he yanked her by the arms, pushed her over in one swift move till she was on her back and he was perched above her.

With a graceful tilt of her head, she raised one knee to allow him to enter. He pressed his erection up along the apex of her thighs, marveling at the heat and splendor.

With a soft groan, she took him in and stared into his eyes as he drove in further till he was totally inside. They were a tight fit, and he was awed by the feel of Genevieve.

Moving in and out, he rocked her, gently lifting her leg up and over, watching her breasts and pinkish nipples jiggling with his thrusts.

He rolled her over to her knees and she seemed to like the change in position, going along with whatever he wished to show her. With her on her knees and he behind her, he reached over her thigh and urged her to ride his fingers.

The combination of his fingers and his erection inside of her, and his other hand cupping one dangling breast made her move rhythmically again, faster and faster beneath him until together, they released. He pressed his forehead into her spine and allowed the deep throb of satisfaction to roll over him, through every fiber of his body, loving the turn of her hips in the sunshine, wondering if he could ever get enough of Genevieve Summerville.

They dozed in and out for hours. Genevieve wasn't sure what time it was when she finally awoke from their lazy slumber, nestled in Luke's warm arms. Enough time had passed that the streams of sunlight pouring from the window had moved off their bed and were now hitting the far wall of the barracks.

Naked and slightly chilled, she nudged in closer to Luke. Her breasts rolled with her movements and sandwiched the side of his body. He moaned and stroked her arm.

"Luke, wake up."

"Hmm?"

"It must be getting close to dinnertime. Wake up."

She felt him jump. He leaped for the pocket watch resting on his night table. "Four o'clock. Lots of time."

He turned his attention back to her, lingering on her bare breasts.

"Haven't you had enough?" she whispered.

"No..."

She giggled. "Neither have I."

"Are you sore?"

"Not too much."

His hands slid down her waist. She marveled at how quickly the two of them had fallen into place with each other. Did he feel it, too? The aching inside his chest, the fluttering of nerves and anticipation at how they might spend their next moments? Their next weeks?

But her doubts crept in. What was she doing, giving herself completely to a man she'd feared only a short while ago, a man who wasn't sure being with her was the right thing to do.

She was so much more certain about it than he. She wanted Luke.

His kiss upon her neck magnified the wonder of their nakedness. When he arched himself on top of her, she pressed her body willingly against his. As he cupped her face in his large palm and wove his fingers down the path of her hair, down her arm and side of her breast, she forgot everything except the slow deep throb inside her body. She let the tide control her, and wanted to show him how much she felt for him. Rising to her knees, timid at first but gaining confidence as his eyes roved her body and his mouth twitched with a sensual response, she spread her knees to either side of his body. He was lying down; she was perched in a sitting position and lowering her hips onto his erection.

He reached up and stroked the underside of her breasts. She rubbed her intimate area against his, and when the feeling came again, the urge that began as a slow hum inside her center and built into a thundering ache, she pushed her hips down and slid him fully inside.

Luke closed his eyes, giving himself completely.

For the first time in her life, she understood the power women had over men.

When he palmed her breasts, she couldn't hold back any longer. Rocking deeper and deeper, giving herself to this man who held her heart as much as he held her body, she wasn't aware of the hour. The magic of his touch held her prisoner.

He pulled and tugged on her hardened nipples, causing the waves inside of her to come crashing, causing that delicious burst of white-hot excitement and ultimate release of tension.

At the same moment, he kissed her breast, doubling the sensations and causing her to gasp aloud. She couldn't stop moaning, louder and louder as the contractions deepened. The strength of it was like nothing she'd ever felt before.

She was amazed at her own boldness, her awakening to the energy between them.

Perhaps it was her loud exclamations that excited him, for she felt him suddenly give way to his own shudders. His arms shook, his thighs rocked into hers and he clasped her hips.

Moments later, damp with perspiration and drenched from their lovemaking, she finally collapsed on top of him. He trailed his fingers up her backside, resting on her buttock.

He gave it a playful slap and whispered into her tangled hair. "You're so good at this, Genevieve. So good…"

Chapter Twenty

Luke found it strangely shy of Genevieve to want to bathe alone after all they'd done together, but she was nervous, she said, that another officer might come knocking. So he hauled out a tub and set it in the other bedroom, heated water over the cast-iron stove, and she immersed herself.

It was nearly six o'clock when he rapped on her door. "Are you all right in there, Genevieve?"

She came out fully dressed, her long hair plaited into a single braid, wet black hair framing her face as she did up the buttons of her sleeves. "Like new."

With a timid glance, she stepped past him. He marveled at how innocent and timid she'd looked to him these past two weeks, but how delightful and daring she turned out to be as a lover.

He tempered a smile as he slid into a fresh shirt. "How can you be evasive? Don't you remember what we did ten feet from here?"

She blushed clear to her ears. "Of course, but…but now it's over and nothing has been said of…of…"

"Ah, yes," he teased, "…of the future."

She didn't smile, simply studied him, as though unsure of what to say in case she upset him.

"Genevieve, when this investigation is over…and we have time…*I* have time to sort it out…"

The sheen in her eyes told him how much it hurt.

But what exactly could he say? He could try to make light of what they'd done, but lightness wasn't going over well. If he tried to pull her into his arms and kiss her, he'd perhaps make her feel that's all he cared about.

He anchored his arms around her and simply spoke the truth. "When I'm with you, Genevieve, my world catches fire."

Her shoulders eased then, and her mouth settled into a comforted expression. Whatever retributions were running through her mind, she was able to set them aside.

"I'd like to go back to my house before we go for dinner," she said. "I'd like to change."

"What's wrong with what you've got on?"

"I'd…I'd like to wear something nicer for you."

"Genevieve," he said, stepping back to appraise her blouse and skirt. He kissed her hand. "What you're wearing is beautiful. It's like an artist's framework for the lovely woman beneath."

She smiled in confusion, pressing a palm against her cheek. "But these are such old things."

"The white blouse is pretty against your skin."

She tilted her head, black braid pressing against her bosom. "I really don't know whether to take you seriously."

He drew her to his waist and kissed her damp cheek. "Any man would be busting with pride to dine with you, just the way you are."

"Now that's the nicest compliment anyone's ever paid

me. But please, I insist. It won't take me long to run home. I'll meet up with my aunt and uncle, and meet you at the restaurant."

"All right, if it would make you happy. I'll have one of the constables escort you home. I've got to speak to the commissioner."

They packed her wedding mementos in a wooden crate he'd found, along with things forgotten—chamomile tea belonging to her aunt Abigail, and two squares of white felt scraps from her hat-making enterprise.

They reached the top of the slope, near the commissioner's cabin, where Luke called for a constable. Wary of her reputation, he wasn't going to kiss her goodbye in front of witnesses. He only cared to protect his wife.

His wife.

"I'd like to kiss you," he whispered, "but I don't think—"

"It's all right," she said, but glanced away so quickly he couldn't read her expression.

Then she was gone, leaving him standing on the hill staring after her. She looked back one last time with such longing and pleasure in her eyes, it seemed to slug him in the gut. A new feeling crept through him, terrifying him more than he'd ever admit. The feeling that perhaps he couldn't live without Genevieve.

"Here's the list." Minutes later behind his desk, Commissioner York handed Luke some notepaper.

Hot sunshine sizzled on the desk between them. Luke glanced at the names. "Nothing unusual."

"I've got some big news, though, regarding the robbery of Orman's jewelry store."

Luke spun up. "You caught the thief?"

"Thieves. Just got word they're in custody, hundreds of miles upriver, in Whitehorse. Two juveniles who've been roaming up and down the river stealing every bit of gold that flashed before their eyes."

"So they're not linked to Orman's murder."

The commissioner tapped the sleeve of his red uniform. "No connection whatsoever. You guessed that already, though."

"Yeah. They couldn't have physically killed him, because they weren't present. They could have ordered him killed, but I never found any evidence linking his murder to the store break-in." Luke turned back to the property list in his fingers. He scoured the names again to be sure he wasn't missing anything.

There were no surprises in the property deeds. Clyde Orman was the first person who'd been registered to own his home and his jewelry store.

Judge Donahue had bought his home from a gold miner who'd struck it rich the year before and was moving back to San Francisco.

Vince Cliffton was the second owner on his casino. The first had been his brother Ripley, as Miss Norris had explained.

Ripley and Burt owned their own homes, and in Burt's case, a saloon as well.

The Thornbottoms had bought their modest log cabin from the Langstaffs next door.

Kurt Kendall owned a large home and barn beside the livery.

Penelope and Genevieve didn't own any property.

Luke released his breath when he saw Genevieve was

in the clear. For some reason when the commissioner had asked about her properties earlier, Luke had been overcome with dread.

"Nothing suspect in any of this," Luke said. "Only the question why Ripley sold the casino to Vince."

"It happened quite quickly, as I recall. Ripley inherited it from some old man he befriended, but decided he would rather pan for gold. Sold it to his brother."

"They don't like each other, do they?"

"Nope." The commissioner bit into a dried apricot.

"Why not?"

"Don't rightly know. Maybe it's got something to do with how profitable the casino became. Soon as Ripley sold it, Vince added the restaurant and business took off for the sky."

Luke shoved the paper into his pocket. "I'll keep the list, and I'll let you know how dinner goes this evening. Much obliged on the two constables you're sending over with me."

"You expecting trouble?"

"Not at all. Otherwise I wouldn't be taking…taking my wife."

The word sounded strange, saying it aloud to another person.

The commissioner's eyes lit with a curious sparkle.

A cool trickle of sweat meandered down the back of Luke's neck. He was her husband. He'd never imagined himself as anyone's husband. Taking care of a woman and perhaps a family down the road was difficult to envision. Wasn't Luke just like his father, roaming the country from coast to coast looking for adventure and women to share the finer things in life? Luke had been thrilled with that much—or that little—so far.

The white-hot passion he felt for Genevieve today

might fade, turning into friendly conversations, then polite nods, until they had fewer and fewer things to celebrate between them. Until the only way they communicated was as his parents had, through anger and bitterness at life's disappointments.

How does one sustain love over a lifetime?

Luke stumbled out of the commissioner's office and into the street toward the casino, thinking about her. He strode up the few steps of the boardwalk and leaned against the splintered handrail.

Genevieve was not guilty of anything. She'd opened her heart to him, and he'd readily taken everything she offered.

What did that make him?

Other women had known what he wanted and had agreed to the unspoken terms of no promises right from the start, but Genevieve had a more virtuous nature.

"Luke!" Someone hollered from the other side of the street, startling him.

He looked up to see his dark-haired brother, Colt, and pretty blond wife, Elizabeth, bustling down the boardwalk carrying wrapped parcels.

Luke nodded.

Waving, Elizabeth fanned the air with a billowing blue sleeve. "Buxton, where are you off to?"

"The casino."

Colt gripped his holster. "Have you heard the great news?"

"What's that?"

"Your new judge has arrived. He was spotted going into the Digs Hotel. You'll be getting that annulment soon!"

Luke straightened at the rail. His heart raced.

With a jaunty pace, Colt and Elizabeth waved goodbye and headed into the butcher shop.

After a moment of stunned silence, Luke slumped against a post, unable to move.

"For heaven's sake, you look fine. Stop fussing at the mirror." Aunt Abigail frowned in exasperation at Uncle Theodore, who was turning and patting his long white ponytail. "Your hair looks good. Let the women have a go at the looking glass."

Aunt Abigail shoved him out of the way as Genevieve pressed a hand to her nervous stomach and watched the family squabble.

"I think it's wonderful you're joining us." Aunt Abigail addressed Genevieve. Her aunt ran a brush through her thin hair. Milly would be dining with the friends she'd missed the most during quarantine, Cora and Rose.

"The food at the casino is superb," chattered Aunt Abigail. "Mr. Cliffton said he'll give us a reduced rate on everything on the menu. Can you believe our good fortune?" The older woman squealed in delight. "I mean, perhaps being pent up for two weeks will turn out to be in our favor. Mr. Kendall has offered us a reduced rate at the livery stables, too. Of course, we do have to buy livestock before that pans out, but I daresay a mule is not entirely out of the question."

"I can't see myself on a mule," said Uncle Theodore. "A large black stallion, now that I see."

"What in heaven's name would we do with a stallion? Do you know how much those animals can eat?"

As they continued with their difference of opinion, Genevieve scooted behind them in the mirror and patted her hair. She'd braided it in two and had pinned both braids above her ears in large elegant circles. She'd changed into her black blouse and matching lace skirt, nothing fancy, but clothes Luke had never seen before. In the mirror, Genevieve could barely look herself in the eye. If only her aunt and uncle knew what she'd been up to with Luke this afternoon. All blessed afternoon.

If only they knew how befuddled she felt. They would tell her how big a mistake she'd made. They'd tell her she was inexperienced and stupid for trusting a man before marriage, and what would she be able to say to that?

That her heart felt a thousand times different? That her heart urged her to press forward when all reasoning seemed to point the other way?

She nervously smacked her lips, moistening them for the tenth time, and pinched her cheeks to create a blush.

"Why must you always bring my sister into these arguments…" Uncle Theodore was saying.

"Because she kept those two mules till the day she died and they never gave her any headache—"

"She was fortunate and married rich…"

"All's I'm saying is if we sell enough corn-husk brooms this fall, we may be able to swing a couple of goats and—"

"Couple of goats! How did you slip those in!"

Genevieve quietly interrupted them. "Shall we go?"

Their eyes met in the mirror. Uncle Theodore removed his top hat from the rack and bowed to his two women. "Yes, let's."

On the breezy boardwalk, Aunt Abigail looped her arm through Genevieve's and they dodged pedestrians—folks going into utility shops, diners into the corner café, and customers crossing to various tented businesses sprawled between the storefronts.

The older woman gave her niece a sideways glance and

bit down on her lip. "Perhaps we'll have the good fortune of bumping into Joshua McFadden."

"Oh, Aunt Abigail…you didn't."

Her aunt shoved her tongue into the pocket of her mouth and didn't meet Genevieve's burning gaze.

Uncle Theodore tapped his hat. "He's a good man. Will strike it rich one day, and then perhaps you can buy your aunt all the mules and goats she'll ever need."

He looked to his wife and she burst out laughing.

"And you your fancy stallion." They nudged each other, pressed shoulder to shoulder, laughing. Aunt Abigail removed her arms from Genevieve to anchor herself lovingly next to her husband.

Genevieve sighed. It was endearing to see their arguments always end in such affection. So different from Genevieve's folks.

A breeze whispered past her ears, cool air blowing from the river and cooling her heated temperature. She was anxious to see Luke again, eager to look into his eyes and see the tenderness returned. Across the way, the sounds of a piano drifted from an open saloon. Men called in the street to each other from the livery stables. A gentleman in a white suit, using a cane, hopped up the steps to the Digs Hotel. Genevieve tried to keep her focus ahead of her, on the shoulders of her aunt and uncle, for every time she turned there was another stranger gawking at her. Land's sake, the men outnumbered women tenfold, but had these men never seen a member of the more delicate sex before?

"Ah, here we are." Aunt Abigail twisted her shawl around her thick shoulders and stopped at the BlackJack Casino.

When Genevieve came to an abrupt halt, her dangling

earrings tapped against her cheeks. She fingered the fine gold chain at her throat and wondered if Luke was here yet.

Uncle Theodore held open the door. His wife passed through, followed by Genevieve. It was the most elegant building in town. Gold leaf stenciling in the interior plate glass windows read, Welcome to the BlackJack Casino and Restaurant.

Sunshine lit the foyer. Tall ceilings, double story, echoed their voices as they said hello to the pretty woman who was hosting the entryway. Plush red carpeting bristled beneath Genevieve's boots. Walnut paneling, which must have cost a heavenly fortune to import, gave weight and substance to the space. An opulent lantern with a pewter base and etched glass flickered its lighting across their keen faces.

"Table for three, please."

"Oh, Uncle Theodore, I must tell you. Inspector Hunter invited me to sit with him this evening."

Her uncle drew back his shoulders, assessing her, and seemed to grow two inches in the process. "No young niece of mine will go chasing after any gentleman this evening."

"But Uncle—"

"If he wishes to speak to you, or enjoy the pleasure of your company, he can approach our table and ask."

She swallowed firmly and twined her fingers together. The black satin of her gloves rustled. He was so terribly old-fashioned. And he'd be so disappointed if it was confirmed how far she'd gone already with Dr. Luke Hunter. "Yes, sir."

"Now then," he addressed the hostess again. "Table for three. We're Vince Cliffton's guests this evening."

"We have a lovely table upstairs with a view of the gardens and river behind us."

"Sounds perfect," Aunt Abigail cooed. "We dined there yesterday."

They took the stairs and Genevieve scoured the rooms on either side of them, looking for Luke. All she saw were dozens of cigar-smoking men lined up at a roulette wheel and tables filled with men playing poker. The hum of voices, the clatter of drinks and the spinning of wheels made it almost impossible to hear any conversation.

She took the top of the stairs and turned left.

They entered the most magnificent drawing room. The front wall contained a massive pine bar, as glossy as ice. A huge mirror spanned the entire wall behind the bar, lined with crystal drinking glasses, champagne flutes, wine goblets and rows of rows of liquor bottles. She caught herself looking in the mirror as she and her family crossed the dense carpeting and wove through the packed tables to the window. In the mirror, she spotted another pair of eyes watching her.

Luke. Luke was here already.

He was seated alone at the far wall, drinking. In the mirror, he lifted his glass and silently toasted her. She couldn't read his expression, but he seemed somewhat withdrawn. A flurry of nerves cascaded through her stomach. Was it just that he *appeared* more solemn, reflected backward in a mirror?

She turned to look at him directly, the way she normally did, and his eyes glistened in a friendly way. There, that was the Luke she was accustomed to.

She smiled in return. Unfortunately, Uncle Theodore was eyeing her in the mirror, too.

"Have a seat, Genevieve." But before she could, to her complete horror, Joshua appeared.

"Good evening, everyone."

He was dressed in a very fine suit with a golden cravat. Aunt Abigail looked at him adoringly, but Genevieve was curt. "Hello, Joshua."

"Please, won't you join us?" Uncle Theodore extended the invitation to Joshua at the same time Luke appeared on Genevieve's other side.

She groaned.

Luke held out his hand toward her uncle and they shook. "Good evening, sir, ma'am. Genevieve." With a strained voice, he said hello to Joshua. "How are you this evening, McFadden?"

"Fine. I was just about to sit down and—"

"Genevieve and I had planned—"

"Do have a seat, both of you." Aunt Abigail's declaration stunned everyone.

Stuck in the middle of this mess, Genevieve stood rooted. She wanted to go with Luke, but it would be terribly rude to do so at this moment. Luke reacted with gentlemanly instinct.

He pulled out Genevieve's chair. "Thank you, Mrs. Thornbottom. Very kind of you."

Genevieve caught her skirts and lowered herself onto the seat. Luke sat down beside her.

Pinching his mouth in disapproval, Joshua sat to her other side. As they shuffled nervously to look at the one-page cardboard menu they'd been given, a barmaid appeared. Not Penelope, for she no longer worked here. Aunt Abigail had informed Genevieve of the gossip an hour ago. Penelope had gone off with Mr. Kendall.

This barmaid looked so thin and made up and new to the Yukon, Genevieve felt sorry for her.

"Good evening, folks," the young lady said. The men asked her name. "It's Alice Purdue. May I get you something from the bar?"

"A bottle of wine would be nice, Alice," said Uncle Theodore. "Wine for all. And please make note we are guests of Mr. Cliffton's."

Luke interjected, "Please bring the corked bottle to the table and we'll open it here."

Genevieve eyed him. It would be one-hundred-percent safe to drink if they witnessed its opening. Were they carrying this a bit too far? If anyone had wanted to poison them—specifically, Vince or Ripley Cliffton—they'd had plenty of opportunity during two weeks of quarantine. Unless, perhaps, they felt more threatened if Luke was indeed closing in.

A male waiter, lean and dapper in black vest and pants, brought a loaf of bread to the table on a cutting board. He placed it in the center and sliced. Its rich aroma filled the air. The loaf had come in its entirety, and had been baked before they even got here, so was likely safe. Its outside crust didn't look as though it'd been smeared with anything.

Luke must have been thinking the same thing, for he nodded at her. They placed their orders—baked salmon for Genevieve and Joshua, halibut for Luke and ham—likely canned—for her aunt and uncle.

They ate bread and Genevieve enjoyed every morsel.

"It's busy tonight." Aunt Abigail leaned closer, pressing her large bosom onto the table. "Our meal will likely take some time in this lineup."

"We can always dance while we wait," said Uncle Theodore.

His wife smiled. "They are playing a polka."

And off they went, leaving the other three guests awkwardly peering at each other.

Luke lifted his wine goblet. "To your future success in the gold fields," he toasted Joshua.

It wasn't a toast Joshua could refuse. They sipped.

"Would you like to dance?" Joshua asked her.

Good heavens, not this again.

"All right." Perhaps she could tell him once and for all.

The polka ended and a waltz began. She placed her hand in Joshua's. When he placed his other hand at her waist and stroked her gently, she squirmed. He twirled her, and she noticed in the mirror that Luke was watching them.

They didn't dance well together. Joshua stepped forward and so did she, knocking knees with him. When he went to one side, she went to the other.

"I'm sorry," she whispered.

"Don't keep saying you're sorry."

A few more minutes of it and she couldn't take any more. "Joshua, this isn't going to work. It's never going to work between us. Please, can't you understand?"

Not knowing what else to do, she left Joshua on the dance floor staring after her as she stalked toward the powder room.

Bursting through the door, she set her tiny purse on the counter and tried to catch her breath. She stayed a reasonable amount of time and then exited, nearly bumping into Luke.

"I've been waiting for you." With dark hair tumbling on his forehead, shirt straining at his shoulders, he whisked her onto the dance floor. His hand pressed against her spine in a delightful way. It felt good to be in his arms again. To soak in his presence and have her heart pounding against her ribs.

But suddenly Uncle Theodore was glaring at her from the mirror, Joshua was downing his wine and Luke wasn't speaking.

What was he thinking? Why such a sullen face?

When the dance was over, without a word he gripped her loosely by the wrist and led her back to their table.

Joshua was talking to their pretty new barmaid, Alice. "What claim is that?"

"Two hundred yards up from Bonanza Creek."

Joshua whistled. "Lotta gold in that area. Good luck to you, miss."

Genevieve didn't feel hungry anymore. She felt scared and worried and unsure of what they were all doing here tonight. Her skin pricked with apprehension. What if she'd led her aunt and uncle into harm's way tonight, with a poisoned meal?

There hadn't been any sign of Vince Cliffton yet, so perhaps they'd come for nothing. She rose.

"Where are you going?" asked her aunt.

"I'm—I'm not feeling well, Aunt Abigail."

"What is it?"

"A—a headache."

"But we've ordered our food already."

If the meal wasn't safe for her and Luke, it wasn't safe for any of them. "I think we should all leave."

"But our food."

"I'm really not feeling well, and if you could please walk me home…".

"What is it?" asked Joshua, joining them.

Luke drew to her side. "Genevieve?"

"I'm not feeling well. I'd like to leave."

"What's this?" Vince Cliffton said behind them. She

jumped when she heard his booming voice. "Sit down. Sit down, please. Please have a seat, all of you."

Genevieve trembled at the sight of him, hair slicked back and surrounded by two bodyguards. Was this the man Luke suspected of killing two people? Or was it his brother, Ripley, following right behind?

Chapter Twenty-One

The son of a bitch was guilty. The problem was, thought Luke, gritting his teeth and staring at the two brothers before him, Luke wasn't sure which one.

Ripley. Or Vince.

Wall lanterns flickered behind them and reflected in the mirror above the bar. Everything twinkled. The clatter of knives and forks and glasses swirled around them.

Luke shook their hands, trying to suppress his outrage. "Pull up a seat and join us."

Ripley squeezed in beside Joshua, Vince beside Genevieve.

"Wine?" offered Theodore.

Vince fingered his fine cravat. With a grin at Genevieve, he ordered the barmaid, "Bring the table another bottle." He smoothed his hand over his satin vest. "And I'll have my usual."

"It's like old times." Abigail peered around the table. Her long earrings bobbed against her fleshy throat. "Well, not the bad. Just the good, I hope."

Ripley glanced away when the initial laughter faded to

more of a perplexing moan. They seemed to realize that someone here might be a murderer.

Greta Norris and her parting words drummed in Luke's mind. The judge had drawn up the deed for the casino, and the brothers had had a row over it. They'd even argued with the judge, and Luke was itching to know what the argument had been about.

"How's business?" Luke asked Vince.

"Mighty fine. Feels good to be back."

"We ordered the ham," Abigail boasted. "I haven't had ham for three months." She lowered her voice and didn't move her lips, as if she was a ventriloquist. "And we told them to put it on your bill." Then she laughed.

Vince nodded. "I just checked on your meals. I told my chef nothing but the finest for you folks."

He'd been to the kitchen, in close quarters with their plates? Close enough to add poison? Luke didn't like the sound of it. Neither, apparently, did Genevieve, for she gave Luke a heated glance.

Luke turned to Ripley. He wore a blue plaid shirt and black pants, not nearly as spiffed up as his brother. "How are things with you?"

A look of annoyance crossed Ripley's face, as if he was through answering questions from Luke. "I'll be heading out in the morning, if you must know. There's a new gold strike on the river just north of the creek."

Joshua leaned in, eager to hear news of gold. "You don't say. Whereabouts?"

Ripley swung his chair closer to Joshua and the Thornbottoms, and the small group quickly got lost in their own private conversation—gossip on who in town had recently struck the biggest vein. Joshua seemed keenly impressed with the new barmaid and her apparent gold claim.

Their discussion left Luke, Genevieve and Vince staring stiffly at one another at the other end of the table.

"How's the investigation going?" asked Vince.

"Can't seem to get a grip on anything new."

"That's too bad."

"My men did pay a visit to the Land Claims Office earlier. That brought up some interesting questions."

Vince strummed the table, as if he didn't rightly care. His eyes glossed over the other diners. But a telltale sheen of sweat glistened on his forehead. "How so?"

"I was wondering if I might ask you a question."

"You can ask three," he said, laughing, "then I'm going to dance with Miss Summerville."

Genevieve coughed and rearranged her skirts.

Luke pressed on with Vince. "Why did Ripley sell you the casino?"

Vince's jaw flickered. The light in his eyes glistened. "He's sitting right beside me. Why don't you ask him?"

"I intend to. But I'm getting a lot of different opinions. Thought I might ask you both."

Vince's mouth twisted. "Different opinions?"

"Everyone in town heard the ruckus when it changed hands. Miss Norris. Commissioner York."

Vince clawed at his tight cravat. "He sold it because he wanted to go gold prospecting. He wanted to buy his outfit with the money he made, and hire a few men to dig for him."

Luke nodded sympathetically, as if he cared. "Right."

Distracted by a movement outside the window, Genevieve peered through the glass. Luke followed her gaze to the flower gardens below. A man in a long apron, rubber gloves and tall boots was making his way through a bed of red tulips. They made a colorful splash on an otherwise green horizon. Luke turned back to the more important task. "Why did the judge disapprove of your deed?"

Vince's eyes narrowed in the lantern light. "He didn't disapprove of anything. He drew up the papers like we asked."

That was a downright lie. Miss Norris had said the judge had argued with them. The brothers had also lied initially to Luke, in quarantine, when they'd told him they'd never talked to the judge much.

"Ripley," Luke called.

The man broke away from his discussion with Joshua and the Thornbottoms. "Yeah?"

"What made you want to sell this place? The business is overflowing."

Ripley's eyes shot to his brother. "Gold fever, mostly."

"Along with something else?"

"Vince made me an offer that was hard to turn down."

"Ah, I see."

Clearing his throat and sitting up in his chair as if he'd had enough questioning, Vince turned to Genevieve. "Care to dance?"

Luke stopped him. "I've got two more questions, don't I?"

Vince eyed him, then fell back against his seat and laughed weakly. "Go ahead."

"This one's for the both of you." The men gave him their undivided attention. "Why did you travel separately to the Klondike? Two brothers—make that three—you'd think you'd come together. Help each other out. Keep each other company."

Vince remained silent, tapping his fingers nervously on the tablecloth.

Ripley squinted at the wall, then stared absently through the window. "Vince went first. Burt and I didn't want to leave our jobs on the railroad till we'd been paid. The checks amounted to two thousand dollars of back pay. Vince here was itchin' to come, so he headed out two weeks ahead of us. He'd found himself a business partner."

"By two weeks."

"Right," said Ripley.

"With Orman," said Luke. "Anyone else?"

Vince remained impassive. "Just Orman and me. We were going to blaze the trail for my brothers and set up a casino when we got here."

Their drinks finally arrived. Another bottle of wine, and a cup of coffee for Vince. He took it like he always did. With evaporated milk.

Evaporated milk.

The thought hit Luke with a powerful thud.

Holy hell.

He slumped back against the hard rails of his chair and let it sink in.

Vince was the son of a bitch. Luke was looking at the killer.

But how the hell had he done it? With what poison? Without a damn murder weapon, Luke still didn't have a case.

"Thanks, fellas," Luke said calmly.

With some apparent relief, Vince turned to Genevieve. "May I have this dance?"

Actually," said Luke, rising to his feet. "Miss Summerville was just telling us, before you arrived, she's not feeling well."

Genevieve took his lead seamlessly, rising slowly to her feet, exaggerating her imaginary symptoms. "Headache." She pressed her fingers to her forehead and swayed.

Across the table, Abigail made a face. "But, darling, our meal is almost here. Couldn't you hold out a little longer?"

Genevieve moaned. "Absolutely, I'll just sit down..." She hunched over the table.

"We must get her home." Luke touched her elbow. Under no circumstance did he want anyone at the table to be eating anything that Vince Cliffton had checked on in the kitchen. "I'll walk her, sir," Luke said to Theodore. "May I have the keys to your house?"

Just as Luke was hoping, Theodore burst up from his chair. "If she needs taking home, for heaven's sake, we'll be the ones to do it."

"But your meals..." Flabbergasted, Vince rose to his feet and motioned to the empty settings.

Ripley scowled. "You can't leave five minutes before the plates arrive."

"I'm...so...sorry..." Genevieve tried to stifle a wave of what appeared to be nausea, good actress that she was. "You all go ahead and eat. I'll try to stomach...I'll sit here and rest my head on the table."

"We can't let you do that," said Luke. "What kind of gentlemen would allow a lady in distress to sit and watch while we ate?"

"But the meals..." moaned Abigail. "The ham and the mashed potatoes. The pickled beets and...and the raisin pie I was going to order..."

"I'll have the meals sent to your home," said Vince. "Tonight."

"You do that," said Luke. By the time the dinner arrived at their home, he would have had time to explain the dangers to the Thornbottoms.

Poison. What goddamn poison had Cliffton used? No charges would stick until Luke could answer that question.

"Goodbye, then," groaned Genevieve, stumbling to her feet.

On her way past the group, Vince grabbed her arm, pulled her toward him and took a good long look at her face. Genevieve averted her eyes, mumbling weakly.

Luke clenched his teeth and tried to resist his urge to punch the bastard in the mouth.

Hands off. Hands off, you bloody lying killer.

Genevieve stumbled down the carpeted stairs of the casino, panting to exaggerate her symptoms. Her aunt and uncle fussed in front of her. Luke took her elbow on one side, Joshua on the other. Sandwiched between her two suitors, Genevieve was truly beginning to feel nauseous.

As much as she wanted to be alone with Luke to sort out their private affairs, their situation in the casino was dangerous and all she focused on was escape. Luke had definitely narrowed his scope on either Vince or Ripley, she wasn't sure which one.

She turned to her left. "Thank you, Joshua, there's no need for you to follow further."

"I insist. Perhaps it's Luke who needn't follow. I can deliver you quite nicely to your door."

"Yeah, I'll bet." Luke, towering above them, gripped her arm more firmly.

Joshua sneered. "What's that supposed to mean?"

"She didn't come with you. She's certainly not going to leave with you."

"She didn't come with you, either, Hunter."

Uncle Theodore clicked his tongue as they bustled out

of the front door and fled into the fresh air of the boardwalk. "That's enough. Both of you. Can't you see my niece is ill?"

Whatever doubts the Cliffton brothers may have had about her illness, thank goodness they weren't following them down the street.

The group stopped in the busy road for a moment. The men released her arms and she ran her hands along her sleeves and adjusted her crooked shawl. Feeling the Yukon wind in her face soothed her nerves.

An elderly man she'd seen earlier, in a tailored white suit with a magnificent cane that was carved into a cobra, approached them. A clerk from the Digs Hotel across the street walked with him.

The clerk pointed to Luke. "Here they are, Judge. Miss Summerville and Luke Hunter."

She stopped cold. Judge?

Luke reeled back to take a second look. "Sir? Are you looking for us?"

The gent held out his hand. "Pleased to meet you. I'm Judge Hillroy. Just got into town."

Genevieve's knees locked. The cold shock rendered her speechless. Here was the man they'd been waiting for.

In quarantine, the minutes and days had passed so slowly and now…and now…she was unwilling to face him, yet unwilling to turn away.

He was no longer a figment of their hopes. He was as solid as a mountain standing in front of them.

Luke, paler than she'd ever seen him, stumbled forward and shook the gent's hand. Luke fumbled for wording. "Your Honor, welcome to Dawson."

"Thank you."

"How was your trip?"

"Took me longer than expected because I broke my ankle on my way to Alaska. Had to wait it out for a few months. But I'm here."

"Thank heaven." Aunt Abigail clasped her hands together and peered at the sky. "You don't know how long and hard we were praying for your arrival."

The judge shook hands with the Thornbottoms, Luke and Joshua, then finally settled his gentle eyes on Genevieve. "You must have been astounded at the turn of events. Thinking you were marrying one man, yet on paper, married to another. I had dinner with Commissioner York an hour ago, and he explained your unfortunate situation."

"Yes," she mumbled, aware all eyes were upon her.

"Must have been quite traumatic for a young bride. Not to mention the intended groom."

"It was me," Joshua said. She'd almost forgotten he was still here. "I'm her intended."

With her mind swirling with the legal implications, and her heart trembling with sorrow and fear, Genevieve closed her eyes. When she opened them again, Luke was looking at her.

The breeze lifted the dark hair above his temples. Fading sunlight played on his tanned cheeks. His lips, pressed so solemnly together, displayed no hint of what he was thinking. His stance, once so riveting, seemed to harden.

"There's good news, here, folks," said the judge.

"What?" Uncle Theodore squeezed his wife's trembling shoulders. "Tell us, please."

"I'll have to have a look at the document, of course. But if it's a standard marriage license, the way the commissioner has explained, then this marriage can be dispensed with very quickly."

"How quickly?" Aunt Abigail held her breath.

"I'll have an answer as soon as I see the marriage license. But perhaps right on the spot."

Aunt Abigail gasped.

Joshua grinned.

Luke said nothing, but the fine scar beneath his eye throbbed softly.

Genevieve had difficulty swallowing.

"We could do this tonight, then?" Uncle Theodore peered at the judge.

Genevieve and Luke were the only two who hadn't said a word. Now the time came for them to speak.

All eyes turned to Genevieve.

"It *is* what we wanted," she said. "From the moment it happened."

"Precisely," said Joshua.

Luke said nothing. The air around him crackled. His face was stone.

Why wasn't he saying anything? Surely he would stop the judge from proceeding with the annulment until they'd sorted through their feelings.

"I didn't know we could fix this so quickly." Aunt Abigail almost sang the words. "It's all working out so well in the end."

Uncle Theodore patted Joshua's shoulder with approval.

Furrowing his brows, the judge looked from Luke to Genevieve. "I know I almost don't need to ask this—" He peered around at the inquisitive faces of the strangers who'd collected on the boardwalk, and lowered his voice. "It's only a formality, and please forgive my forthright question. This is, of course, provided there were no marital relations between you."

Aunt Abigail gasped and drew her hankie to her mouth.

Uncle Theodore cleared his throat.

Joshua slipped his hand under Genevieve's elbow, as if giving her support.

The judge eyed the married couple again. "I said provided there were no marital relations."

Luke coughed.

Genevieve looked down at the ground and twisted her fingers together. Heat rose up her neck and basted her cheeks.

Aunt Abigail gave her a gentle shove from behind. "Tell him."

Uncle Theodore narrowed his eyes at Luke. "Speak up, please. And remember whose reputation is at stake here."

Genevieve couldn't raise her eyes. The sounds of the boardwalk drummed down her spine. Shuffling feet, whispering that grew louder, and most of all...Luke's deadly silence.

"What are they waiting for?" she heard a stranger whisper.

"To annul their marriage," answered another.

Genevieve finally looked up, perspiration dampening her temples and her face still scorching.

The judge looked from her to Luke with dismay, then with dawning recognition. "Well," he said softly, "this changes everything, doesn't it?"

Loud murmurs burst from the crowd.

"It'll be a divorce we need to consider then," said the judge.

In Luke's quiet stillness, when it was finally clear to her how much he wanted this parting, she decided to end the torture for both of them.

"Yes, Your Honor. It's a divorce we'll need."

To her utter humiliation, Luke still didn't speak. She didn't think it was possible to feel any more degraded, but before she could stop Joshua, he stepped out and punched Luke in the face.

Blood rushed to Luke's muscles. His jaw throbbed with the pounding. His eyes grew focused and his temper unleashed.

"Goddammit, McFadden, why are you still here?"

The comment inflamed McFadden more. He lunged at Luke, swinging and missing, but Luke belted him in the stomach. McFadden fell. The physical release felt good.

"Get him, Luke!" someone from the crowd shouted.

"Luke deserves the thrashing. Look what he did to McFadden's bride!"

Abigail Thornbottom shrieked.

Uncle Theodore cupped her and Genevieve by the back of their waists and pushed them through the crowd. "I've had enough of this bloody fighting."

Luke noticed that Genevieve didn't look back. Her slender shoulders caught the wind and her face dipped out of sight.

Joshua rose to his knees.

"It's over, McFadden," Luke told him. "It's over."

Everything was over for Luke. Not only his marriage, but the whole damn investigation if he had no murder weapon.

After two of the toughest weeks of his life, he had nothing. There was nowhere else he could turn to, nowhere else he could look. He'd uncovered everything he could think of and it hadn't been enough. He had a murderer but no proof.

"It's over," he said again. Everything was over.

"Like hell." McFadden leaped and tackled Luke to the ground.

Luke was losing a woman he'd never really had. His life. His bride.

But it's what he wanted, wasn't it? Freedom.

Freedom to pound the living daylights out of Joshua McFadden. Freedom to live the rest of his life alone. Freedom to avoid marriage and all the headaches that went with it.

It's what he wanted, he told himself, lying facedown in the dirt with blood crackling from his lip. He stumbled to rise, shaky on his feet, and tackled Joshua again.

It's what he wanted.

Chapter Twenty-Two

"Divorce." Genevieve whispered the dreadful word.

It rolled bitterly on her tongue.

Three days had passed, and she was still keeping to her room. Aunt Abigail continued to call her for meals. Genevieve helped tidy as she always did. Uncle Theodore spoke briskly about the weather and the store, avoiding all mention of the dastardly night. Milly played with Nugget and ensured the pup was taken out for walks, knowing something was amiss but not privy to the intimate details. No one mentioned the spectacle in the street, nor the implications of what Genevieve had done with Luke and what it meant to her reputation.

She already knew.

She'd been loose with her morals, and there was no way she could explain herself.

The one thing Luke wanted most was his liberty.

Well, she had given it to him. Divorce it would be.

She'd tried so hard to overcome her past, to overcome the bickering and the physical arguments she'd witnessed between her own parents, yet here they were.

Luke slugging it out in the dirt.

And she, a failure at the very thing she cherished most. *Marriage.*

If it was what Luke truly wanted, why did he feel such despair? His misery plunged lower with each passing day as he groomed the horses, slept alone in the bed he and Genevieve had made love in, and spoke to the commissioner about the failed investigation.

"It's not enough." Commissioner York leaned back on his chair and propped his boots onto his desk. "So he drinks evaporated milk. So what?"

Luke removed his Stetson and leaned against the far counter. He adjusted the holster on his hips. "I've never seen him touch any sweets. So it doesn't make sense that he'd bust up his partnership on the trail with Orman over a jar of honey."

"So he lied about the honey. So what?"

"He hated the man's guts. Enough to poison him."

"You've got no witnesses to the crime. No weapon. No motivation."

"But he did it. As sure as hell. When we were in quarantine, after Orman was poisoned, no one would eat the food the cook brought. I gave a speech on why I thought the food was safe. Vince was the first one to dig in. He's the killer, he knew the food wasn't poisoned."

"What else have you got?"

"When I announced the quarantine was over, Vince was the first one out the door. He couldn't wait to get out from under my watch. And I felt his eyes on *me* from the first moment of the wedding ceremony. Watching to see what I'd do."

"Show me. Get me one solid scrap of evidence that points to him."

"I've got the motivation."

"What is it?"

"Blackmail was involved."

"Why would Vince blackmail the judge?"

"Something the judge knew about him and the deed to his casino."

"What about Orman? Why would he poison Orman?"

"They hated each other almost from the minute they started on their journey to the Klondike. They likely fought about their partnership. Maybe Orman wanted to open a jewelry store but Cliffton wanted a casino."

"Why didn't his temper explode on the trip, when they were arguing?"

"Separation worked at the time, I guess. Later, the blackmail got out of hand. I think Cliffton was blackmailing both the judge and Orman."

The commissioner spread his fingers and then pressed them against each other as he studied Luke. "All you've got are maybes. Come back when you've got positives."

Luke sighed. The commissioner rose, tossed his Stetson on his head and grabbed his leather gloves from the peg. "I'm taking General out for a gallop. Come back and see me when you find something new."

Luke exited the cabin and watched the commissioner stroll to the stables. Blue skies and green grass framed the man's figure. Luke's gaze lowered to the commissioner's brown leather gloves.

Gloves. *Gloves.*

He let it sink in. Images danced through his mind.

Three nights ago in the casino, Luke hadn't known it then, but he'd taken a good long look at the murder weapon.

A smile came to him slowly. Dammit. It had been under his nose the entire time.

With a nod at the two constables beside the fence to follow him, Luke calmly made his way toward the center of town.

Two hours later at two o'clock in the afternoon, Luke found Vince Cliffton behind the glossy bar of his casino, pouring a whiskey for himself. The last of the lunchtime diners, a tableful of customers, got up and left. That made the place deserted except for the two bodyguards finishing their lunch at a table near the entry.

"I'll have one of those," Luke said, moving to the bar. His pulse pounded as he tried to control the disgust he felt for this man.

Cliffton glanced up in surprise, bottle in midair. He smiled slightly and pulled out another glass. "What brings you by?"

Luke steadied his rough voice. "Came to see the view."

Cliffton took a swig of his drink. "The view."

"Yeah." Luke picked up his whiskey. He swirled the golden brown liquid and took a shot, enjoying the burn down his throat.

"Nice shiner you got there."

"McFadden got in a lucky punch." Calmly, he rose, taking his drink with him to the windows. The weight of his Enfield revolvers swung at his sides. He was ready for the bastard.

Cliffton joined him by the window, looking out. Luke took note of the Colt revolver slung on his skinny hips.

Luke tipped back on his boots and assessed the grounds below. Part of the river gushed by in the distance, but sandwiched between the river and the casino were the colorful flower beds belonging to Denny Prinz.

The Dutchman was hoeing in his garden, wearing his tall boots, apron and long rubber gloves. *Gloves.*

"Did you know that flower, there, the tall purple one Prinz is weeding, is called foxglove?"

"Foxglove? Nope."

"Yeah. He just told me apothecaries make heart medication from it. A tiny dose is enough to strengthen the heart. Beautiful flowers, don't you think? No one would ever suspect that a larger nibble is deadly poisonous."

Cliffton stopped moving.

"That's why he wears the gloves. Even a simple scratch could blister for days."

"Did you come to talk to me about flowers?"

Luke, trying to contain the fury that had been building for two and a half weeks, took another swig of his whiskey, slapped the empty glass onto a nearby table and faced Cliffton head-on.

"You son of a bitch, you did it."

Cliffton's eyes turned as black as granite. "What are you talking about?"

"Lily of the valley can affect the heart in the same way as foxglove. That was the murder weapon. You used lily of the valley as the goddamn poison. Genevieve's wedding bouquet."

Cliffton stared, not a hair moving out of place.

A chill rose to the back of Luke's neck, rustling the fine hairs. He was aware of it all—the bodyguards lunging for their guns as soon as Cliffton nodded in their direction, the two Mounties rushing from the stairwell to take care of them, and Cliffton reaching for his gun and pulling the trigger at the same time he dove behind the bar.

Luke dropped and hit the floor for protection. The

bullet missed. He gripped his gun and fired as he fell behind a chair.

To his left, the two other Mounties were wrestling the guns from the bodyguards. Sounds of kicking and punching and gunshots boomed through the air.

Bullets ripped through the long mirror behind the bar. Wineglasses shattered. Liquor bottles smashed. Cliffton fired back.

Rolling along the floor, Luke took careful aim along the base of the bar, guessing Cliffton's position. After a long second, Cliffton's hand appeared silently from around the edge of the bar, taking aim at Luke.

Luke fired first, hitting Cliffton in the wrist. Cliffton shrieked in pain as his revolver hurled through the air. It landed with a heavy thud five feet away from Luke.

Cliffton clamped his bleeding wrist with his other hand and fell against the bar, cursing.

To Luke's left, the other two Mounties were apprehending Cilffton's bodyguards.

Luke made his way over to the bar and, seeing no signs of other weapons, yanked the coward up by the belt of his pants.

Cliffton swore. "You're gonna pay for this."

"Is that right?" Luke clenched and released his jaw. "I was thinking you're going to tell me all about the blackmail. Right bloody now."

Genevieve couldn't believe the news herself.

Rays from the late-afternoon sun streamed through her new shop window, around the painted sign that said Genevieve's Hats and Suits. Such a mix of emotions ran through her. When she peered at her sign, pride filled her. When she thought of the recent quarantine, she shivered with a sadness for the departed men, and when she thought of Luke, well…her stomach pitted into a firm rock.

She'd already decided she wasn't going to run from gossip, but face the town head on. Her uncle, God bless him, had taken out a small loan from the bank on her behalf to rent the shop. If all went well, she'd be able to repay him within six months.

"Is it true?" Milly scooted around the cash drawer to capture Nugget, who'd run off with a stray ribbon. The young lady was dressed in her Sunday finest to serve customers, with glossy brown hair, trim figure and a ready smile. Genevieve had Uncle Theodore to thank for the space, too—several days ago he'd arranged for the spot next door to his own shop.

"Yes, honey. Vince Cliffton was arrested late last night."

Several women packed the shop on this opening day, trying on hats in the mirrors and running their fingers along the checkered wool jacket Genevieve had finished stitching only last night.

Aunt Abigail fanned her face as she walked by the fireplace. Logs gently crackled and spit, warming the room, scenting it with wood smoke and casting a cozy glow. Although it was summer, the evening would chill soon. "I can't believe a fine gentleman would use such a horrible poison. With the very wedding bouquet we bought for you!"

Dr. Elizabeth Hunter slanted a straw hat onto her head and adjusted its plume in the mirror. "Most folks don't know how poisonous some of these plants can be. Even soaking the leaves and stems of lily of the valley makes the water poisonous. Mr. Cliffton then brewed coffee from it and gave it to Mr. Orman. It caused the skin rash on his throat, similar to measles."

"What about the judge?" said a heavyset woman, pulling out her billfold to pay for a gentleman's bowler. "How'd he die?"

"Garlic soup the night before," said Elizabeth. "Lily of the valley was taken directly from the Dutch gardens Vince Cliffton raided that evening. The roots of the plant are sometimes mistaken for garlic. They look similar. I've heard of accidental poisonings in the mountains. Apparently, Mr. Cliffton mixed it with real garlic soup."

Aunt Abigail murmured. "Land's sake."

Elizabeth brought her straw hat to the counter to pay. "From what my brother-in-law Luke tells me, Mr. Cliffton thought the judge would succumb the night before the wedding. He wasn't supposed to live to the following day."

Which meant, thought Genevieve, if all had gone according to his plan, her wedding to Luke shouldn't have happened. Perhaps that would have been best.

"Luke was right about the blackmail," said Elizabeth. "But it was the judge who was blackmailing Cliffton."

"Why?" asked Genevieve.

"He'd lost ten thousand dollars' worth of gold the night before, gambling. He wanted it back from Cliffton in exchange for keeping silent about the deed to the casino. It seems Vince had coerced Ripley to sell it to him at less than half its worth. Ripley was so desperate for money to buy an outfit and go for gold, he wouldn't listen to the judge's advice."

"So that's why the brothers dislike each other."

"Sorry to say. Better news about Miss Norris, though. The commissioner hired her as a permanent cook for the Mounties. She'll have work as long as she needs it, and a place to stay."

"That's good news," said Genevieve, grateful to the commissioner but saddened for the Cliffton brothers.

"Such a lovely straw hat." Elizabeth tapped the brim. "The mosquito netting will be a godsend."

"Two dollars, please." Genevieve was still trying to absorb all the information.

Taking out a small satchel of gold dust, Elizabeth pushed her long blond braid off her shoulder. She watched Genevieve measure out the equivalent of gold on her portable scales. Every merchant in town bought and sold with gold dust or nuggets, for there was such an abundance.

"Luke and Colt are very similar," Elizabeth whispered. "Both as stubborn as sin. It sometimes takes a while for them to come around. And…in your case…well, let me just say that Buxton—Luke—is one of the most hardheaded men I've ever come across. When we were first introduced, he fought tooth and nail for Colt to leave me behind in British Columbia."

"Sounds like him." Genevieve's lips twitched with heartache.

Elizabeth smiled, but Genevieve couldn't muster friendly feelings for the man who'd left *her* behind.

It was time Genevieve got on with her life. She would say yes to one of the merchants who'd come calling on her yesterday. She'd find a new husband, hopefully, one who'd treat her kindly.

It seemed that Joshua had finally gotten the message they weren't meant to be married. After her disclosure of her lost virtue, and his ensuing fight with Luke, Joshua had taken off for the gold fields again. Rumor had it he'd been seen with Alice Purdue, the new barmaid from the casino. They were working together to find a fortune.

Joshua was the type of man who'd always be chasing a fortune, and it would never be enough.

Genevieve, on the other hand, should be grateful for what she *did* have. An aunt and uncle who accepted her, despite her transgressions. A cousin who adored being with her. A new shop to fill her time and, hopefully, her pockets with enough earnings to support herself. Only when she sold these hats, repaid her uncle for the rental space, and turned a bit of profit would she then buy fabric for new clothing for herself.

The afternoon flew past and Genevieve, thankfully, didn't have a lot of time to think of Luke, nor to suffer through the pain that had settled around her heart. Three hours later, at closing time, the final customer left when the doorbell jingled again.

Pleased with how many hats she'd sold in just one day—six—Genevieve whirled around with a smile. "I'm sorry, we're just clos—"

Luke stood before her in his striking uniform. In the red wool tunic she'd sewn him. The crisp cut of the cloth fell beautifully against his wide shoulders. The lapel sat flat against his chest and cut his thighs at just the perfect length.

She stood in her best clothes, burgundy blouse and skirt mended ten times over and worn so often the cotton stitching was tearing through, but today, she wore them with pride.

Looking around the empty shop, Luke removed his broad police Stetson and swiped his dark hair with his fingers.

Gripped by emotion, Genevieve waited for him to speak.

He seemed to drink her in. His attention lingered at her throat, fell upon her cheeks and trailed along her mouth.

Then he took his time, walking among the hats, touching the brim of this one and flicking his long fingers along the feather of that one. The reflection of his jacket moved along the tiny wall mirrors. One by one they reflected the image of the polished uniform and the handsome Mountie in it.

It hurt to look at him. Her throat constricted.

When at last he came to stand at the shop window, staring up at the sign and nodding in acknowledgment at what it said, she was ready to burst with sorrow. She still yearned to touch him and he wanted nothing more to do with her.

"I suppose you've come to tell me you've shown the judge our marriage license. That things are underway for the...the divorce."

Luke's lashes flickered in profile. When he swallowed, his Adam's apple moved up and down. Then with a quick move to the door, he turned the dead bolt and lowered all the blinds.

The room dimmed, but sunlight still reached them from the cracks. Golden light from the fireplace lit his face.

His words were slow and gruff. "I've come to say I'm wrong."

She gulped past the hurt, wondering how long it might take to get over this man. "About what?"

"About how much I need you. About how I can't live without you."

Her heart contracted. She could almost hear it beating in her chest. The words didn't fully register.

"Don't you feel it, too, Genevieve?"

"What?" she whispered, too afraid to hope.

"The pounding of your heart?"

"I think it's terror that makes my heart pound."

"It *is* terror. It's terror *and* hope *and* love. I think it's all the same thing."

"Love and terror?"

He nodded, lips parted. "Terror that you'd leave me. Terror that I would never be enough for you. Terror now that I've found you, I will do or say the wrong thing and never hold you in my arms again."

There was such power in his presence and his words she couldn't speak. Breathless, limbs aching from the heavy air, throat clamped with tears about to spill, Genevieve watched and waited.

A clock on the wall ticked loudly. It echoed through the room.

Luke lowered his hat and played with the brim, his mouth quivering, his dark eyes glistening with sentiment. "I never knew what I wanted from life until I met you. I want you, Genevieve. I want you to be my wife."

When he looked at her with such promise and hope in his eyes, the world stopped. The air stilled. Fire crackled.

Genevieve stepped toward him, laughter bursting forth until it became a soft sob. He pulled her into his arms and rocked her, holding tightly as if he would never let go.

"I love you, Genevieve," he whispered into her hair, kissing her head and her ear and her temples. "Say you'll be my bride."

The release of longing she'd held back from the moment she'd met him made it difficult to answer. She'd never expected that he'd come back to her, that he'd propose marriage when he was finally free to go his own way.

Her voice shook. "Luke, I have never known a man like you. You're my love. Yes," she said, kissing his mouth, basking in the feel of his power. "Yes."

They held each other for a long time, murmuring their declarations, unable to get enough of touching and kissing. "But Luke, we're already married."

He cupped her face in his hands. "I'd like to make it official so there's no doubt in anyone's mind—in your mind. Forget about what anyone else might think. I'd like to marry you in the church."

"Hmm," she moaned, smiling at the wonder of it all. "My aunt and uncle will like that."

He stroked her arm. "I apologize deeply for the scene in the street with Judge Hillroy. Everyone in town knows what we did during quarantine, but now we can explain we were married all along. Your reputation will be restored."

She stared at his handsome profile. "That's true."

He kissed her eyelids. "It's interesting...the other thing you said..."

"What's that?"

With a rumble of laughter, he kissed her throat again. "That we're already married...maybe this means we're allowed to head straight to the honeymoon...."

Gently, he led her toward the fireplace and she, warming in the heat, laughed as he softly kissed her mouth. "I know just the place. Sheepskin blankets and all."

Hours later, with the blinds still drawn and the midnight sun clinging to the skies, Luke turned toward her on the sheepskin, as naked and beautiful as Mother Nature had carved him.

Genevieve rolled on the blanket, loving the feel of soft fur on her naked breasts. Loving the feel of her husband's hands cupping her and sliding his palms down her backside.

"You're a remarkable woman," he whispered. Firelight lapped against the curve of his cheek. "You made me want to run screaming from marriage."

"I recall." She kissed his nose.

"Yet you protected me...respected my opinion...gave

me my freedom...and in the end showed me freedom is living with you."

She lifted her face and memorized the intensity of his face, the way his hair fell across his forehead, the way his hand felt upon her breast. She would always carry this moment in her heart.

"You are by far," she said with teasing laughter, "the best proxy husband a woman could ever want."

Epilogue

Two months later

"They're here!" In the October chill, Luke closed the back door of Genevieve's shop and strode to the front room to tell her. In his long leather duster, cowboy hat pulled low over his brow, he was ready.

Genevieve stood at the display rack, adjusting the peacock feathers on an extravagant red felt hat. It was closing time. Milly had swept the floor and left, and Nugget lay at the fireplace, sleeping.

"I'm coming, I'm coming. Almost done." Soft laughter cooed from her throat.

"Hurry up, woman, you'll miss them. They're in glorious form tonight."

And so was she. Luke took a moment to relish the vision. Genevieve, dressed in a splendid new suit made of royal-blue linen, twirled around her colorful hats. Her hemlines skimmed the floor. She swished when she moved. He loved that swish. Fabric draped softly against her full bosom, narrow waist and wider hips. He'd always been drawn to her, like a lost sailor searching for a light from shore, for any signs of hope and life.

He sighed and glanced around at their warm corner of the world.

Her shop was already the most popular one in town for women. Her new contract with the Mounties kept her busy, and a captain from one of the paddle wheelers had also commissioned some uniforms. Genevieve was training Milly as her apprentice to keep up with all the work and she had almost repaid her uncle for the bank loan.

Luke leaned against the counter and watched her humming as she gave the hats final adjustments.

At her request, their church wedding had been small and private. On her side, only the Thornbottoms had been invited; on his, Colt and Elizabeth. The wedding had finally stopped the wagging tongues about what had taken place during quarantine.

Penelope Wick and Kurt Kendall had also been married, and Luke was pleased for them. Kendall wound up with Judge Donahue's horse because he hadn't fully paid for it. Joshua's barmaid, Miss Alice Purdue, had struck it rich on her gold claim. Unfortunately, Joshua was trying to fight her in court that he was part owner. The law was on Miss Purdue's side. Luke shook his head at what gold fever did to some people.

Vince Orman had been dispatched to a Vancouver penitentiary to serve his life sentence. As stunned as his brothers were to discover he was guilty, they were trying to move on past the anger and sadness. Ripley had taken over the BlackJack Casino, and was working with Burt on expanding his saloon.

Luke watched Genevieve twist around to pull down the shade on the front door. She locked it. Her sensual movements captivated his eye.

She'd blossomed into someone extraordinary—from the naive woman he'd first met, to a resilient one who had more strength and determination in her than most folks twice her age.

Pride filled him. She'd never lost her optimism. That had been the difference between them from the very start. Her upbringing with her folks had driven her to strive for more in her marriage; Luke's witness to his parents and their bitterness had pained Luke so much he'd wanted to run away. He *had* run away, from making promises to everyone in his life. Including, most painfully, to himself.

How could two people, he and Genevieve, who'd come from such similar upbringing, react so differently to it? She'd shown him that the broken family he'd come from was not one he had to recreate.

And the secret of sustaining love over a lifetime was to take it day by day. Or in this case, by the evening.

He marched over to his wife, kissed her cheek and pulled her by the hand.

"Luke…just one more pinning…"

"I'm hauling you out right now. Get your coat."

Nugget yawned and stretched out her full seven pounds.

Genevieve laughed and reached up on tiptoe to kiss his mouth. "Have I ever told you how much I love you?"

"Never once," he teased. "I think I might be falling for you a little bit, too." He warmed to her strokes, wrapped his long arms around her, and playfully tapped her backside. "I love you, too. Now stop distracting me. Come."

She grabbed her fur coat by the back door and slid her arms into the beaver pelts.

Luke popped the back door and they stepped out into darkness.

Darkness. After months of never-ending summer sunshine, they basked in the natural feel of having the sun set behind the ridge. Soon, autumn would end and they'd be steeped in almost round-the-clock winter darkness.

He pulled cool air into his lungs. The snow was already three feet deep, rivers and lakes iced up and not navigable. The town of Dawson would be isolated from the rest of the world for the next seven months.

Around them, lantern lights glittered from shops and barns. Piano music from the saloon down the road tinkled in the quiet. Their own log cabin, modest but welcoming, a home they'd built together last month, sat beneath the hills.

"Where are they?" Genevieve whispered, tugging her gloved hand under his elbow.

He glanced up at the sky and pointed above the line of cedars and spruce, to the left of the quarter-moon, above their cabin. "There."

Northern lights danced across the black canvas. The wispy patches were backlit with golden lights, tinted in creamy shades of rose. After a moment, those flickered into nothing. They were replaced by a brilliant twirl that covered a quarter of the sky. Then the northern lights vibrated with hues of cream and turquoise.

They stood in awe.

He looked down at the rich curve of her cheek. He'd never get enough of the sight of Genevieve in moonlight.

"Luke, sometimes extraordinary things can happen, can't they?"

He braced an arm around her, pulled her close and buried his face in the sweet smell of her neck. He kissed her throat and recalled how it had pulsed beneath his lips the very first time he'd touched her there. "I met you."

* * * * *

For a sneak preview of Marie Ferrarella's
DOCTOR IN THE HOUSE,
coming to NEXT in September,
please turn the page.

He didn't look like an unholy terror.

But maybe that reputation was exaggerated, Bailey DelMonico thought as she turned in her chair to look toward the doorway.

The man didn't seem scary at all.

Dr. Munro, or Ivan the Terrible, was tall, with an athletic build and wide shoulders. The cheekbones beneath what she estimated to be day-old stubble were prominent. His hair was light brown and just this side of unruly. Munro's hair looked as if he used his fingers for a comb and didn't care who knew it.

The eyes were brown, almost black as they were aimed at her. There was no other word for it. Aimed. As if he was debating whether or not to fire at point-blank range.

Somewhere in the back of her mind, a line from a B movie, "Be afraid—be very afraid…" whispered along the perimeter of her brain. Warning her. Almost against her will, it caused her to brace her shoulders. Bailey had to remind herself to breathe in and out like a normal person.

The chief of staff, Dr. Bennett, had tried his level best to put her at ease and had almost succeeded. But an air of tension had entered with Munro. She wondered if Dr.

Bennett was bracing himself as well, bracing for some kind of disaster or explosion.

"Ah, here he is now," Harold Bennett announced needlessly. The smile on his lips was slightly forced, and the look in his gray, kindly eyes held a warning as he looked at his chief neurosurgeon. "We were just talking about you, Dr. Munro."

"Can't imagine why," Ivan replied dryly.

Harold cleared his throat, as if that would cover the less than friendly tone of voice Ivan had just displayed. "Dr. Munro, this is the young woman I was telling you about yesterday."

Now his eyes dissected her. Bailey felt as if she was undergoing a scalpel-less autopsy right then and there. "Ah yes, the Stanford Special."

He made her sound like something that was listed at the top of a third-rate diner menu. There was enough contempt in his voice to offend an entire delegation from the UN.

Summoning the bravado that her parents always claimed had been infused in her since the moment she first drew breath, Bailey put out her hand. "Hello. I'm Dr. Bailey DelMonico."

Ivan made no effort to take the hand offered to him. Instead, he slid his long, lanky form bonelessly into the chair beside her. He proceeded to move the chair ever so slightly so that there was even more space between them. Ivan faced the chief of staff, but the words he spoke were addressed to her.

"You're a doctor, DelMonico, when I say you're a doctor," he informed her coldly, sparing her only one frosty glance to punctuate the end of his statement.

Harold stifled a sigh. "Dr. Munro is going to take over

your education. Dr. Munro—" he fixed Ivan with a steely gaze that had been known to send lesser doctors running for their antacids, but, as always, seemed to have no effect on the chief neurosurgeon "—I want you to award her every consideration. From now on, Dr. DelMonico is to be your shadow, your sponge and your assistant." He emphasized the last word as his eyes locked with Ivan's. "Do I make myself clear?"

For his part, Ivan seemed completely unfazed. He merely nodded, his eyes and expression unreadable. "Perfectly."

His hand was on the doorknob. Bailey sprang to her feet. Her chair made a scraping noise as she moved it back and then quickly joined the neurosurgeon before he could leave the office.

Closing the door behind him, Ivan leaned over and whispered into her ear, "Just so you know, I'm going to be your worst nightmare."

Bailey DelMonico has finally
gotten her life on track, and is
passionate about her recent career
change. Nothing will stand in the way
of her becoming a doctor...that is,
until she's paired with the sharp-tongued
Dr. Ivan Munro.

Watch the sparks fly in

Doctor in the House

by *USA TODAY* Bestselling Author

Marie Ferrarella

Available September 2007

Intrigued? Read more at
TheNextNovel.com

HN88141

HARLEQUIN® *Romance*.

New York Times bestselling author

DIANA PALMER

Handsome, eligible ranch owner Stuart York knew
Ivy Conley was too young for him, so he closed his heart
to her and sent her away—despite the fireworks between
them. Now, years later, Ivy is determined not to be
treated like a little girl anymore...but for some reason,
Stuart is always fighting her battles for her. And safe in
Stuart's arms makes Ivy feel like a woman...his woman.

Winter Roses

Available November.

REQUEST YOUR FREE BOOKS!

 Harlequin® Historical
Historical Romantic Adventure!

2 FREE NOVELS PLUS 2 FREE GIFTS!

YES! Please send me 2 FREE Harlequin® Historical novels and my 2 FREE gifts. After receiving them, if I don't wish to receive any more books, I can return the shipping statement marked "cancel." If I don't cancel, I will receive 6 brand-new novels every month and be billed just $4.69 per book in the U.S., or $5.24 per book in Canada, plus 25¢ shipping and handling per book and applicable taxes, if any*. That's a savings of close to 15% off the cover price! I understand that accepting the 2 free books and gifts places me under no obligation to buy anything. I can always return a shipment and cancel at any time. Even if I never buy another book from Harlequin, the two free books and gifts are mine to keep forever.

246 HDN EEWW   349 HDN EEW9

Name _____ (PLEASE PRINT) _____

Address _____ Apt. # _____

City _____ State/Prov. _____ Zip/Postal Code _____

Signature (if under 18, a parent or guardian must sign)

Mail to the Harlequin Reader Service®:
IN U.S.A.: P.O. Box 1867, Buffalo, NY 14240-1867
IN CANADA: P.O. Box 609, Fort Erie, Ontario L2A 5X3

Not valid to current Harlequin Historical subscribers.

Want to try two free books from another line?
Call 1-800-873-8635 or visit www.morefreebooks.com.

* Terms and prices subject to change without notice. NY residents add applicable sales tax. Canadian residents will be charged applicable provincial taxes and GST. This offer is limited to one order per household. All orders subject to approval. Credit or debit balances in a customer's account(s) may be offset by any other outstanding balance owed by or to the customer. Please allow 4 to 6 weeks for delivery.

Your Privacy: Harlequin is committed to protecting your privacy. Our Privacy Policy is available online at www.eHarlequin.com or upon request from the Reader Service. From time to time we make our lists of customers available to reputable firms who may have a product or service of interest to you. If you would prefer we not share your name and address, please check here. ☐

HH07

COMING NEXT MONTH FROM

HARLEQUIN®
HISTORICAL

- **CHRISTMAS WEDDING BELLES**
by **Nicola Cornick, Margaret McPhee and Miranda Jarrett**
(Regency)
Enjoy all the fun of the Regency festive season as three Society
brides tame their dashingly handsome rakes!

- **BODINE'S BOUNTY**
by **Charlene Sands**
(Western)
He's a hard-bitten bounty hunter with no time for love. But when
Bodine meets the woman he's sworn to guard, she might just
change his life....

- **WICKED PLEASURES**
by **Helen Dickson**
(Victorian)
Betrothed against her will, Adeline had been resigned to a loveless
marriage. Can Christmas work its magic and lead to pleasures
Adeline thought impossible?

- **BEDDED BY HER LORD**
by **Denise Lynn**
(Medieval)
Guy of Hartford has returned from the dead—to claim his wife!
Now Elizabeth must welcome an almost-stranger back into her
life...and her bed!